Merik

Merika's Story
Copyright © 2016 by M.A. ABRAHAM
www.maabraham.com

Acknowledgements...

I would like to take this time to thank my editing team, Eniko, Fran, Morganna, Candice and Sarah for their continued support and efforts in correcting my poor grammar and literary efforts. Without them my books would be unfit for reading. A good backup team is priceless and I hope to one day be able to find a way to repay each of you for your support... and Becca... what can we say, you continue to be my foremost reason for being out in the public eye, your talents are endless. And, last but definitely not least, I would like to thank Cora Graphics for the wonderful job she did on my cover. A good cover is priceless and you have made this one as masterpiece.

Merika's Story

Dedicated to those who dare to dream

A small whimper of distress was the only sound Merika made as she noticed the car next to hers speed up to pass hers. The driver was exceeding the speed limit, and not being very careful about how he was maneuvering between the other cars. He swerved, as he changed lanes directly in front of her, and barely missed her front fender. Another pulled up from the other side, and a third followed the second. The last one cut her off, and the rear of his car skidded and swayed, before it was controlled. It was clear these people were racing in heavy traffic, which was illegal, but it looked like that wasn't about to stop them. They missed hitting her car, but it was a close call. None of the drivers paid any attention to the trouble they were causing. Instead, they sped up again, to repeat their performance with other cars on either side of the highway. The recklessness of their driving forced her to move over, to narrowly miss the back bumper of a vehicle that did the same rather than cause an accident. It was an ill-fated move on her part, as she quickly noticed, she was stuck in a turn off lane. Well, she reflected, it fit in with the kind of day was she was having. Her whole week had been a total nightmare.

Merika decided there was nothing she could do about it, as she followed the heavy traffic off the turnpike. She would have to find her way back on to the freeway again, as soon as it was possible. The question was how? She had no idea where she was, and couldn't find the on ramp. She was going to have to wing it, and hope for the best.

Merika's mind wandered to where all her problems had started. The month before she had received a cable from her mother, telling her about a medical problem that had suddenly popped up. She immediately took a couple of weeks off from the television show she was acting in to rush to her mother's side. As her character in the series was due for some vacation time anyway, she figured her absence wouldn't be noticed. She knew she would be coming back to a full schedule, which meant she would have to work hard when she returned, whether she was in the mood or not. She didn't care, her mother was more important to her than any job. She had always come first to her mother in the past, now it was her turn to show that she felt the same about her.

Merika was an actress, and for the past seven years, she had played one of the young soap opera beauties on television. Despite her great success, and mounting wealth, she failed to put down roots. At twenty-three, she had few physical possessions, other than her car, and a couple newly acquired kittens, which her mother had talked her into adopting soon after arriving. As her mother had also bought a few kittens of her own, which she had left for her to care for, she was feeling overwhelmed. She had gone from having no one in her life, except her mother, to having four furry bundles of attitude.

Often, Merika questioned what she perceived as flaws in her character. She had no close friends, though people flocked to her wherever she went. Her popularity made her feel unsafe, and that insecurity made her back away from others in ways that most people mistook for conceit. It wasn't difficult to understand why they might think that; she was petite, blonde, blue-eyed, bright, intelligent and pretty. She realized her looks attributed to her success in the entertainment world, but there was more to it than that. It wasn't her beauty that kept her in the show, she was a good actress, and she worked hard at her job, perhaps too hard, and that gave her little time to be with others. Her lack of interest in anyone special didn't help. Instead, she gained a reputation of being a snob because of it. Men fawned on her to no avail and, although she smiled and was cordial to everyone, she continued to form no attachments. For the first time in her life, there was no one left in the world that meant anything to her.

As far as Merika was concerned, her mother had made a brave

show of living during her last few days of life. She must have somehow known that despite her actions and appearance the end was near. They had gone shopping, and then spent hours cooking together. These were the type of things, her mother told her, that memories were made of. She explained that in her youth, they had spent a lot of time baking, and she shared all her special recipes with her. Merika found it strange that she couldn't remember the times that her mother was talking about. In fact, she had few memories of moments spent with her mother at all. To the best of her recollection, she had spent most of her life either in boarding schools, or on a television stage set. The rest of her life was a blur.

Merika was so focused on the memories of the last days she had shared with her mother that she failed to notice when the landscape changed. The car moved onwards, traveling from paved highways, to gravel roads, and then to a dirt trail, that seemed to run into a forest. Her progress was ignored by her, until her car coasted to a stop. Merika blinked in surprise, as she looked at her surroundings, and then glanced at the gauge on the dash, that told her she had an empty fuel tank. It was then that she realized she was in trouble.

"Great, just great." Merika talked to herself, a habit she had gotten into years before. She always used this method to memorize her lines and to make decisions. For her, the verbalizing of any situation gave it clarity.

Getting out of the car, Merika looked around, pulled her suitcase and the kitten carrier out of the back seat, and continued to go in the direction she had been driving. She didn't know why she was going there, but for some reason, she seemed to be drawn in that direction. She hoped there would be someone further up the road that had a phone, because hers wasn't working. In her grief, she had forgotten to recharge her cell phone. There had to be some form of civilization nearby, after all, she was on a road, and all trails led somewhere. Right?

CHAPTER I

The matriarch of the homestead could feel a trace of power heading towards them from across the distance, and she knew someone was coming. She decided they had the time to finish what they had started. Whoever she was feeling had not entered the valley yet. She studied the essence of the signals and could sense a feminine signature. There was something about this woman's power that made her think that the peaceful existence they were enjoying in the clearing was about to come to a temporary end. It wasn't a malicious spirit; it was more of a restless one, which was looking for its roots. She was curious to see where that would lead.

"Sephra!" The matriarch looked up at his mate as his thoughts touched hers. "Should I be able to feel her this soon?"

"No, my love, she has not entered the valley," Sephera answered

"She is powerful!" The thought reflected the Patriarch's awe.

"I noticed, and I have a feeling our lives are about to become very interesting. We are going to be very busy for a while. Tara, set the table, the meal is almost ready." Sephera noted, as she turned to pass on her next order.

The sound of voices floated from the household kitchen, followed soon after by the clink and clatter of dishes and cutlery. In only minutes, the table would be set and ready for the steaming platters of food that were sure to follow.

"The meal is ready," a voice replied from the kitchen area, and within five minutes, those not serving the meal were washed up and seated in their places at the table.

Sephra was pleased at how orderly everything was working out. It had only been a few months since she had turned over the running of her home to her daughter, Serena. It was all a part of Serena's formal training, for every girl in the valley was expected to be able to run a household properly. Young ladies with higher evolved powers were expected to be able to handle jobs better than the others. Serena had taken to the task as if born to it, which was a very good thing because she was expected to make a very good match, as she was very powerful.

"Father, you may say grace," Sephra spoke in unhurried tones. She was the ancestral head of this particular homestead as her family had lived here as long as anyone could find recorded information. She met her mate at a gathering, much like what would happen when their new member arrived. She wondered if any of her sons would catch the young lady's interest, then decided that was unlikely. None of them had the kind of power it would take to match the strength the woman who was coming exhibited.

After the prayers had been spoken, and the meal had been set upon the table, they sat and began to eat. It wasn't long after when Serena jumped to her feet with a gasp, knocking over her chair as she did. "We are going to need Rodan, mother," and her face reflected her fear.

Sephra, in contrast, was the picture of tranquility. She continued to eat calmly as she responded. "Rodan's power is but a myth. You are right about one thing though, Serena. We will need a serious counter force to face this young woman, because, whomever she is, she does not come without a form of protection, for she brings the storm."

"Are you sure, Sephra?" Her mate asked, more for the benefit of their offspring than his own. He knew that if Sephra said so, then it was real. In matters like this, Sephra was never wrong.

Their children, however, were still learning. Serena was young in her knowledge of the recognition of the power of their people, and their sons still needed direction. The Matriarch's mate followed up his question with an order directed at his sons.

"You are familiar with the routine by now. The circle will need to be struck around the stones and the fire needs to be lit, to create a focus."

"I will lead the focus," one of the twins spoke.

Looking to Serena's fear filled face, Sephra spoke as she heaved a sigh of resignation. "You will never manage to hold it against the power that comes. We will have to use extreme caution this time, or things could turn ugly. The person who is approaching us has not been trained to harness it as we have. Simply put my son, you do not have the strength it will take to control her. You will find that few have the talent to do this."

"Then it will have to be Daffyd. He is the male Alpha of the family after father." The twin answered.

Serena interrupted. "I think we need Rodan, and yes I know you have doubts about the full extent of his talents, but I believe in him. I also have a very bad feeling about what is going to happen here tonight."

Daffyd, who had been concentrating more on the food that was cooling before them, then the subject being discussed, spoke. "I am able to sense this woman's strength just as well as you can, Serena. She is half the night away, so we have time to eat and do whatever needs doing before she arrives. So, with this in mind, I suggest we eat before Angela's culinary efforts go to waste. As Angela is the best cook in the family, it would be a shame to let something like that happen. Right Nigel?"

Nigel tossed his brother a smug, self-satisfied grin, and replied. "You are just jealous. Admit it, I married a great cook, not just a beautiful woman."

Angela, who had been sitting before a huge platter of lamb chops decided that this was her time to intercede. "Would you mind if I asked Taylor to reheat the food, or would it be a waste of energy that would be needed later?"

Sephra paused to consider the matter, then replied: "Warm up the food, Taylor. We will eat and everyone can help clean up after. Tara, you will stay as far away from this matter as possible. We want nothing to affect the child you are carrying. You are too close to your delivery time to chance an accident."

Serena sniped back, "This is not an accident that is coming at us, mother. It is a runaway freight train. I have never felt anything like it in my lifetime."

"Considering the fact that you are barely out of childhood, that says nothing for your experience." Serena's father spoke up.

"Father," Serena's voice grew whinny, and Sephra spoke, to put an end to it.

"That is more than enough, Serena. There is enough unrest surrounding us for tonight, without your causing more. Let us eat in peace."

To show that she had some use, Tara warmed the food and everyone ate.

They were a striking looking family; the men were all handsome, their hair color in various shades of brunette, and they were robust in physique. The women were feminine, beautiful and graceful as butterflies, being blonde, brunette and redheads. Only one of the young women wasn't married. The single female was sister to the horde of men assembled about them.

The women, who had married into the family, had come into the valley in much the same way as the stranger was now. They had made their choice of mate from the men who had greeted them upon entry, and none had found reason to regret their decision. Each girl felt they had made the right choice and was pleased with their lives. They were a family, and each and every one of them felt loved, supported, needed, wanted, cherished, and complete. They belonged, and were happier than they had been in the outside world. Each and every one of them had their own talents and powers, and felt themselves growing and expanding every day.

For Sephra and her husband, it had been love at first sight and, even as the years had passed, their relationship had remained froth with passion. Rayjan had been the first of their sons to be born, a mere ten months after they had met and wed. Daffyd had come second, then Nigel, Taylor and Anton, Everitt and Devlin. Terrance and Gerald had followed four years later. When they had thought that there would be no more children, Serena had come into their world. Serena was the only daughter, the family sweetheart. Each and every child was made to feel special, the pride and joy of their parents and siblings, and each knew the strengths and weaknesses of the other and had learned to compensate for one another. As a family unit, they made a formidable team. That they were able to work well together boded well for the area where they lived, for their home was not far from the outside edge of the Valley. Anyone, who entered their world had to go through them to gain full entry.

As the family had grown and matured, there had been warnings of other people of power stumbling into their world. Angela had come from the outside world. She had been lost and scared, as most were when they first arrived. She had taken one look at Nigel and fallen in love. They had gotten married two weeks later. Tara had arrived a few months later, acting as if she had known what to expect. She was a born flirt and, as she was a female of above average looks and power, her presence had brought several interested suitors to their homestead. It hadn't taken her long to decide that Taylor was whom she wanted and needed.

Several other people had arrived since, both male and female. Each showed signs of developing various stages of strength and power. Merydith had powers so weak it was questionable whether she belonged in this world. It had taken a while, but Sephra had taught her how to direct those she had, and eventually her talents grew. Even after she had been trained, it had taken their Alpha to determine that her specialty was in blocking. It was the sole reason they had trouble discerning what she was. Alycia had followed so close behind Merydith that the family had wondered if they might have been traveling together.

It seemed interesting that everyone who came to the valley seemed young, alone, gifted, and destined to form an attachment to a member of the Valley population. Once they gained confidence, they moved deeper into the valley, where they found the one they were meant to be with.

What Sephra's family was about to face now, however, was beyond the realm of their collective experience. This young woman was broadcasting a power so strong that they were surprised everyone in the valley hadn't heard her approach. With that in mind, they wondered how many of the community would respond to the possible danger, for most of the men who were present had felt that Serena's comment had been quite accurate. The newcomer had gifts that were not under control, and that could create total devastation, unless someone could get her to settle down.

Their evening meal had been eaten, and then cleared away in uncustomary silence. Everyone had done their part, working as a unit, to save as much collective energy as they could. When everything had been cleared away, the men had gone to the standing stones near the entrance of the Valley to form their circle of power.

Serena had watched the men go about their task with a frown and a sad sigh. It hardly seemed fair to her. She was every bit as powerful as any of her brothers, being the known female Alpha of the area, but because of her gender, she was expected to stay home. To be fair, she knew that if the men needed back up power, they were only minutes away, but it was not the same as being in the front line.

Merydith walked up to Serena's side, and grinned as she commented, "For a person who is more than five hours away, she sure is coming in loud and clear." Then, to change the subject, she added, "We have finally decided where our house is going to stand. I can see it in my mind already."

"We will all miss you when your home is finished and you leave us," Sephra replied as she walked over to Merydith to give her a hug. " But, we will still get to see you every day." She paused with her head cocked to one side for a moment as if listening to something for a moment, then added, "We are about to get some unsolicited help from the neighbor. Antoine and Andre are on their way. They say that they have also alerted Kodac by wind carrier." She seemed to think that amusing as she smiled.

Serena tossed a look of awe at her mother and quizzed. "Do you really think he will come? Kodac goes nowhere!"

"Kodac goes where he knows he is needed. He has just never had reason to come here before." Sephra answered.

"I heard he became a recluse since his wife died, when she gave birth to Rodan. It is one of the reasons he is reputed to be so obscure." Angela relayed, only to get a frown from Sephra for her pains.

"Repeating such rumors gives them credence. You know better than to listen to what gossip other people spread. Kodac has so many responsibilities, he needs to pick and choose whether something deserves his attention or not. He tends to the things he knows only he can do."

"I hear he has another son besides Rodan, although I have never been given a name. People don't talk about him. He is supposed to have dark hair, while Rodan's is so fair that he is compared to a living, breathing Adonis. Rodan is so powerful and talented that he shines like the sun." Merydith breathed in awe and wonder.

"The name of Kodac's other son is Tyrus, and I have seen him myself. In fact, there was a time when I thought he was interested in me. I, however, only had eyes for my Taylor." Tara purred as she preened.

Angela just sniffed in disbelief and exchanged a look with Serena, who appeared wide eyed at the thought that someone she knew might know all the premier Alphas in the Valley. She had heard things, and in her mind, she had romanticized about the stories people talked about the most. Steeped in mystery and awe, she, like most of the other girls her age in the valley, could only fantasize about the fair Rodan. That her mother knew she had placed Rodan on a pedestal to worship meant she must agree with her analysis, and approve. What she didn't realize, was that her mother thought that if her daughter ever met the man, reality would knock him from his post and give him that much further to fall.

Sephra tilted her head as if to listen closer to something then interrupted the girls' chatter.

"Pull up your blocks tighter girls, things are about to get worse. Whomever sent the warning to Kodac, also touched a part of our visitor's psychic makeup. She is reacting out of fear and doesn't realize what she has called upon in her subconscious search for protection from what she thinks is danger. Remember the storm I spoke of? Look at the sky. The clouds continue to darken even further. If there is no major lightning strike before this all comes together, I will never know what saved us."

CHAPTER II

Sephra walked out of the house and onto the deck as she raised her head once more to listen for a few moments. She then ran for her cape. "Girls, follow me. We may know about our world and the powers we wield, as well as the reasoning behind it, but she does not. Her actions are purely defensive. She has no idea of the scope of what she is about to unleash. We don't dare interfere with the integration process the men are initiating, but we have to assume that she is going to need help when this is all over. We have to be prepared, in case the men need help as well."

"Why should the men need help, there are many more of them than there is of her?" Merydith spoke, puzzled how one lone girl could overpower a circle of so many men.

Sephra appeared pleased with Merydith's question, as it meant her girls were thinking on their own while they searched for answers. "It is not a question of numbers, Merydith. It is all about power. You will see what I mean when things break loose. For now, however, we need to prepare ourselves to do what we must just as our men do, for it is every bit as important."

Several hours later, the women had set up their own area. It was more of an infirmary than anything else, and Sephra set up a teaching circle, so she could explain more about what they could expect to happen, as well as why.

"In a battle, such as the approach of this woman looks like it may become, there is a greater chance of casualties. Nor am I speaking only about our visitor. The men are just as prone to injury as she can be."

"Has this anything to do with the lightning that you spoke of earlier?" Merydith asked.

"Partly. For the sake of those still learning and those needing to refresh their memory, I will expand upon what I have already told you. Lightning strikes can happen just about anywhere, unless the wielder has the training to direct it. In this case, the person who has called up this storm does not have this control, nor does she understand what she has done. She is untrained, although she must know something, or she would have never been able to gather enough power to release a maelstrom.

"Perhaps there is something we can do to calm her." Serena suggested.

"Never interfere in an action taken by another, unless you know you have the strength and energy to do what needs to be done to control the situation. This type of power takes an extreme amount of training and knowledge. Anything less is apt to cost someone a life. Do not think for a moment that I am warning you to exercise caution just to exercise my lungs. I am deadly serious. Any ill advised move could cost you your husband, your family and your life." Sephra explained.

"I feel nothing strange or out of the ordinary. Are you sure this is not a natural storm?" Merydith wondered.

"You power and talent is very limited, Merydith. Think. Feel the wind as it increases in velocity? Hear the message it carries? Heed the warning, for it is a threat, if not a promise of things to come." Sephra explained.

"Why would she wish us harm?" Angela asked.

"Hurting us is probably not her intent. At this moment, she is only aware of her uneasiness. As we feel her, she can feel us. She has no idea what she is sensing and is reacting to her fears. By the time she reaches us, this storm will be a palpable thing. She doesn't understand what she is scared of; she only knows that she is. She doesn't know about us, but she feels our power, as it reaches out to touch her and control hers. You went through the same thing albeit with less force, so you should remember what she is feeling," Sephra pointed out.

"I do not remember being afraid." Merydith stated.

"I remember being petrified, but I have no memory of creating a storm." Angela spoke, as a new and stronger gust of wind whipped through her hair and she tightened her grip on her cloak.

"Even collectively, none of you have the power it takes to create something like this, and before you feel too bad about that, I would have you consider the repercussions before giving thanks to the creator for his great blessings." Sephra advised.

Serena, tired of being quiet while her mother taught her lesson, piped up. "We should all be aware that power comes to us with a price."

"Exactly. Serena is capable of creating a storm of considerable strength should she feel threatened enough, but it wouldn't be so intense. She would know how to direct anything she created, as well as control the power involved. She would also know how to reign it in, when the need for it was over. Unlike the person directing this storm." Sephra continued.

"Storm?" Serena scoffed as she repeated her mother's last word. "You mention something as tame as a storm when we are about to face power that could challenge a hurricane?"

"I used it as a comparison daughter, as well as a way to give you a clue about how much power we are about to face. This girl, and I say girl because she has yet to become a full woman, has much more power than you have, my darling daughter. To compare hers to yours would be comparable to talking about this of a storm versus a maelstrom. Nor would I call the kind of storm you would generate an evening shower. Whoever this person is, she is just that powerful." Sephra warned.

"Good Lord mother!" Serena breathed in fearful awe. "We are in trouble. How in the world could she have gone undetected or free for so long?"

"Someone with great power must have been shielding her." Sephra sighed. "It is the only solution. The person who had her controlled must have died recently, or, it could be someone who, for some reason or another, decided to withdraw their protection. Because of this, we have suddenly become aware of her. Either way, she is alone and vulnerable." Sephra noted.

"Is that why we are seeking to bind her? To control all she is?" Angela asked.

"The men seek to bind her because it is the only way they can integrate her into our world quickly. They do realize they may not have the strength it takes to tame her power. For them, it is a matter of safety." Sephra continued.

"Is there anyone who could do this without forcing her to bend to their will?" Serena asked.

"Perhaps Kodac. Probably Kodac. It would take a supreme male Alpha like him. To make this clearer, I will try to explain more. As I read her signature in the atmosphere, I would have to say that she has had some formal training in handling her powers, but not enough to understand just what she is doing, or the extent of her strength. I doubt if she has enough power to withstand the combined forces gathered here tonight, at least I sure hope she doesn't. Sometimes it is a psychological thing. There are times when a strong emotion like fear can lend a person power and strength beyond their capability. Believe me, by the time this person reaches us, she had better be bound and harmless, or under the control of something. If she isn't, that fear could create a series of circumstances that I shudder to think about." Sephra added.

"Something tells me that none of us are going to come out of this night the way we went into it. This experience is apt to change all of us in some subtle or catastrophic way." Angela prophesied.

"Be that as it may, my children," Sephra took charge once more in attempt to settle down their fears with a touch of the normal. "Nothing is about to happen for the next few hours, so I suggest we all get a little rest."

"How are we supposed to rest with things looking the way they are, and the person who is causing our unrest getting ever closer?" Merydith shuddered. "Even I can feel the growing threat, and I have almost no power to feel her with, at least not that kind."

"Merydith, might I suggest that you not start to panic now? There is no reason for it. Our biggest enemy might be our own over active imaginations. Now rest, you are going to need every iota of energy you have in your body in the next few weeks. Anyone who packs the punch this lady does, is going to attract a crowd as big as a small city. We all know who is going to have to act as hostesses."

Saying that, Sephra and the girls settled themselves onto the thick grass and she whispered a light incantation to the wind. Within minutes, all those who were to act as her backup team had curled up close to her and had fallen asleep. It was more than she could do.

CHAPTER III

The further Merika traveled from the car, the spookier everything seemed to get. She kept berating herself for her over active imagination, but it seemed to make things worse. There was something in the air, something almost tangible, something reaching out for her. She put the case that held the sleeping kittens down, and rested for a moment, telling herself as she did, that she had spent too many years in television.

As far as the world knew, Merika's name was Tanya Wade. No one knew her real name, not the private school where she had spent much of her formative years, not her co workers, not the government, not even her agent knew her by any other name than the one she acted under.

"Keep your real name to yourself." That piece of advice had come from Merika's mother, and it was a rule she lived by as far back as she could remember. "Your name is a bond between the two of us, something only the two of us share. It is special. Tell no one and none can ever have a hold on you or control you. Your name holds power over you. Hold it close and tight. Never forget my words." Her mother had cautioned her.

It was one of many childhood memories Merika had. It seemed that many of those held a touch of fear in the telling, which had made it a paramount of importance. She remembered her mother sending her off to boarding school while she had still been a tiny child, and it had broken her little heart. She had felt as if her beautiful but elusive mother no longer loved her, even though she knew better. She could also remember brushing the tears from her mother's cheeks, as they ran unheeded while she held her before they parted.

Memories of her mother; although fleeting, were filled with love and closeness. She remembered how she would brush her mother's long hair, so soft and golden. Her mother called it her crowning glory, and it fell to her hips in a riot of curls, just as Merika's did when she wore it down. Silky and so full, the handling of it had made her feel so close to her, so much a part of her. When her mother would talk of how much she resembled her as a child, it filled her with hope that she might grow up to look like her mother.

Thoughts of her mother followed Merika, as she moved further into the depths of the forest. Those memories were like a sore tooth, constantly reminding her of the spirit that no longer guided her every move. In the past, everywhere she went, and everything she had done, had seemed to be under the guidance of her mother. She had not done this in person, but in spirit. She couldn't be with her child the way she would have liked, but her presence had been there nonetheless.

In her mind, Merika remembered sharing conversations about life and living she had with her mother. They spoke together about loving, and the timing involved in giving. Her mother had taught her about respecting her body, about what not to take seriously, and what should be. When her opinion of herself got over inflated, she found her mother's words in her mind, and they put her back in line. When she felt down, the love she sensed from their connection lifted her up. The lessons she was taught were harsh and demanding at times, but there was never any doubt that there was love behind the teaching. Deep within her mind, there were also subtle hints that there had been more than her immediate memories of her mother, but that is all it amounted to, hints of something held deep in the recesses of her subconscious.

Moving ever onward, Merika remembered the first time she landed a role on a television show. She had been only twelve at the time. By the time she had turned fifteen, she had turned what was supposed to have been a short-term character into a main story line in a popular soap opera. Now, seven years after that, she was one of the headliners in that show. She had also held staring roles in three movies, to add to her credit, and she commanded major attention wherever she went. None of it impressed her, as she had grown used to her life's accomplishments over the years.

Merika remembered the first indication that something was wrong with her mother. It had not come by messenger or telephone, in the way it had this time, but with a premonition. She had quickly taken a leave of absence, to see to her ailing mother. At first, there had been nothing to indicate that her sickness was serious, as she had returned to work. Her mother didn't get better, though she never said anything. A year later, there were complications that caused her condition to worsen, and she lost her fight against the disease. It had been during the last few weeks of her life that Merika had come to be with her.

Tears flowed freely down Merika's cheeks as she walked and remembered her mother. She missed the presence of her essence by her side and within her mind. No more would she pause to listen to some unbidden piece of advice, or to cough to hide secret laughter at some comment that crossed her mind, something her subconscious told her came from her mother. She would miss all of that. The warmth of the comfort she felt when she was alone, the shared laughter, and the knowledge that she was loved. Really loved.

It was in the midst of these warm, but painfully healing memories, that Merika felt the first waves of a powerful compulsion. Coming out of the dark, and through the waves of apprehension as it did, took Merika by surprise. Someone was out there, someone was trying to lead her towards a location not too far away. The thought sent a shock through her, and her mind immediately grasped for reasons and possibilities.

Who was behind this? Why? What did they want from her? Was it real, or something from her imagination? All of her instincts screamed warnings at her. Someone or something was threatening her safety, and she had no idea how to react. Was it a threat? Did anyone really mean her harm? Merika was alone and without guidance for the first time in her life and she felt lost and defenseless. She might not need protection, but what if she did? How could she protect and keep herself safe? She needed to get away from here, needed to move on. Most of all, she needed her mother's reassuring presence surrounding her once more, but that was not possible, her mother was gone. There had to be some place safe, someone she could rely on, but whom?

As Merika moved through the forest, the clouds overhead grew darker and the wind grew stronger as it pushed her onward and she grew even more scared and panicked. She had to get out of the storm or she was going to be in trouble for it was growing in strength and getting violent. She needed shelter.

A sudden dull glow appeared in the distance, shining through the darkness like a beacon, and Merika stopped. She could only wonder what she was seeing. Was it real? As she rested, she considered her situation, while she checked on the kittens, smiling at how cute they looked cuddled up together. She could only wonder how many more hours it would take for the sedative the vet had given them to travel would wear off. For now, she felt grateful that they slept. She sat on her suitcase, as she nibbled on a granola bar, and considered how smart or stupid it would be to approach the first signs of civilization she had seen in over seven hours. She was tired and had no idea whether the fire she saw ahead was going to lead her to the safety she craved and needed, or whether it harbored the reason for the danger that she had felt broadcasted at her.

While Merika rested and pondered her immediate future, the

storm seemed to stall and weaken a bit. The men, who were monitoring the situation, sealed the circle of power around their focus, as they stood by the fire and waited for her to come to them.

Earlier in the evening, two of their neighbors had arrived to offer their assistance. Andre and Antoine were brothers and, being young, more than just a little confident of their success. After all, they were not only good looking and personable, they were invincible.

Daffyd felt Merika come closer, and then she seemed to stop as if to regroup and rest. Considering the power and energy she was expending, he figured she probably needed to. He rose from his place by the fire and moved to the center stone, where he began to prepare to cast his spell.

While the men forming the circle waited for their moment, Andre gave voice to his confidence. "There is no way anyone will be able to break our power. We are twelve and she is one. No one female could ever hope to have the kind of power it would take to transcend that."

Sephra's husband snapped back. "I would advise against ignorance or over confidence. Either could get us all in trouble. As for this girl not having the power to break our circle of power, I would question that. Just look at the size of the storm she brings, and although it seems to have abated slightly, I would not count on that being the case if I were you. Our battle with her has yet to begin. Might I suggest you turn your attention back to the task at hand and forget about the possible glory and rewards of success until after it has been achieved."

Andre felt the sting and embarrassment of the elder Alpha's words and turned his attention back to the focus. Daffyd was feeding his energy to the fire so he could build up the flames enough to show everyone where she was in the shadows, as she approached them with caution, and more than a little reluctance.

"Come closer, we will help you," Daffyd's voice floated to where Merika had stopped to set down her load one last time.

Merika took one look at the scene before her and her breath seemed to catch in her throat. Just what had she stumbled in on!

"What is your name?" Daffyd's voice seemed to enter her mind. "We seek to find out if you are a friend or foe. To show you that our intentions are friendly, I offer you mine. I am Daffyd."

Merika turned as she sent back a hesitant reply, passing out her stage name, as she would normally do. "Tanya, Tanya Wade." She then found the fortitude to move forward another fifty yards or so, though she left her luggage behind this time.

With her standing as close as she was and his possession of what he thought her real name was, Daffyd decided it was time to act, and his voice shot across the distance to where Merika stood.

"Tanya Wade, I bind you and with the power contained within this circle, and that amplified by this set of the standing stones, we seek to contain your talents so you can do no harm or cast no spells without our permission."

Daffyd's voice cut through the sudden scream of wind, as it blasted through the area and Merika screamed in terror, as she felt the tentacles of their combined power reach for her.

"No!"

Merika's memories of her mother's last words ripped over and over through her mind. "When I am dead, they will hunt you. They will try to control and contain who and what you are, and you will know whom I speak of when the time comes. Merika, my beautiful darling daughter, I have done all I can to shield you and, in doing so, I hope I have not made a grave error. I cannot, in all honesty, say that they are an evil people, any more than you and I. Their intent is for peace, and they work for the good of all mankind, as much as they can. Those who I am talking about keep their existence a secret, and no one can blame them for doing so. The average person would never understand what they are, what we are, Merika. Our talents would cause us to become persecuted, and even killed out of superstitious ignorance. It has happened in the past, and mankind has not changed so much that things would be much different now. History is filled with examples of what I speak of. Who knows, maybe I made a mistake by keeping you away from the world where we belong. God knows I did what I felt was the best I could for you. You are my life and the extent of everything I hold dear and love."

Merika had been left to make her own judgment of her mother's words, but right now she was so scared she had no hope of thinking straight. So she reacted to what she perceived as a threat, in ways she could never have imagined. Never in her wildest dreams would she have imagined herself capable of using atmospheric elements in the fashion that she was doing at the moment. A small portion of her mind, however, wondered how much control she had over what she appeared to be doing. She also began to worry about the effect that such a weapon would have on everyone about her, even herself. It was not the foremost concern in her mind at the moment though, for she feared the battle she faced could be a matter of life and death.

Merika felt the wild force of the foreign power close in and around her and felt a sudden bout of claustrophobia. She was being crushed! Her lungs felt strained as they fought for oxygen. A large portion of her body felt as if it was being weighted down with lead. She gave a helpless little whimper, before an uncontrollable urge to escape the bonding forming in her subconscious mind surged through her. It seemed to build from the ground, rising upwards through her body, as it took over her senses. She raised her arms to the sky, as if to signal her freedom and independence. In exultation and celebration, she threw her head back, to give a wild keening cry to the heavens.

As if the shout was a signal, everything around her seemed to break loose at the same time. The skies lit up with several jagged bolts of lightning, the air crackled with power and electricity, the heavens resounded with an eardrum shattering intensity of thunder. The spell, which had threatened to overtake Merika's powers, shattered and she gave a laugh of pure exhilaration.

She was free! No one was going to hold her prisoner. The men who had been in charge of the spell scrambled to regroup, and Merika could feel the change in the air as she sensed them attempting to recharge their power. She snarled back at them in challenge and, with a fist, she directed a strike of lightning to land upon the ground, landing in the center of the fire in the circle, right in front of the male focus of the circle.

The force of the resulting explosion scattered the flames, blew the circle of power apart and knocked Daffyd off of his feet. He landed over six feet from where he had been standing.

"Enough," A new voice cracked over the sound of resulting thunder, and all attention centered on a triad of men who had just dismounted from identical horses.

Another bolt of lightning flashed overhead, illuminating the scene below, and an audible gasp was heard from amongst the women as two names were barely breathed aloud. Kodac and Rodan. The third male remained anonymous, but it was he who stepped forward to form the new focus. There was no doubt in anyone's' mind that his was a new direction and a very powerful challenge to Merika's power.

"Merika," the new focus spoke as he moved forward to direct her attention away from the others and towards him. Unlike the others, he didn't seem to be afraid of her. He was blonder than his other two companions, his hair just short of platinum. His features were harder and his every fiber affirmed his strength and talent. He was, without the doubt of any of the people who were standing around him, one of the most powerful alphas their people had ever known.

This man's voice was deceptive, something Merika immediately noticed about him. She knew what he was doing; she had used the same trick when she acted. The softness of the tone he used belied his power, his voice seemed soft and soothing, his forward movement little more than a steady glide, moving him ever closer to his quarry as he worked to capture her full attention. "You have no reason to fear us, Merika. You know this deep in your heart and mind. We mean you no harm. You, however, have done much damage, Merika. Think of what you do."

All it had taken for this man to do a quick assessment of Merika's character and intent was for him to look at her. It took no great intelligence to understand that what she was doing was fed by fear. He also knew enough about her in the outside world, to know she was not a spiteful, destructive or cruel person. She was an intelligent humanitarian, according to everything he had ever read about her. It was something he would call on to refocus her attention with.

As he had looked at Merika, he had also taken note of more than just her reputation and state of mind. Even as tired and drawn out as she looked at the moment, she was a beautiful woman. Slight of figure, yet with curves all in the right places. He found he had to work to keep his mind on the job at hand. He could not afford to let his mind linger on those cornflower blue eyes, that pert little nose, or those tempting lips so full and inviting. He pushed all this into the back of his mind and concentrated on what he was doing.

Merika was shocked when she heard him use her given name, and she asked. "How can you know my birth name?"

The man read the danger signals in her narrowed eyes and smiled, as he continued to pull her attention towards himself. "How can I not? You are the daughter of my father's friend. He knew her as Teryka. I have seen pictures of her when she was young. You have inherited her coloring and her beauty."

As Merika made eye contact with the stranger, the storm began to lose power.

"Let me help you through this, Merika. Let me guide you. There are things you need to do, to bring this storm under control before it hurts someone. Reign in your power, Merika. You are tired, and the elements draw even more of your energy as we speak. Power has its price. Your mother must have told you that. It is the first and foremost rule that we live by. Look around you, Merika, see the price that some have already paid? Only a few will be able to do their chores tomorrow, and you have expended infinitely more energy than they. Very much more and you could cause a few deaths. Could you brush that aside without regret? Could you leave a woman mourning a husband, force a mother to bury her child, or a child to wonder where his or her father went? You know what it is like to lose a parent when you are young. Think about that. You remember the sense of loss you always felt, and the sense of longing you never lost."

"How do you know these things about me?" Merika cried in bewilderment, while the storm continued to rumble around them. She had not even felt him enter her mind to help her control her fears and kill the ensuring elemental connection. Her subconscious, however, had lunged to grab the touch his offered. Her instincts had noted the colors of his inner essence and she had felt the comfort ensured by his touch that he had not even known he was projecting.

The storm calmed as the wind quieted, and only a few electric flashes still lit the sky above them. The male Alpha now standing before Merika, spoke to answer her unspoken questions as he filled her mind.

"Your mother did not realize how much she broadcasted. Merika, understand, your mother feared for no good reason. She was young and alone after the death of your father. She was afraid she would lose you to her husband's family. We would never have let that happen. She was a good mother, a powerful member of the community. She didn't need to waste her life as she did in the outside world. In the end, she died for no good reason. We could and would have helped her."

That was the thought that broke Merika's will to feed and sustain the storm any more. She collapsed on the ground in a sobbing heap, with her hands pressed against her face. The man before her just stood there, watching her for a few moments. He then turned to Daffyd.

"It is over. As for the rest of you, after having been born, raised and trained in the valley, I would have thought that any of you would have had more brains than to consider trying to bind a woman you collectively have no more than half the power needed to succeed. Could you not have waited a few more minutes until we arrived, or do you all have a death wish?"

His voice was neither kind nor soothing now, it was harsh and filled with contempt.

"That is quite enough, Tyrus," Kodac snapped. "They did what they thought they had to, just as anyone else might have. Even you. No one could have forecasted just how powerful Merika could have been."

Tyrus did a quick mental sweep of everyone present, and being in no mood to be reprimanded, responded. "Serena knows. Sephra suspected. The men present should have paid attention to the warnings of the women. Especially so if they were unable to read the situation for themselves."

"Easier said than done son," Kodac continued. "And that is the last any of us are going to say about this matter."

Serena glanced at Merika, as she cried on the ground for only a moment, before her gaze focused on the third man that had shown up, and she whispered his name to herself. "Rodan."

As if he had heard her speak, Rodan looked at her and smiled. He noted how her gaze immediately fell in modesty, and how pretty she looked, as his attention brought a blush to her cheeks. His immediate impression was a combination of what he had just heard about her, the aura she threw, and the picture she presented. Together they presented her as a young, powerful, intelligent, down to earth, and extremely beautiful girl. True, she was not blonde as the woman his brother had brought under control, but few were, and he preferred the cultured look of a brunette. Which made Serena perfect for him.

Rodan had smiled at her and it had seemed as if he could no longer breathe. Serena had never seen such a beautiful man, so strong, so virile, and so presentable. He was Adonis in the flesh! How could someone like her hope to begin to catch and hold the attention of a man like him?

Sephra noted it all and frowned at her daughter. She knew what was going through Serena's mind. She, too, had been young once. Despite all of her misgivings, she said nothing. Serena had always harbored a crush on the myth of Rodan, ever since she had heard it, and Sephra thought that there would be no real harm in her looking. She knew her daughter well enough to understand that she would be quick to realize that he would fall short of his reputation. Most men did, and it was obvious to her how. To her mind, the brother to watch was Tyrus. Now there was a man that would take time to get to know, and he would be worth every moment it would take. But neither he, nor her daughter had even noticed the other was alive. She also doubted if they would. Tyrus, in his own way, would be too much man for her daughter.

The problem that could have been Serena and Tyrus was not even a concern for Sephra. She had seen the look in Tyrus's eyes when he had looked at Merika and, although his actions were contrary to what she had witnessed of his feelings, she knew which woman would win out in the end. Tyrus would choose Merika, whether he wanted to or not. Nature had a way of bringing what it wanted together. Merika was harder to read. Her mind had reached out to Tyrus', however, it had been out of the need for comfort and guidance. Merika's was a soul in need of healing, and right now she was very vulnerable. Sephra could only wonder if Merika would grasp at the first man to offer her solace, or if she would prove to be more elusive than anyone would expect. She showed signs of not being able to trust very easy.

CHAPTER IV

After Sephra sent the ladies off to see to the welfare of the men, she moved to tend to Merika on her own. There was something about this young woman that reached out to her, as if she sensed that some part of her needed more than just a little comforting. What had it been that Tyrus had said, she had grown up without a father, and now her mother was dead also? That meant the young woman was alone in the world. Not only did she have no one to offer her solace, during her time of grief, but now she was amongst strangers that she had no reason to trust. Merika needed a shoulder to lean on, and someone caring who she could talk to, and she needed it badly.

Sephra searched her memory in hopes of remembering who Merika's mother was. Tyrus had mentioned her name, and it was vaguely familiar, though she had never known anyone called Teryka. She remembered hearing about a distant relative to Kodac, who had a daughter called Teryka, but that had been many years ago. Could Merika be her daughter? Tyrus had seemed to know her and her history just by touching her mind, but then again he was the Valley chronicler, so he should be familiar with all the individual histories.

Tyrus was another mystery, as far as Sephra was concerned. He had magnified her curiosity about him by calling Kodac his father, just as he in turn had been called son. Sephra had heard that Kodac had more than one child, but so little was known about his personal life, that few realized that even Rodan was even more than a rumor. The ruling Alpha led a reclusive life when it came down to family, and not much about him was common knowledge.

"Merika," Sephra spoke, sounding every bit like a mother trying to offer comfort to a heart broken child. "You must not cry like this, you will make yourself sick." She bent over the distraught woman and placed a hand upon her back to display her empathy.

Merika was not about to accept any part of Sephra's sympatric offerings. She pushed away from the motherly figure before her, as if she had just been burned. "Never touch me, I do not need your pity. Leave me alone." She snarled, although she didn't intend it to. She didn't want to hurt the woman who was offering no more than to be a friend, and yet she couldn't accept that offer, not yet. It reminded her too much of something her mother would do, but she wasn't her mother. Her mother was dead, and the pain of her loss continued to wash over her. She needed to escape so badly from the hurt, and those who could see it in her. She sprang to her feet, and began to run.

Merika's reaction took everyone by surprise, except Tyrus. He had been expecting further reactions from her, and had been watching for something to happen from the corner of his eye. He knew that both his brother and his father had dismissed her ability to act further. They thought that, as she had exhausted her energy supply, she wouldn't do anything else. He didn't share their optimism. In their overconfidence, they had moved on to other matters, something he considered carelessness. People, in his experience, often found reserves of great strength and durability when you least expected it.

Tyrus could understand Rodan ignoring the young beautiful Merika. His brother had taken one look at the equally beauteous Serena and a spark of natural attraction had not only flown between them, it could have ignited the whole forest with its intensity. He couldn't blame Rodan for thinking as he did, especially when the young lady looked to be equally besotted.

Tyrus felt that Kodac shouldn't have been fooled by Merika's actions. He should have been aware that there would be more to face from the spirited beauty, for Merika still shone with the residue of the power she still held in reserve. Tyrus had noticed that Kodac was leaving him take over more situations like this, along with more of the responsibilities of his station, since he had come to the Valley. He had, however, still maintained leadership. To Tyrus, it was a telltale sign that he was being groomed to take over his father's place in this world, a position he would rather not be in.

When Merika bolted, Tyrus was ready for her, and with a flick of his fingers, he tripped her. As she fell, he walked over to her side to offer her a hand up. She just tossed him a hostile glance, as she rose unaided, and surprised him by freezing him where he stood. She then sprinted away, in an attempt to escape.

Merika managed to run the full length of the clearing before Tyrus broke free from her spell, and started to run after her.

"You are playing a dangerous game with your weak efforts to escape, Merika," Tyrus growled a warning into her mind, as he formed another spell, which he found her capable of blocking somehow.

Tyrus gritted his teeth as he raced after her. He found it frustrating that he had to resort to chasing her down physically. He knew that Merika had spent little time with her mother; he had managed to pull that much out of her mind. He questioned how Teryka had found the time to teach her daughter the complex spells she threw at him, even without taking the time to think about what she was doing. She acted as if she had used the magic that she had been born with all of her life. Sure, he knew that Teryka had been a strong telepath, but could she have planted all this information in her daughter's mind over a great distance and do it in a way that it would remain dormant in her subconscious until it was needed? It was something he had every intention of asking his father about.

Merika could feel Tyrus giving chase, and was hot on her heels, so she ran faster, thanking her stars as she did that her body was in the shape it was. Her feet seemed to fly, as they carried her over the ground, taking her out of the clearing and into the darkness of the woods. Here, she reasoned, she might be able to find a place to hide in the shadows. At the same time, she fully understood that her natural coloring was not conducive to blending into the background. She was sure there were things she could do to camouflage herself to make it work.

Thinking, as she ran deeper into the forest, Merika considered the different things she might be able to do to help herself. She started by reaching back, to pull the hood of her jacket up to cover her hair, for she was every bit as blonde as the man who was now hunting her. She could feel him behind her, hear him, and she chose to ignore him.

"Bothersome female," was the least of Tyrus's thoughts, as he continued to chase after Merika. He gave her credit for being fast, but he was confident that he would catch her in the woods. Her hair shone like a beacon in the night, bright as any flashlight, and he felt he could count on that to guide him. As he continued to follow her trail, he had to admit a bit of admiration for her, after all, she had been exhausted. He could not begin to figure out where she was getting the energy from to make this new run. He could almost understand why the men had considered taking the risk to try to bind the girl. Binding, when successful, solved many problems, when it came to controlling the unintegrated, unfortunately it was neither practiced nor approved of by the members of his family.

His family, in Tyrus' estimation, had the dubious honor of having the strongest powers, and they considered it their duty to make sure those were not abused. The Alpha males of the Valley were not allowed to use force to control other people around them.

That meant absolutely no talent used in the binding of a subject. In principal, he agreed. People deserved the right to exercise their own freedoms. Nor was their leadership based on the ways of a dictatorship. Tyrus, in fact, did not even consider his family the rulers of the Valley, though there were others that would be willing to argue the point.

As one of the premier male Alphas in the Valley, Tyrus ran a mental tab through the loose rules that bound them. It was their responsibility to protect the people who depended on them, and sure, it sounded feudal, and perhaps many might consider it that way, but that was the way it had to be. The powers that served them dictated this, and most people understood why.

"Merika!" Tyrus' voice carried through the muffling effect of the foliage that surrounded them. He tried to magnify the clarity of the sound, however, that did nothing to disguise how winded he was feeling. He had always been proud of how well endowed his body was, but running was not one of his better sports, not as it seemed to be with Merika. At this moment, he was finding her talents very frustrating.

The sky was beginning to show the first signs of the breaking of dawn, as Merika heard the signs of Tyrus crashing through the undergrowth of the trees. He was closing the distance between them fast, and with the encroaching light, she knew he would be able to see her better. This thought sent a jolt of alarm through her. She needed to find a place to hide and quickly. Someplace he would never look, but where? What could she use that would serve her purpose? She had no idea what to look for and no time to do it; the forces around her seemed to be plotting against her. She felt she was losing the battle, and it was only a matter of time before she would be caught.

Merika realized that she was running out of energy. Her legs were beginning to tire, and she felt the telltale signs of a stitch growing in her side. She chanced a quick glance over her shoulder to see if anyone was closing in on her, and gave a loud gasp of shock when she tripped over some minor obstruction on the ground. A moment later, she felt a set of arms lift her from the forest floor, to hold her as one would an injured child.

Merika had nothing left to fight with. She was exhausted, and tripping had been the last straw. Her limbs felt like lead, and what wind she had had left, had been knocked out of her by the impact. The fall had made her hood fall off, and her hair came loose, to cascade down and around her. The strange thing was, despite the fact that she had no idea who now held her, she felt no sense of danger.

Merika felt the upward momentum of whoever was holding her. She heard the creak of leather, and the snort of a horse, as the man settled, before repositioning her so they would both be more secure and comfortable. She barely had the presence of mind to acknowledge where she was, or the shock that she was on a horse, a place she had never been before in her life. She heard the man, who had been following her, as he arrived at the side of the animal, and that was the last she remembered before she passed out.

"Father!" Tyrus gasped as he leaned against his father's horse. He looked as if he was holding himself up, as he fought to catch his breath.

Kodac shifted, as he allowed Merika's cascading hair fall over his arm, to cover his son's head and shoulders. He grinned at the sight, and then leaned over to see how his son would react to the touch and scent of their new guest. He smiled, as he noted how Tyrus tensed, the moment her hair fell to surround him with the scent and texture of that shimmering sun fall, and how his eyes took on a haunted look.

Tyrus couldn't help but notice how Merika's hair smelled of lemon, and felt like satin. It was all he could do to stop himself from burying his face in the sunny riot of curls that fell about his head and shoulders. He feared she was going to be more trouble than he might be able to handle and he vowed to put a lot of space between the two of them. In his experience, women were often trouble and he wanted nothing to do with them, at least nothing that might trap him into a long-term relationship. With most women, the thought of forming such a bond would not even come into the picture, so the temptation to do so was nonexistent. He, however, had touched Merika's mind with his, and there had been something in that exchange that captivated him. He found her essence haunting, even now, and feared he would never be the same, now that they had met. Now that they had been connected in their minds, he might not be able to find the strength needed in him to sever the connection that allowed him entry into her thoughts, something only couples shared. He shuddered inwardly, as he wondered what he was going to do about that. He had created a monster within him, and it was only beginning to take shape. He could only wonder how it would fully manifest.

Kodac could feel the battle going on within his son's mind, as wave after wave of mixed emotions rolled through and over him. Tyrus was more than just attracted to the young woman; a part of him wanted her for his own. The problem with that was that Tyrus had few favorable experiences with women on any level. Tyrus' mother had been a master manipulator, and it had left him scarred, and in need of someone like Merika, someone who needed him as much as he needed her. Kodac was aware of all of this, as he had touched both of their minds while they were joined. He had noticed how the auras, that signified that the two were an ideal match, had swirled around each other in harmony. It had met with Kodac's full approval.

Kodac grinned as he replied. "We will speak of it at length my son. You understand that you still have a lot more to learn, which tells me, I have a lot more to pass on to you before I move on in life. So far, I have found you have done very well. You learn your lessons well, retain them over time, and have a good sense of judgment. I am proud of you."

Tyrus nodded in acknowledgment of the praise. He was touched by his father's willingness to share his feelings with him. He then motioned at the comatose Merika, and asked. "What are we going to do with her? With such raw power, do we dare release her to be on her own, or do we take her home with us, to teach her proper control?"

"While that might be convenient, it would not be fair to the young girl. To begin with, I cannot believe that Teryka would leave her daughter in ignorance, it would not be like her. Teryka was nothing if not one of the most conscientious people I ever knew. Right now, Merika is exhausted. She will need time to rest and heal from the pain of losing her mother, amongst other things. That will take time. It will also allow us to figure out where she will fit in the scheme of things, and find out where she belongs. I have a feeling that won't take long in the discovering."

"She is bound to have a hard time of it," Tyrus stated his opinion.

"Then we are going to have to help her." Kodac responded.

"Figures," Tyrus commented, as he frowned. "She would have to be difficult."

"She could be worth the trouble," Kodac pointed out.

"Think so? I have yet to see anything about her to give me that impression," Tyrus answered, along with a derisive snort of disbelief.

Kodac almost gave a bark of amused and disbelieving laughter.

He had seen the struggle Tyrus had with his instincts to reach out to this young woman. So, instead of challenging his son directly about his comment, he shrugged and replied. "Perhaps you see nothing in her to attract you because she is not meant for you, but she might be perfect for another man. Anyone who looks like her won't be alone for long. She deserves to know life to it's fullest. She needs a home, someone to love her, and a family. Now, do you want a ride back to the clearing, or have you called your own ride?"

"He comes," Tyrus replied.

Kodac then nodded, as he relayed his short-term plans. "We will need to stay close to the clearing for the next while. Sephra will take care of Merika, until she is back up on her feet, and has begun to show signs of healing. Sephra's talent is strong in that field. When Merika has had time to recover somewhat, we will be in a better position to make a decision about her future."

"Sephra, father? Are you sure?" Tyrus was not so sure he liked his father's choice, though there was no doubt that Sephra's talent was perfect for the job. She had several sons who were young and very eligible, who would be very eager to make a match with this young woman.

"You think she is not up to the challenge?" Kodac asked as if he were unaware of exactly what his son was thinking.

"That isn't the problem. Sephra has the talents Merika's condition calls for, but it would seem she already has her hands full," Tyrus pointed out.

"Well, they are about to become even more so. Besides, she has a daughter to help her, as well as the wives of some of her sons. She knows how to delegate responsibilities very well, with all the practice she has had over the years. You will see what I mean as things unfold." Kodac responded.

"What do you mean?" Tyrus asked suspiciously.

"If you remember, my son, we were able to feel Merika's coming a long time before we were told about it. You can bet that more than a few of our people are also aware of her presence, especially the male alphas that are looking for a suitable wife. Sephra, and her family, are about to become hosts to a lot of curious and young suitors. I am willing to bet they won't come alone. They will bring other members of their families, and this will become a small meeting of our people. This clearing is about to become very crowded," Kodac, answered with a knowing smirk. He wasn't disappointed, when he noted Tyrus' frown, along with the thoughtful expression that crossed his face. This was something his son had not considered, at least not yet, but now that the seed had been planted in the back of his mind, it would take time to form. He hoped Tyrus wouldn't fight his attraction so much that he would allow this chance at a happy future pass him by.

Tyrus frowned, as the image of Merika in another man's arms crossed through his mind. He then shook his head in disgust, as he dismissed the possibility. If another man wanted her that badly, here she was for the picking. He was determined he wouldn't be the idiot making such an ill-advised decision. "I had a feeling this woman was about to make our life complicated. I just had no idea of how much that would entail."

"As I said, this could turn into the equivalent of a small gathering of our people. As Merika's powers are great, we can expect some of the prime alphas to attend this time. They will all know that, and they will be bringing sisters and other female relatives with them, to capture the attention of other suitors who they would have to compete against otherwise for Merika's hand. We will all be busy, but it will be a time for us to enjoy ourselves also." Kodac continued, as he pressed the idea of many other suitors for

Merika's hand at Tyrus. He was trying to figure out a way to make his son become more protective of Merika, and possibly even a little possessive of her. Again, he was not disappointed with the reaction he got from his son.

With a voice chalked full of irritation, Tyrus snarled, almost to himself, "I think this whole matter is being blown out of proportion. She is nothing but a female who has more power than what she knows how to handle."

Kodac gave a loud snort, almost loud enough to equal the one that erupted from Tyrus's horse, as it sidled up to his son. He then spoke his thoughts aloud as he watched Tyrus mount.

"My son, your experience with the right type of women is almost non existent. I realize your mother, although beautiful and powerful, was one of the worse manipulators known to mankind, but you cannot paint all of the fair sex with that same brush. The other men will know what they are looking at, the moment they set eyes on Merika. She might not know what she is capable of doing yet, but I can guarantee that there isn't an alpha in our lands that won't be willing to teach her. You can be sure, they will enjoy doing it when the time comes, if it comes."

"Perhaps I don't have the right experience, but I don't happen to think I am wrong," Tyrus replied, as he mounted his horse. "Even when I was a child, I understood why you refused to marry my mother, even though she carried your child. I can assure you, that growing up under her tender care was a nightmare I will never forget. I also know that there was nothing you could have done about that. A man has to know about something to be able to change things."

That said, Tyrus moved his mount closer to his father's side, and held out his arms, in an offer to take Merika from him. His father just laughed at him, as he teased.

"Getting Merika into your arms will not be that easy, my son. If you want her, you are going to have to earn her."

"A statement like that isn't even worth commenting on. I only thought to relieve you of a burden," Tyrus defended his actions.

"I am not that old and decrepit yet and we both know it, just as we both are aware that she weighs less than nothing. I must admit it is no hardship to have something so delectable this close. You will have to try it sometime." Kodac teased.

With that, Kodac tossed his son a smile, as he nudged his horse into action with a controlling knee. A few moments later, both Tyrus' father and horse were gone, and Tyrus was left behind, as he watched them ride out of the forest towards Sephra's homestead.

Tyrus laughed at his father, and followed in his wake. Lord he loved how his father taught him about life. It was a challenge. His only regret was that he hadn't gotten to know him earlier, before he had become bitter about the world that surrounded them in general.

CHAPTER V

Merika woke cocooned in the warmth and comfort of a feather bed. She looked around, in an effort to get her bearings and took note of her surroundings. This was a room meant for a woman who enjoyed being one. Merika gave a sigh of relief, as she remembered her last waking moments, and she smiled. She had not been sure of what she would wake up to, but she had been sure it would not be to the lacy frills that decorated this room. Everything was decorated in pink and white, in a fashion she thought would have done justice to almost any home decorating magazine spread. It was a room most girls would have killed to own, though she could think of none that she knew who would have the courage to admit it.

The sound of the turning of a handle and the opening of the door, heralded a tray-bearing attendant, and Merika raised a hand to her chest, to make sure she was properly covered. She felt the soft chiffon of one of her own nightgowns, and gave a little smile, as she stretched like a cat, wincing only a bit at the discomfort the movement caused by the stiffness and bruising of her muscles. That, at least, had been no less than what she had expected. The events of the night before had left memories she would rather have not woken up to, for she felt as if she had just lived through some horror movie.

The attendant turned out to be one of the young women Merika remembered seeing in the clearing of the forest the night before. She had only a vague recollection of her, and what she recalled was that this person had been more interested in a very handsome young man who had appeared, than what was going on around her. That thought made her smile widen even further. It had looked to her, as if the young man had seemed every bit as impressed by the young woman, as she had been by him. Upon inspecting the girl, Merika decided that he should have been.

The young woman had light brown hair with natural golden highlights. Her skin was creamy smooth, her mouth was full and held a pleasant welcoming smile, and her eyes sparkled with youthful health. There was an impression of good humor shining through those pretty eyes, as if lit from within, and they were the brightest green Merika had ever seen in any person. It made her look more as if she was very pleased with her lot in life.

"Well," the young woman's voice sounded as pleasant as her demeanor, with just a hint of huskiness. "It is about time you woke up and joined the living. My name is Serena."

Despite her friendliness, and the way she looked, Merika still fell back on old habits, and replied as she always did. "My name is Tanya." She found she could not fully suppress the wariness that had always been so much a part of her. She had lived with it all her life after all.

"I know, it is your stage name. Tyrus explained it to us. He seemed to know quite a lot about you, considering that he never met you in person before. I thought that rather interesting. He told us that your real name is Merika. I think I like that name better than Tanya."

Serena chattered as she bustled about the room, setting down the tray she had brought into the room with her. She then got Merika to sit up in bed, while she plumped up the pillows to place them behind her, before placing the tray over her lap.

"You are not to get up until mother has had a good look at you. In the meantime, I want you to eat each and every bite of this, though you might not find much to chew on. There is just some broth, a small fruit salad, toast and tea. Mother says that if you show signs of having regained some of your strength, she will probably let you get up for a while."

"Am I allowed to ask questions too?" Merika asked.

"I would wonder about your state of mind if you showed no interest in your new circumstances." Serena admitted.

"Well then, let's start with one of my questions. Where am I?" Merika wondered.

"In my room. Like it?" Serena replied, as she looked around the room with a obvious sense of pride.

"It is amazing. Very feminine, though not something I would choose for myself." Merika admitted, as she praised Serena's taste in décor. She continued to speak, as she picked up a spoon to scoop up some soup. The smell of the food before her was tantalizing, and her stomach quickly let her know how hungry she was. "Tell me, how did this Tyrus person know my real name?"

"Tyrus, at the moment, is the territorial chronicler. If anyone would know about your parentage, it would be him. As far as his knowing about your stage name being no more than just that, Tyrus spent the better part of his life in the outside world, just as you have. I assume that your name is documented differently in our records than it is on stage." Serena pointed out.

Merika nodded her understanding, although it didn't answer her question. She hadn't been born here, her mother had given birth to her in San Francisco, so how did they get her name? Could they have known about her even in the outside world, without the knowledge of her mother? That would make more sense, as far as it went. She knew she looked enough like her mother to be identified as her offspring, as anyone who had ever met the two of them together had been quick to point out. Also, she assumed that as both her mother and father had been born in this area their names would be in the public records. As far as knowing about her in the outside world, her television career was well publicized; she was a headliner. It would hardly be brain surgery to put these facts together to come up with all sorts of connections.

Serena carefully sat upon the edge of the bed, as she watched the play of thoughts run through Merika's mind. "You must have more questions than that. I would if I were you. I know I am curious about your life, so what do you say about an exchange of information?"

Merika warmed up even more to Serena, as she made her feel like they were fellow conspirators in some minor plot. People who were friends would play out the type of game that wouldn't hurt anyone. She tossed her a grin and replied. "I am game if you are."

"Alright, as I am hostess here, you go first." Serena offered.

"So, now that I have rejoined the living, what will happen to me? How long was I out?" Merika asked.

"Well… you have become one of the main reasons for a gathering of sorts. The curiosity that was caused by your show of power has attracted nearly half the population of the valley. There are signs that a good portion of those people are now journeying to our clearing. I am not quite sure what to think about that yet. In some ways, it is exciting to see so many people together in one place. In other ways, it is rather intimidating. Kodac took command of the situation and quickly set order to the meeting." Serena informed Merika.

"Order? Merika asked. She could only wonder why this had to be done.

"Granted, it has just been two days since you showed up, but as that was the last anyone saw of you. It made people wonder what was happening, and things threatened to get out of hand when they weren't getting any answers. There were accusations that you were being kept secreted away, and when Tyrus tossed out a few derogatory remarks about the general atmosphere of the crowds who were asking those questions, Kodac decided to take action." Serena reported.

"I gather this Tyrus can be caustic when he chooses, which comes as no surprise to me somehow. What did Kodac do?" Merika wondered.

"Tyrus can be more than caustic, he is downright rude. Worse than that, however, is when he is right while being so. He has a way of cutting right to the meat of the matter. Kodac settled the situation by putting the men to work. The groundwork for five houses has been sectioned off, around the borders of the clearing. It is more than our family needs at this time, but they will fill fast, and then we will have to build more. Tyrus took to the woods with whoever would go with him, to harvest the lumber that will be needed to build the houses. The rest are getting ready for when it begins to arrive," Serena continued to tell Merika about what was going on outside of the house.

"Was Tyrus the young man you were so interested in the other night when I arrived?" Merika enquired.

Tara walked in, as Merika phrased her question, and teased. "That was Rodan, our Valley Adonis. Tyrus doesn't bother with females. Rodan, on the other hand, loves women. That man can charm birds from the trees with a smile."

Speaking through a furious blush, Serena snapped back. "Only if he could spare the time to take his eyes off of his own reflection long enough to try. I have never had the misfortune to meet a man so full of himself. Rodan thinks he is God's gift to women."

Tara just laughed and teased all the more. "So do most of the women I know. Admit it Serena, you are smitten."

Feeling a need to show a little support for her newfound friend, Merika spoke up in her defense. "If Serena is, it sounds to me as if his charms wore off rather fast, or is it that Serena has little patience with clowns and fools no matter how good looking they are?"

Serena was grateful for the support, and even happier when the subject was dropped. A short time later, she watched with interest, as Merika seemed to squirm under the blankets, soon after she had finished with her meal. She didn't need to be told what the problem was, she knew. She rose to take the tray from her lap, tossing her a smile as she spoke. "You finished all of it, good for you. Now, if you will give me a minute to get rid of this I will help you up. I think mother will understand why we didn't wait for her."

"I think I can manage this on my own, after all I am not useless." Merika declared, as she swung her legs off the bed, to place her feet onto the floor. She wasn't about to let anyone know how weak she felt, and figured that the effort she made would give her strength. She was going to stand and walk on her own, it was a matter of pride. She didn't need help to go the washroom.

Serena wasted no time, as she shoved the tray she had been holding into Tara's hands. "Take the tray, Tara. Merika, I have a feeling you have no idea what you put yourself through. You burned up a lot of energy when you built and maintained that storm. What they say is true, Merika. Power does have a price, and over the last few days, you have been paying it. You are not quite recovered enough to do much yet, no matter what you think."

"So you keep reminding me, over and over." Merika spoke in her frustration. She then surprised both girls as she stood and made her own way to the washroom, where she washed and relieved herself. She returned to the bedroom, to find Sephra waiting for her. A new dress had been laid out for her to wear, and Sephra watched her from the doorway, for any signs of weakness.

"You look a bit pale, but outside of that, I would say you appear to be no worse for wear. Come, I want to check you out and if you are up to it, we will see about you getting dressed. It will do you good to leave the room for a bit of fresh air." Sephra decided.

Merika was led to a chair, where she sat down, and Sephra placed her hands on either side of her head, while she closed her eyes so she could focus her full attention on the signals she would be able to pick up from her patient. When Sephra had finished, she nodded her satisfaction remarking as she did.

"Your recovery time has been nothing less than astounding child. What should have taken you weeks to bounce back from seems to have been accomplished in mere days. That is very impressive. It shows how healthy you are and in how good of shape you are." Sephra looked thoughtful for a few moments, then broached another hurdle, one she knew would have to be taken care of at some time, one way or another. Considering the lack of time and circumstances surrounding them, she was quick to decide that the problem could be settled at this time, but only if Merika was willing.

"Your mother has left you a wealth of knowledge tucked away in the recesses of your subconscious. Many, many years have gone into those teachings, and in case you wonder just how I know, Kodac told me your mother was the most conscientious person he had ever met. A person like that would not leave her only daughter to face the world ignorant of her talents. She would arm her with all the information she could, to survive in the outside world after she was gone. That is exactly what I think your mother did, she then locked it deep within you, until someone like me could come into your life to release it. Now, I want you to think about this carefully, Merika, because there is a lifetime of information hidden in your head, and it could overwhelm you if it gushes into your consciousness all at the same time. Do you believe that you are strong enough to receive the lessons your mother left you at this time, or would you rather wait for a while? I want you to consider carefully, because this will affect you more mentally than physically." Sephra warned.

"Do you think you can release these memories safely?" Merika asked.

"It is within the parameters of my talent, so yes, I can do this. I can trigger the memories that your mother left for you, and all the lessons and time you shared while she taught you about these things. I can only imagine the thought and energy it must have taken for her to do what she has done and for the reasons she did it, to keep you safe. I admire her strength of will, for fighting for what she believed in." Sephra declared.

"Correct me if I am wrong, but I have a feeing I am about to get very tired again, am I right?" Merika tossed Sephra a crooked smile, as she asked her question.

Sephra smiled back, impressed with how quickly Merika was grasping what she was trying to explain. "Not in the same way as you were. When this is over, you will find yourself knowing things you never realized you knew. You may find memories of time spent with your mother that you had no knowledge of. Anything is possible."

"What are the side effects?" Merika wondered. She wanted to know as many of the details as possible.

"In the beginning, it will scare you. You will find yourself pensive at times, apprehensive at others, and perhaps even a little emotional until you have become comfortable with what your brain has stored in it." Sephra admitted.

"Very well then," Merika replied with a nod, and sigh of resignation. As far as she was concerned, there was no time like the present to get this done. "Lets get this over with."

"Are you sure you have thought this through enough? You could find it more overwhelming than you expect, especially so soon after your recovery?" Sephra warned.

"I have it figured this way, there is no time like the present. Also, I believe that if you would not have believed me up to it, you would never have suggested it to me in the first place." Merika admitted.

"True, and somehow I think I knew what your answer would be. In fact, it could hardly be anything else, for I believe you are every bit your mother's daughter. She taught you well. Now, to further explain things. Your mother will have placed a trigger within you for me to find. When I do, you may find yourself more than a little disoriented, or it may not hit you right away. She may have set it so that things would be released inside of your mind a little at a time. That is my hope." Sephra explained.

With that said, Sephra placed her fingertips over Merika's forehead, and delved into her mind with hers. Moments later, she gave a cry of satisfaction. "Ah ha, there it is."

It only seemed to take a moment to Merika and suddenly the world around her spun. She sunk to her knees, as she held her head between her hands, as if to stabilize it. When her world righted, she looked up at Sephra and spoke her awe aloud.

"I have never felt so complete. For the first time in my life, I know who I am, what I am." The amazement in her voice was palpable, and Sephra almost cried, as the waves of happiness that came from Merika washed over her.

Sephra realized that Merika would need help sorting it all out, and was amazed to think she had not even considered this. She thought it would be a good time to begin now, so she spoke out to her to form her first controlled focus.

"I think you are going to have to spend some time thinking over the knowledge your mother hid in your mind, as soon as you can. To begin with, you are broadcasting on a very wide level. Everyone will be able to read you for miles. I wouldn't be surprised to learn that one of your greatest talents is as a telepath, and it is very, very powerful."

Not being used to anything when it came to her newfound powers, Merika looked dumbfounded, and being called upon to exercise some control on her own, triggered the beginning of a panic attack. Just as she feared she was going to lose control, a male voice seemed to reach in her mind to stabilize her. Calm. Cool. Collected. The man's voice spread a soothing sense of control through her.

"Take a steady breath, Merika, and pull up your blocks. You remember how it is done." The tone of voice the man used was warm, as if in approval, as Merika responded in a positive and favorable fashion. Before leaving her mind, he sent her one last message. "You should be fine from now on. Just remember, the first time with anything is usually the hardest, and you have already taken that step."

The mental touch of the man's mind had been somehow familiar, yet Merika could not seem to pinpoint the source. She knew she had felt his connection with her somewhere before, but placing it was beyond her at the moment.

Sephra noted the look of preoccupation on Merika's face, as she received her message. She watched her deal with her problem, then tried to sort out whatever else was going through her mind. When whoever it was that had contacted Merika had removed his or her thoughts from the young woman's mind, Merika made short work of putting up a block. Sephra didn't know who had come to Merika's aid, but she recognized the work as being that of some of the people she knew. Merika, she decided, would never be far from a helping hand. She waited for Merika's face to clear, and she discerned that her guide had withdrawn, she then paused a little longer, until she felt sure that Merika had a firm grip on herself and was ready to move on.

"As you continue to use your powers more, you will find the process more natural and easier to do." Sephra assured Merika.

"That is more or less what the voice told me just a few seconds ago." Merika admitted.

"Did your advisor tell you his or her identity?" Sephra asked.

"No. He just told me to take a deep breath and pull up my blocks. He gave me the impression I would know how. He also said that I would be fine from this point on as the first time doing anything was usually the hardest."

Sephra smiled to herself as she reflected on what could have been a cryptic message. All things considered, it narrowed down the field of helpers to just a few. Sephra liked to know what was going on around her, as it made life easier to deal with, so she tried to figure out who was helping. Whoever it was, had to have known a great deal about her, for not much about their guest was common knowledge.

Kodac had gotten Sephra to do a mental and physical examination of the young woman, while she had slept, and when she had reported her findings there had been only five people in the room. Only the people who had been present during her report knew all the details. They were aware of that fact that Merika was chaste, and what it had taken for her to keep herself pure during her life in her chosen career. They had thought that gem of discovery astounding, considering the lack of morals in the outside world. Whoever had sent Merika that tidbit of reassurance, had known about the examination, it was the one thing Sephra was certain of.

Merika herself was unaware of what they had done while she had slumbered. She did not know that they had delved into her mind just as deeply as they had examined her body. There was little that they had not discovered about her. Kodac had agreed that it was important to leave nothing to chance about her, not when she was capable of using the kind of power she had. They had found her surprisingly well adjusted, stable and normal in all ways important.

They had decided that the easiest way to integrate Merika into their society would be to allow her to find her own way. Often, young people had the resilience it took to make great changes in their lives, if left to do so, without outside interference. To make sure that she met the right type of people, they sent Serena, to serve as a guide and, with luck, friend. It was a starting point. Sending a summons to her daughter, Sephra set up the connection, as she prepared to send Merika into their world.

"You seem to have made a remarkable recovery, Merika, more than I could have hoped." Sephra praised her, then spoke further to set her free. "I would have you remember that you are still weak, and probably even a little shell shocked from all you have recently learned. I think you would be better if you are allowed to interact with other people. Company often has a way of invigorating the young, and making alien customs seem familiar. You will note that most people are essentially the same no matter what their culture. I have asked Serena to take you around, as you two seem to have hit it off, and to introduce you to others.

Serena walked into the room during the conversation and smiled a greeting as her eyes sparkled in anticipation. "You called for me mother?"

"Yes, I want you to show Merika around, introduce her to others and whatever. Might as well enjoy yourselves as you do it so take your time," Sephra instructed.

Serena tossed Merika a wide smile and made a come-a-long motion with her head. "Come on, Merika, time to change. We are about to become the center of attraction."

"Grab a sandwich or something before you leave. Merika hasn't eaten much in days, she will be starved." Sephra pointed out.

The girls tossed each other a conspiratorial grin, before Serena went to the kitchen to grab a quickly made up snack.

Sephra chuckled as she left the two young women alone. She knew that they would work out the rest together, and it would be good for them both to get out amongst the others.

The moment they had finished eating, Serena went into her closets and pulled out an attractive dress to change into, while Merika watched and took close notice of the style. They both had taken a look at the dress that Sephra had laid out on the bed for Merika earlier and had laughed, as they wrinkled their noses at it in distaste. This was not the type of clothing they had in mind for their walk, this was much too plain. The moment Merika saw the dress Serena had brought out of hiding, she knew she wanted something like it, if she could get it.

"Is this what most of the other girls will be wearing?" Merika asked.

"More or less, though I thought to dress up a bit more than they will be. I suggest you do the same. After all, the idea is to have a good time, and it would not hurt to garner a bit of attention from the men while we do. I so assume, you enjoy male admiration, am I right?" Serena asked mischievously.

"Guilty as charged. There is nothing like making some guy drool, no doubt about it," Merika looked at Serena, then added. "The trick is to do it while not making a spectacle of yourself. I must say I do like your outfit. It suits you so well."

"Something like it would suit you as well." Serena admitted, as she whirled around to show off the dress. It had a close fitting bodice, with a full skirt that showed off her figure to perfection. She shook her long hip length hair loose until it hung in sheaths around her shoulders and back, then smiled as she commented.

"I love to wear my hair loose, though it is impractical with the type of duties I do in everyday life. It would be in the way."

Merika smiled back at her and, not to be outdone, she closed her eyes to visualize a dress she had once seen, liked, but would never have worn in the outside world. Here it would fit in, with an understated elegance that would still stand out. With a slow steady movement of her hands she moved them from her shoulders down past her hips, and a pretty multi hued blue dress slowly formed around her. When the spell was complete, she flicked her wrist, and a brush appeared in her hand.

"Let me do it." Serena spoke as she took the brush from Merika's hand and with a wiggling movement, she sent Merika's hair cascading down her back in a riot of curls and waves to her waist. Serena sighed, as she ran the brush through the satin softness of her curls. She had wanted to feel the texture of Merika's sun colored hair from the moment she had seen it. This was her chance. "I wish my hair curled like this. Is it natural?"

"Yes, and yes it did cause a lot of jealousy amongst my class mates when I went to school. It is not near as beautiful as my mother's. My mother was so breathtakingly beautiful, men used to stop in mid sentence when she entered the room. I thought it a shame that she hid herself the way she did, but she always told me that she was happy in her life and as she acted the part, I left it alone,"

Merika shared a part of her old life with her new friend.

"Was she able to do the trick you did with the dress?" Serena wondered.

"Yes, but quicker. A few hours ago, I would not have been able to tell you anything about these memories. I am grateful that your mother was able to release them into my consciousness when she triggered the lock my mother had placed on them. There is so much that my mother taught me that I never realized was waiting for that moment. There are some I still need to remember, but I can sense them waiting to emerge." Merika informed Serena.

Serena turned her friend around, and fingered the material of the wide collared dress. "It is nearly as soft as your hair. You are going to wow all the guys we run into."

"I agree, the dress is a keeper, but it is no lovelier than your own and you know it. Now, I believe it is time for me to make my first very public appearance, so, shall we?" Merika suggested.

That said, both girls left the house, and did their best to blend into the crowds outside.

CHAPTER VI

Serena and Merika wandered about the homestead clearing for over three hours, while they checked out the progress being made on the houses that were being erected. They also looked at the excavating that was going on at the future sites, the entrance paths into the main forest, and even the fresh trails that were being made by the logs that were to be used to make up the buildings.

It was an afternoon of bonding, and building a friendship as they shared individual memories, hopes, dreams and fears. Like other girls before them, they giggled together as they commented on the different people they knew and had met in the past. Serena filled Merika in on all the gossip about the men who had come in from other parts of the valley to help, or because they had felt Merika's arrival. Not even Serena's brothers were exempt from their scrutiny and comments.

Eventually, the girls headed back towards the main house, and they would have gotten to their destination at a decent time, if Merika had not noticed a building that seemed to be attracting a lot of attention. Of course, she had to check that out too, especially since most of the traffic going in and out of the building was female.

Serena frowned, as she failed to divert Merika's attention from her newest point of curiosity, and tried something different to accomplish her goal. Thinking to turn her away from the building, she tried to dismiss it through a cutting remark. "That is more or less Angela's domain at the moment."

"I want to see what the attraction is," Merika explained refusing to be swayed.

"You should rest for a while, before we do anymore exploring. We have been gone a long time." Serena objected. She didn't particularly like the Kitchen area, even if she knew how to use them.

"I am fine, Serena, give me a break." Merika pushed her friend's concerns aside.

The girls had reached the building by that point, so Serena just shrugged her shoulders and gave in gracefully. She knew her mother was not going to be pleased about her not being able to rein Merika in, even when she was beginning to show signs of getting very tired, but Serena was willing to bet that her mother wouldn't have fared any better.

Merika gave an audible cry of delight, as she entered the room. "My mother would have been in heaven here. Mom loved to cook and bake, she was a cordon bleu chef." Merika explained, as she walked around in the room. The kitchen made up three quarters of the building and housed dozens of stoves, cabinets, counters and supplies.

"Your mother was a chef in the outside world?" Angela spoke, as she made her way to Merika's side. She had heard what Merika had said, and wanted to know more.

"She said it was one of her gifts. Scenes like this are like a walk through memory lane. A few hours ago, I would have known there was something familiar about the place, but I would never have been able to tell you what." Merika explained.

"Did your mother ever take you along with her to see her work?" Angela wondered.

"Yes, she also taught me how to cook and bake. I mean, I was never as good as she was because she said it was a lesser talent in me, but I remember how we used to have baking contests and the laughter we shared as we talked and worked. Our times together were much too brief, but they were always productive." Merika reminisced.

"So you are telling me that you know how to bake? What?" Angela asked.

With a shrug, Merika answered. "The usual. Breads. Cakes. Cookies. Pastries. All sorts of different things, why?"

"Because baking is not my strong point. I mean, I can cook a decent meal, but I am way over my head with what I have to do this time. I never learned to cook for large crowds, it wasn't needed at home where there was only four of us. There are fifteen hundred people who need to be fed daily out there, and I am out of my element, even if I am supposed to be in charge." Angela admitted.

Merika, becoming suddenly more alert and definitely more animated, responded. "I would be more than willing to lend a hand if you want."

"I could care less if you were to say that you were going to take over, just as long as you know what you are doing, and what you are letting yourself in for." Angela admitted.

"I know, and it will be like carrying on my mother's work, so it will make me feel close to her. Now, show me where the supplies are kept, where the pans are, and would someone get me an apron?" Merika talked, as she quickly tied her hair back, while she moved deeper into the kitchen area.

"As you know what makes a kitchen like this run under crowd type conditions, perhaps you should take over." Angela offered up her position, her voice wistful. She was more than willing to admit to her shortcomings, and Merika looked like a way out. She could see to the cooking part, while Merika took over the baking part of the meals and lunches.

It was not to be, however, as Merika just tossed her a smile and replied. "This is your domain, Angela. As the chief talent in your family, your job is to reign as Queen of this kitchen. It would not only be an insult to you and yours for me to take over your position, but the ultimate in poor manners. If you wish, I will offer my support and expertise, such as it is."

"At this point, I will take what I can get." Angela grabbed at the offer.

"Fine, then where do you want me to start?" Merika asked.

"First, I will take you on a tour of the facilities so you know where everything is." Angela offered.

Angela and Merika walked passed the rows of cooking stoves, and rows of pristine countertops. They passed cupboards, filled with pots, pans and utensils. Merika would just nod her approval and move on. There were other rooms, and they were all filled to the ceiling with supplies; things like sugars, salt, flour, spices, assorted fat ingredients, fruits and vegetables. Another room held meats and frozen items. Merika asked about herbs and other stuff and she was taken into the garden area. That area had been given temporary cover to protect it against the encroaching chill of the season.

"I have the evening meal prepared, but we have nothing planned yet for tomorrow. We were going to meet later to set up a menu. It is about as far as we have been able to get in so short a time." Angela brought Merika up to date before adding. "I can cook, but I am the first to admit that I am not much good at organizing. I feel overwhelmed."

"It is called delegating, Angela, and once you get the hang of it, you should be fine." Merika answered Angela.

"Delegating, somehow it seems to sound easier than it probably is," Angela sounded unsure of what she was being told.

"Not really. It is just a matter of noting who best fits in where and putting them to work where their talents are best served. In the meantime, I think we would be smart if we concentrated on getting a head start on things. How many helpers do we have that are knowledgeable and willing to work?" Merika asked. She didn't even think about what she was doing. She had seen her mother do this before, and she followed her example.

"Lots. You were not trained to do what you are able to just because your mother enjoyed it you know. Every girl is expected to be able to take over and run a household when they are of marriageable age. The job of a mother is to make sure her children know what needs doing, when to do it and how." Angela sounded like she was reciting a rule that had been driven into her mind from someone else.

"Nothing like an experienced staff." Merika teased as she voiced her approval, then added. "Now, I will attempt to show you how my mother used to organize these things, then you can take over. I can then start the job that is best suited to me in here. I will begin with the bread products. I will also make pastries, cookies and cakes and the like." Merika offered.

"Are you are sure you have no desire to take over? I really would not mind." Angela assured Merika.

"It would be more than I could handle. I am not my mother." Merika replied.

"Perhaps not, but something tells me you could be, if you wanted to. I know what you said earlier, about your opinions on the matter, but I happen to still believe otherwise. My mother taught me that there is no dishonor in knowing your limitations," Angela admitted.

"Then you should have the chance to discover what your limitations are. I think you have more potential than you give yourself credit for. A little practice will give you the confidence needed to admit this for yourself. Now, to business," Merika ordered, as she got the ball rolling.

Merika set anyone that crossed her path to work, utilizing every scrap of meat that she could find that had already been cooked into stock pots. Within an hour, she had every available pot simmering on the stove elements, and after browning even more meat, she set the beginning of the next batch of food that would be made into soups and stews. When that was seen to, she quickly mixed containers of dough for the pies. She set several helpers to work, rolling out the dough, while she got others to process the fruits that would be needed to fill the crusts. As they finished their initial preparations, Merika took the finished products, and made the sauces that would be needed to join with them, while others were placed in shells. They were so busy with the preparations, that they didn't even notice the passing of time. Before sunrise, they had enough food and baking goods prepared for the next few days.

Sephra put a stop to Merika's burst of energy, as she began setting out more supplies for another round of breads and sweet rolls. It was her intention to make cinnamon rolls and puffed pastry, and she objected to being forced to leave the kitchens.

"I am just beginning to get my second wind. I don't feel tired at all," Merika protested. "Besides, if I leave now, we will fall behind."

"You have dark circles under your eyes. You are pale, and your eyes themselves look too big for your face. I can see, Merika, as well as anyone, and I can tell when someone is overdone. You were allowed out to spend a few hours getting familiar with a part of your new home. You were never meant to exhaust yourself working in the kitchen." Sephra objected.

"I feel close to my mother here, my memories comfort me and I no longer feel alone when I am working. I can nearly feel my mother by my side." Merika explained.

"Maybe so, but your mother would have been the first to tell you that it was time to move on. Now, that said, I will point it out to you that a new set of fresh helpers have just entered the room. You worked through two shifts of such workers, and exhausted the both of them, and you did this despite being tired to begin with. This has gone on long enough. It is time Angela took her proper place, and in case you neglected to notice, she got to sleep last night while you continued to work. You gave her support and confidence when she needed, so she could take over, let her do it." Sephra ordered.

"I am taking nothing away from Angela. She understands that." Merika exclaimed.

"Merika, you are going to go to bed and then you are going to sleep. You are not even going to think about getting up before noon, am I clear on this matter?" Sephra bullied her patient.

"But that is at least seven hours from now!" Merika objected.

"You think this is news to me? Remember, I can keep you out of the kitchen longer if you make me." Sephra nattered at Merika as she herded her out of the kitchen, across the yard, and into the house. She then bullied her into a nightgown and into bed. When she was sure that Merika would remain where she was left, she gave her one last warning before walking out of the room.

"Now go to sleep, if you try to sneak off, I will know."

"What if I am too mentally charged to sleep?" Merika continued to try to worm her way around her hostess.

"Contain it." Sephra returned in a dry tone.

"Sephra, my mind is going a hundred miles an hour." Merika whined.

"Merika, from what I could see in the kitchen, your mind had to have been going a lot faster than that. Your body must have also been keeping pace with your mind because that is the only way you could have prepared all that food in the time you did. What did you intend to do if I would not have pulled you out of the kitchen?" Sephra wondered.

Merika listed off the different kinds of meat rolls, buns, rolls, and puff pastries she had intended to make. She would have added to the list, but. Sephra stopped her, before she got too carried away.

"That is all very good and well, Merika, but for now you need to give the other women time to catch up to you. While you rest, that is their job. Yours is to sleep, so do it." Sephra ordered.

Merika opened her mouth to comment again but Sephra would have none of it. She warned her into silence with a shake of her head and a negative movement of a forefinger. She then turned and left the room, closing the door behind her with a sharp click of finality.

"Sephra is right you know, admit it, you are tired. Nor will you do anyone any good if you allow yourself to get run down." A familiar male voice entered Merika's mind, as it had before, and she frowned in irritation. She had thought that the blocks that she had erected earlier would have been enough to keep whomever this was out of her mind.

As the thought flicked through her brain, the male voice returned with an explanation. "As I said earlier, you are tired, this is why your guards are weak. As for not being able to settle your mind down enough to sleep, I can help you with that."

"Who are you?" Not knowing who was in her mind, really

bothered Merika.

"A friend?" The male voice replied, sounding a little hopeful, a little uncertain. "Either way, I am the one who is willing to give you a helping hand at this time. So, I would suggest you get used to hearing from me. At least until you find your own way. Good night, Merika, have a good restful sleep."

CHAPTER VII

Eight hours later, Merika woke up. It was afternoon and she could hardly believe she had slept so long. What had that horrid person done to her to make her crash as she did? She had fallen asleep so quickly and hard that she could not even remember putting her head onto the pillow. She rose, washed, dressed and went straight out to the kitchen, where Serena was quick to join her.

"You need something to eat, Merika," Serena nagged, getting only a frown back in reply as Merika almost seemed to be making an effort to ignore her. Merika added ingredients to a massive bowl and made short work of mixing it. She then put a cover over the mix and pushed it into a lineup of five others just like it.

Merika mixed another twenty bowls of dough before she turned her attention to Serena, but not before Serena had gotten irritated.

"You are ignoring me, Merika and it will not work. You need something in your stomach."

"Just give me time to finish the first stages of what I am doing here, Serena and I promise to take time to eat something. Just to humor you."

Serena, having procured a promise to comply with her order, left, and Merika continued to make up batters for cakes. Nor did she stop until every pan in the place was filled. As she bustled around, Merika sipped on tea and grabbed a cup of thick broth that was all the time she seemed to think she had to indulge in a meal.

Over the next twenty-four hours Merika worked almost non stop. The cakes were baked, the breads and buns were finished off, she had set others to the task of doing the glazing and mixed enough sweets and cookies to supply a small city. The ovens never seemed to get turned off as platters and pans were switched and refilled, and each time someone was sent to take her back to the house, she was missing. A few times, she had been so deep in a recipe that was fussy and could not be interrupted that whomever had come eventually just gave up. After all, they too, had chores to do.

Angela eventually took up Merika's obsession as a personal challenge and pushed to match her efforts in her area of expertise. It turned into a good-natured contest of wills and the kitchen rang with teasing and laughter. Nobody who worked under that roof was exempt from the jokes and banter that resulted, and it became the place to be; although, the girls never allowed the room to get too crowded. They did, after all, still need to get their work done.

Sephra feeling that Serena's efforts were proving futile, stepped in to exercise her control over the situation, but she soon found herself powerless against the combined powers. Angela only smiled as she nagged at Merika, and Merika seemed only to ignore her and seemed even more determined in her efforts.

Eventually, frustrated with the whole scenario, Sephra approached Kodac with the problem. After all, he was the only one she could think of with the power and authority to make the girl toe the line. He was the Valley Alpha Prime.

"Neither will listen to me," Sephra explained her exasperation apparent. "Serena says she is positive that Angela has been sleeping, but she doubts if Merika has stopped in over seventy two hours. She says she is about ready to collapse but is too stubborn to quit."

Kodac smiled, amused by Sephra's frustration over the young woman's over zealous high spirits. Merika was definitely proving to be a handful. He did understand the problem. Merika had exhibited signs of willfulness right from the start and now her attitude was beginning to spread. In his opinion, Merika needed a guiding, if not controlling hand. To clarify a suspicion of his that this was something that was being undertaken, he asked.

"Has Merika said anything to you about questions she might have concerning a voice speaking to her in her mind?"

"Merika seldom talks other than what she feels need saying to accomplish her goal, that kitchen has become more than just an obsession. I mean I realize that it is her way of dealing with the loss of her mother, but it is overdone. If there is someone out there trying to give her advice she is paying little or no attention to them."

Kodac frowned and closed his eyes as he sent a question to his son. "Tyrus, have you spoken to Merika in the last few days?"

"I tried a couple of times, but she ignored me. I could feel her push me aside in her mind." Tyrus's reply came back to his father voicing his irritation. "That female is more trouble than she is worth and I am busy with other important matters. I have no time for a spoiled petulant child."

"Call her what you want son, but I know you think more of her than that, otherwise you would never have held onto the mind focus you established when you tamed the storm within her." As there was no comment forthcoming, Kodac began by explaining what was going on. "Merika took one look at the kitchens and, in a fit of memory of her mother, she decided to lend a hand. Within hours, she had everything organized, and had turned the place into a beehive of activity. If I were to see how much she has accomplished, I would be willing to bet that she has enough food prepared to feed this crowd for a week."

"She did this all by herself?"

"By bullying those about her to help in the preparations, yes, basically; however, the more important work was done by her own hands. Angela was the other force to reckon with, but Merika gave her a crash course on how to put things together before she was effective."

"And you are contacting me because?"

"We need your help. She is like a woman possessed. She has not slept, eaten or rested in days, and by that I mean days and nights."

"I can hardly say I am surprised. So what do you think I can do?"

"I need you here to create a stabilizing base for her. Someone to ground her and shift her focus."

"No can do father, and not because I am just busy with matters at hand. What you are suggesting is tantamount to playing with fire, not a good idea at the best of times. We all have our priorities. I cannot take the time it would take to travel there and see to the problem as it should be done. I just cannot justify it."

"You have the time if you decide you want it, you know that. To begin with, you are only an hour walk away from here, less if you use your horse, and less yet if you utilize your powers."

"Remember? Power has its price? Admit it father, she might be a pretty piece of work, but who is to say she is worth the effort in the long run."

"It was not so long ago you seemed to think otherwise."

"That was different, I was impressed by the amount of power she could command as a female."

"She commands a great force, even if she were a man rather than a woman."

"I am aware of that."

"I bet you are, just as I am willing to lay odds that you have taken the effort to pass on advise to her since, from time to time, albeit in a telepathic fashion. She does have meaning to you."

"Father, I would not leave anyone or anything as lost as she was to face an uncertain future. She has obviously managed to land on her feet, as any good cat is apt to do. Let her live and learn her limitations on her own. I repeat father, I have work to do."

"If that is your final word, son you just go ahead and tend to whatever it is that you are doing that is so much more important. I will see to Merika myself."

Kodac was in a fury and he blamed it all on his idiot son. The boy had the jump on all the other men when it came to Merika, and whether he appreciated her or not, she was a prize. He growled as he stormed out of his makeshift home. He would teach his son he could do just as well without him. His sons might not be interested enough in her to rouse themselves, but others would be more than pleased to be given the opportunity to secure her. Just see how happy Tyrus would be to see her surrounded by appropriate suitors. He was about to open the field and let the cards fall where they would.

It had been different with his other son, Kodac reflected. Rodan had made his choice of bride known to him as soon as the lad had made it. Rodan had to admit he had been more than pleased when he had learned whom he had picked. Serena had further cemented his opinion that she was right for his younger son by putting him firmly in his place. She had then turned her nose up at the boy and walked away. Rodan had not believed she could be serious, after all, how could she have rejected him when he was all that was charming, and more than a little handsome.

In retaliation, Rodan had decided to make her jealous. Kodac could have told his son that it would never have worked with a girl like Serena. She knew the way men thought too well, after all she did have nine brothers. All things considered, it amused him to watch his debonair offspring make a fool of himself. He never doubted that Serena would eventually take matters into her own hands and whip the lad into line and, he was quite sure, together the young couple would form a solid family unit.

Walking into the kitchen, Kodac snarled out Merika's name as a warning of his presence and intentions, mere seconds before he grabbed her wrist and dragged her out of the building.

"Merika, you are hereby banned from this area. You will eat, sleep and mix with the other members of our company your own age or thereabouts, and you will do it in that order. It is time you made the effort to become a proper member of the community."

"You cannot make me do any of that," Merika snapped back, though the picture she made belied the words as she trailed flour from a mixture she had been working on when he had interrupted. "I am needed here."

"You are needed in several places, not just here. Life is meant for more than just working yourself to death. As for being needed here, the ladies will get over your short absence. As far as not being able to enforce it, just try me."

"But why?"

"Because you have not eaten properly or slept for three days. Now when you are able to exhibit signs that you can show more sense than that to me and prove that you can control your actions, you will be allowed to return to your work. In any case, you will not return here for at least a week."

"I was enjoying myself." Merika retorted.

Kodac was not in a mood to listen to any of her arguments. "You may like what you are doing but you are in need of a break. Everyone does from time to time."

"I refuse to listen to you. You have no authority over me."

"Enough, Merika, you will cease to act like a spoiled and petulant child. You will either begin to listen to Sephra or I will take charge of you myself, and I can, never doubt that."

"That is not fair!" Merika wailed.

"You refuse to listen to advise from any quarter, where it is given in person or telepathically. You ignore the good intensions of the people around you. Girl, you reap what you sow." By that point, they had reached the front door of Sephra's house. He just opened the door without knocking and pushed her through, he followed and wagging a forefinger at her, warned. "If I hear that you have not followed my instructions to the letter, I will take action and believe me I will know whether you have or not. You have my promise. Now. You are going to sit down, eat, then go to sleep. You will not fight me on this young lady, because, I have more than enough power at my command to make you sorry that you tried."

Feeling he had successfully made his point, he turned and left the house, slamming the door behind him as he did.

Merika watched him leave, then heaved a sigh of combined relief and resignation. She had to admit he was at least somewhat right, though not in all regards. She had been making friends. Sure, they were all female but one had to start somewhere, and she had connected. Unfortunately, he was quite right about her being tired, though she had not noticed earlier. It was then that she realized that she must have been running on sheer adrenaline. Her state of hunger was also being brought home to her by the smell of warm food as Angela and Serena entered the room bearing trays. She noted the plate settings and smiled.

"I guess I kind of overdid it. That smells so good, whatever it is."

The two girls just looked at each other and laughed. "We thought that one of the last things you would want to do about now would be to eat alone."

"Or eat something that you had to make for yourself. Sometimes a person can cook so much that they lose their appetite. No matter how good the food would be, it would still taste like sawdust."

"So tell us, what have you discovered during your brief obsession with our kitchen?"

The girls all took their places as they spoke and helped themselves to plates of food, with Merika voicing her gratitude for their thoughtfulness.

"I am so happy you decided to join me. I hate to eat alone, it is something I have done too often in the past."

"That is sad, nobody likes to eat alone."

"So, like I asked," Angela asked as she pushed her for more involvement. "What have you noticed about our little crew? Especially what do you think of Cinnamon? You realize she hero worships you?"

"We will just have to find a diversion for her then. I had enough people fawning over me at work. Promise me that it will be someone who appreciates her though, she is a good kid."

"Notice how well she can lay out those sweet rolls?"

"Nor have I seen anyone named as well. Her hair is the color of cinnamon, her eyes have that hue, she smells like spice, which could be because of her specialty."

"She even sounds rich and spicy, almost like one might imagine cinnamon would. It is uncanny!"

"She is so sweet though, you have to like her."

"I know. Now the big question is, who would make the perfect match for her."

Serena considered the choices for a moment then made her pick. "Dom."

"Really?" Angela sounded surprised. "I was thinking more along the line of Lucas."

Tara walked into the room and, seeing the assortment of food stuffs set out, sat down and joined them, grabbing a bowl of soup and a cup of tea as she did.

Angela just shook her head at her and teased. "Eating again. No wonder you are getting bigger and bigger about the middle."

Tara just tossed her a smile and preened as she patted her stomach, then reached for a slice of bread as she replied. "You are just jealous. So who are we plotting to match today?"

"Cinnamon," Merika chuckled. "Serena thinks her perfect for Dom and Angela has set her bet on Lucas."

"I like her and either man would suit, though Lucas might be a little immature for her. So who is next on the list?"

Angela gave a wicked giggle as she teased, "Merika."

"That would be easy," Serena put it. "It would have to be Tyrus."

"Tyrus!" Tara wrinkled her nose in distaste. "I thought you said you liked Merika. Tyrus is as mean as a rattlesnake and twice as moody."

"Nothing a woman's touch could not cure." Angela said as she wiggled her eyebrows suggestively.

Merika tossed Serena a puzzled look and she, in return, shrugged a shoulder. The exchange caused Angela and Tara to burst out laughing. When the two women had finished having their laugh, Angela gasped out.

"Never mind girls, you will figure out what we are talking about when your times comes."

"Having acted in a soap opera, I can well imagine what you are talking about." Merika defended herself.

"And having nine brothers and a small talent for medicine, I am not totally in the dark either. We know about the physical relationship that goes on between a man and woman." Serena sniffed.

"Just not the emotional ramifications," Tara continued to tease and burst into laughter again, tears beginning to run down her face.

Merika just chuckled and tossed back a flip remark. "Cure or not, we are all in agreement, the thought of Tyrus and I as a couple is definitely worth a laugh."

"Tyrus with any woman is worth a laugh. I think he is inclined towards other areas, though I can only speculate. My knowledge of him is only flighty at best." Tara smirked.

"Meow," Serena tossed back, still thinking she had the right of it. "You mean your experience with him was flighty, not anything else. He would have nothing of it so you are still miffed."

"Do I look miffed?" Tara replied in rebuttal, her mood still high. "As for having nothing to do with me, he refuses to have anything to do with any girl. He is the safest man to be with in the valley. Even if he liked you as a friend, he would never think to move on it."

"So who do you fancy for our fair Merika then?"

"Tudor would make her an interesting mate, but he has not come. So of the men here, I would have to say Rodan."

"Not if my life depended on it." Merika blurted out her rejection. "He is Serena's."

"Mine!" Serena squeaked and flipped back a retort. "Rodan is too busy looking at himself in the mirror to hold any proper female notice for long."

"So talks one who feels neglected," Tara taunted. "He was definitely not looking in the mirror when I noticed. Ever pay attention to how he looks at our lovely Serena, Angela?"

Both Tara and Angela fanned themselves as if they were trying to cool themselves down at the memory as Angela replied. "Of course I have. It is one of the main reasons I think we are having such a warm week so far."

"I had not thought the weather that warm, " Merika replied as she rose to defend her friend from more embarrassment, as Serena appeared more indignant than amused. It just proved to her just how serious it was between the two of them in her estimation.

The conversation turned to other mutual acquaintances after that and for the next several hours the girls continued to gossip, match and tease each other. That was until Sephra walked into the house and put a stop to it. She sent Angela out to the kitchen, ordered Serena to set up for the evening meal, and told Tara to escort Merika to bed and to make sure she not only got to her destination, but went to sleep. Before they all scattered, however, she promised them all that they could have another session like the one they had just had, but in the mid morning when she would have time to join them. The girls just looked at one another and smiled. Considering how well Sephra seemed to know everyone in the Valley, they thought it should be an interesting session indeed.

CHAPTER VIII

It was well past noon before Merika woke the next day, so there had been no get together, like there had been the day before. She dressed, and was almost finished a light lunch, when the other girls of the household rushed into the house. They were all animated and were quite excited, and definitely willing to share their news with her.

"Have we got our work cut out for us, Merika." Angela blurted, as she rushed to her side and sat down. "We are going to have to bake and cook, to get things ready for a banquet. Kodac told me not to make it too fancy, but we both know what is about to happen."

"He banned me from the kitchen, remember?" Merika reminded everyone.

"Well, it looks like has he changed his mind. I told him I needed you. That there was no way on earth I could do what needs to be done in time, without you. There are so many people expected I don't know where to begin, and we only have a few weeks to prepare. Sephra is in even more of a flurry." Angela reported.

As Angela seemed to be in such a rush to fill her in on the news, Merika caught only a portion of what she was saying. She realized that whatever was about to happen meant a lot of work, and that there was a difference of opinion as to how elaborate the menu for a banquet should be. But, beyond that, she was lost and sought clarity.

"Slow down. Now from the beginning, and just tell me what I need to know, starting with what are we to get ready for."

"We are hosting a gathering, something we have never done before. I am not sure how many people will be coming, but I assume there will be about twenty thousand at the affair. Kodac has called a formal high power gathering of all the foremost families in the valley," Angela announced, through her excitement.

"And he told you not to make the meal too fancy! Typical male," Came Merika's dry retort, while a male voice popped into her head.

"Hey, I heard that one."

Merika suppressed a grin, as she ignored whomever it was, and addressed the assembly before her. "So fill me in. Time and place."

"Details in brief you mean," Serena piped in. "The place is here, the numbers are much the same as you heard earlier. The time is in two weeks from now and, out of necessity, it will be quite elaborate, which is what Kodac had hoped to avoid. What makes it an impossibility, is that he has also announced a formal ball for the same evening. Is that the kind of information you were looking for?"

"Pretty much," came Merika's reply. "All the elite of the Valley?"

"Even Tyrus, though considering how anti social he is, I doubt if the prig will even show, and that will really tick his father off. Though the party is not for him. It is for us," Tara added smugly.

"Immaterial either way," Merika could not have been any less interested in Tyrus, as her mind focused on the task before them. They had less than two weeks to prepare for a banquet for a mass of humanity, while still feeding the crowds that were living in the clearing on a daily basis. This task would have been daunting, even for her mother, and Teryka would have known better what she was getting herself into.

"Well ladies," Merika decided that the sooner they got the ball rolling the better off they would be. "We have been issued a challenge. Shall we prove to the Lord and Master Kodac that we are more than capable of rising to the occasion?"

"Not much choice in the matter, is there? The invitations have already been sent out and, the responses are pouring in as fast as Kodac can receive them." Angela sighed in resignation. "I am so over my head, I can never hope to organize this by myself. I am lucky you are here to pitch in."

"As to feeling as if you are out of your depth, move over. We are both in the same boat, lets hope it stays afloat. Now, we need a pen and several sheets of paper. We are going to have to make up several lists of things we have to make. As luck would have it there will be no soups, stews or anything else of that nature, because people are going to have to stand to eat. There is no way we will be able to find enough tables and chairs to accommodate everybody." Merika pointed out.

Even with all the younger women contributing ideas, it still took a couple of hours, before they felt they had a reasonable list of dishes drawn up. They left the house armed with lists, and a determination to see what needed to be done. It was going to be a long, long, two weeks.

Two days short of their deadline, Merika announced that they were ready and, to the surprise of everybody, she left the kitchens voluntarily. She was exhausted. For almost two weeks, she had spent eighteen to nineteen hours a day baking, and she was heartily sick of it. With an uncharacteristic dragging of her feet, she made her way to her bed. When she found she seemed too tired to sleep, she reached for the male's voice that was often in her mind seeking help with her problem. Within moments, she was fast asleep, feeling a deep sense of comfort inside. She spent the next day and a half sleeping, waking only to see to her immediate needs, and grab the occasional sandwich.

The opening day of the event dawned as if in anticipation of the events to follow, and it looked as if it was going to be a perfect day, not too hot, not too cold. A day made to order. Kodac was quick to make his presence known soon after he noticed activity in the kitchen. He looked around at the pristine room, empty except for Merika, who was busily filling puffed mini horns with whipped cream, before placing them on huge serving platters. She had dainties stacked to the rafters, and he wondered how long she had been working to prepare them for consumption.

"Have you been working twenty four, seven again?" Kodac asked.

Merika was surprised at the concern in Kodac's voice, and she shook her head, to indicate that she hadn't. "In the beginning, we settled for five to six hours of sleep a night, but eventually I had to give in. I took a day off. I returned less than an hour ago."

"The birds are just beginning to wake up," Kodac teased amicably.

"They are late, the worm is already gone," Merika joked back, and then smiled as Kodac threw back his head and laughed.

"Perhaps I can give you a hand with those, they look simple enough for me to handle," Kodac offered.

"Mother used to say that most things to do with food processing was. She was so good at it," Merika remembered.

"Your mother was one of the few people I knew that seemed to have it all, beauty, talent, and generosity of spirit. When she fell in love, she fell hard. Your parents were so in love, so happy together, and you were to be the frosting on their cake. When your father died so suddenly, it broke her heart, but not her spirit. I often wondered if she found another she could love, in the outside world. In fact, I hoped she had. She had so much to offer." Kodac told Merika.

"No. Mom surrounded herself with her work and, although she

never mentioned it, memories of the love she had shared with my father. I always missed having a father. She never talked about him, and I understood how much she was hurting deep inside. I remember catching her crying, from time to time, over an old picture. I didn't tell her that I used to sneak that photograph out, so I could see what my father looked like too. He was a very handsome man, but from the look in his eyes, I would say that wasn't what attracted her to him." Merika shared her thoughts with Kodac.

The two talked as they worked, Kodac filling Merika in on her mother's formative years, while they filled the puffed cones. Merika continued to work, as she whipped more cream filling when needed, and helped him when she was free. By the time others began to arrive, they already had several different entrees finished and were involved in pulling more out of the cold rooms, where some space was slowly beginning to open up.

"I never realized how much work I had placed on your slim shoulders." Kodac admitted.

Merika just smiled at Kodac and teased back. "Well, next time you throw a party, you could tone down the guest list a little. The clearing is going to be bursting at the seams."

"I will keep that in mind." Kodac replied, as he smiled back and, taking her hand in his, he raised it to his lips to kiss the back. "My compliments to a lady who does honor to her mother in every way possible. She would be proud of you if she were here."

Looking suddenly melancholy, and very serious, Merika replied, "You give me too much credit. Angela did the hardest parts, and her job has yet to be tackled for the day."

"Will you girls be too tired to enjoy the ball?" Kodac wondered.

"We may be tired when we are finished, but we will find the

energy to enjoy ourselves." Merika assured Kodac.

Kodac left muttering to himself, about sons who didn't know a good thing when they saw it. Seven hours later, he watched, as Merika and Angela inspected the rows of tables that were filled to bursting with foodstuffs. He watched, as Sephra approached them, and smiled as the two girls turned at her order to march straight to the house. Angela, he decided, would be rewarded as was appropriate for her efforts, but Merika, he decided needed something special and he knew just what he was going to give her. She was the undisputed female Alpha of the valley. She deserved the status symbol that went with it. The only thing he hoped that he could give her yet, was the chief Alpha male in the Valley, his son, Tyrus. He could almost envision the children they would create. Beautiful, fair, and talented, their children would be the pride and joy of any grandparent. Now, if he could only convince the two to get together, so his grandchildren had a chance to be conceived, he would feel complete.

CHAPTER IX

With more than three hours to fill in before the beginning of the ball, Merika decided to take a little nap, instead of mingling with the burgeoning crowds. She decided that when she woke, she would create a gown with enough style and grace to make Kodac proud he knew her. In some ways, she felt she had made a special friend, one who had known both of her parents, and he had given her a taste of what it might have been like to have a father. She owed him something.

Right on time, Merika walked out of the house to join the crowds. It was a warm evening with only the slightest of breeze. The sky was clear, with no signs of clouds on the horizon, and she had to wonder if Kodac had been manipulating the weather. She knew he was capable of doing it, if he figured it was necessary, but to her knowledge, he hadn't.

Kodac had been watching for Merika to make her appearance and, when she did, a huge smile of approval spread across his face. She had dressed in a royal blue satin organdy gown, and it made her look like a queen, from out of a fairy tale. The bodice was snug, as it probably had to be to stay up without straps, leaving her shoulders and arms bare. She wore matching gloves, and a four-inch belt, which crossed in front of an impossibly tiny looking waist. From there the skirt of the gown belled out, to float airily about her. A diamond and sapphire necklace, which would have made most society butterflies jealous, encircled her neck to flash against her exposed skin, while matching earrings hung from the perfect lobes of her ears. Her hair had been left to flow loose down her back, except for a piece that had been braided to form a coronet on the top of her head.

Merika walked straight up to Kodac, and gave him a dazzling smile, as she dropped a slight curtsy and sought his opinion. "Am I too dressed up? Or is this good?"

Kodac smiled back as he replied. "You are perfect, the other girls will be dressed much as you are, in an assortment of styles and colors. You have chosen well. In the meantime, I have something for you." With a twist of his wrists, and a flick of his fingers, a three-banded hairpiece appeared in his hands. "As the female Alpha of the Valley, this is yours to wear."

Merika took in the sight of the diamond encrusted hair ornament, and her eyes grew large. "Are you sure that is meant for me?"

"Well, it may not hold a candle to your own jewels, but yes, it is for you. It also means a great deal to us," Kodac informed Merika.

The three bands opened at the top and, were held together on either side of the head, where they would be secured into the hair and when Kodac placed it onto Merika's head they made three small lines of sparkling stones that threaded across from one side of her head to the other.

Kodac stepped back to admire the picture she made and smiled his approval as he hid his thoughts. 'Now to find a way to make her my daughter.' To Merika, he spoke aloud, "Now, go child, enjoy yourself, and dance until the sun rises tomorrow."

At her dismissal, Merika curtsied, and in turning, caught sight of Serena, who was surrounded by a ring of young suitors. Serena motioned for her to join them, and Merika made her way over to her friend. As she walked, it seemed that the crowds parted before her, as if by magic. People watched as she moved as she passed, and they all said the same words. "Alpha Prime." It made her feel like a peach set out for display and sale, although she knew that was not the case. She knew she shouldn't have felt awkward at the attention, for as a successful actress she had garnered crowds wherever she had gone. This, however, seemed somehow different. More real.

"My friend and, the newest member of our community, Merika. By the looks of it, she is also our new female Alpha Prime. Merika, allow me to introduce my friends. Glorianna, Seth, Marla, and Toni."

"Your gown is breathtaking, Merika," the girl called Marla spoke.

"So is yours," Merika returned the compliment. "Everyone is so beautiful. Are all the people so well endowed? I have yet to see anyone who is less that what would be considered drop dead gorgeous here."

"In various degrees, we are known to be an attractive race," Glorianna replied.

The ring of young, attractive and unattached ladies soon began to attract more attention as a few of the young men bore down on them. Within moments, they were surrounded. Each man vied for attention, hoping to catch the eye of one of the inner circle and, for a whole hour before the strains of the first waltz sounded, they were introduced to so many people that none of them could hope to remember all the names.

The girls made their way to the edges of the dance floor, where all but Merika soon were claimed for a dance. When Kodac noticed her standing alone, watching the whirling couples, he decided to investigate.

"Why are you are not dancing, Merika?" Kodac spoke as he reached her side. "Surely you have been asked."

"I have been asked," Merika confirmed, "but not by the right man. I remember mother speaking of the great gatherings. She told me that when the Valley Alpha was in attendance the female Alpha Prime danced with no one, until he opened the festivities by leading her to the floor."

"I must admit I had forgotten that archaic little tidbit. Come,

Merika," Kodac held out his hand for hers. "Shall we show them how it is done?"

"Mother had me take lessons for years. I have forgotten nothing." Merika assured Kodac.

With that, they took their places on the floor and began to dance. They made an attractive pair, despite looking like father and daughter, and by the time the set was over another man approached to take his place. The two men bowed slightly to each other, in acknowledgment, and Kodac made a quick introduction, as he offered up his partner's hand.

"Merika, Tudor. Tudor, Merika." Kodac then left and the young couple swung into the next dance.

Merika suppressed a gasp as a spark of power shot out between them, and Tudor chuckled at her obvious surprise. He explained the phenomena, as he led her smoothly around the floor. "What you felt is the connecting of two major powers. I am the male Alpha of my region. As you are a female Alpha, we are bound to strike sparks off of each other."

Merika tossed Tudor a small smile, and offered no comeback. She was not about to give him an excuse to think she might welcome his advances. She didn't know why she felt the need to keep a distance between them, but she did. She studied his face and although it showcased a combination of good looks, charm, confidence and good humor, she found she wasn't attracted to him. There was something about his eyes that told her that under the veneer of his attractive appearance, he was an arrogant, macho male. The combination was possibly a good one, but not for her.

They made a good-looking pair and Tudor knew it. Together, Merika and he were like two sides of a coin. He was darkly, handsome and virile, the epitome of what every Alpha male should be, and she was so fair and ethereal in appearance that they could not help but compliment one another.

Looking pleased, despite the fact that Merika had refused to respond to his subtle overtures, Tudor continued to add up the reasons she would not be able to resist him. He was, after all, a man who knew his worth, a man of experience who was quite familiar with the effect his body had on most women. He could not begin to count how many women had told him that the aura he exhibited was so compelling that it made them feel weak in the knees. In his mind, she was already his, and he considered it lucky that she had more than only power to offer the relationship. She was a lot more beautiful than the average girl.

Merika was familiar with men like the man she now waltzed with. She could tell by the smug self-satisfied grin on his face, that he felt as if he was being successful as he tried to charm her. In show business, men like him were a dime a dozen. Men like him thought they were irresistible, that no woman could resist them. That all they needed to do was show up on a scene and the women would be grateful he had taken time to notice them.

In her experience, most men like Tudor found the dating game just that, a game. The ultimate goal, was to see how many women they could get to fall into their bed. Merika knew that he would be well aware that she was not the kind of girl that would fall for something like that. She was the kind of girl men wanted to marry, and the idea of marriage to someone like him scared her.

Being the type to run, rather than be caught with someone she was sure was wrong for her, Merika wondered how someone like Tudor would react to her rejection. He struck her as being a man who thought that all he had to do, when he made a choice of wife, would be to crook his little finger and the girl he chose would swoon at the honor she had been bestowed. Not her idea of anything that smacked of reality.

"I have heard many accounts of your multiple talents, Merika, I am intrigued. Why is it that no one has ever heard of you before?" Tudor wondered.

Merika looked up at the Cheshire expression on Tudor's face, and frowned. He looked as if the thought that she might be not all that attracted to him was inconceivable. He was due for a surprise. Her instincts warned her off from him and she always listened to her instincts.

When Merika remained quiet, Tudor poured a bit more effort into his smile and crooned. "Do you know I could feel your power all the way to the center of the Valley? The strength of your storm must have attracted the notice of every Alpha in the Valley, it was so clear. When you were pointed out to me, soon after I arrived, I could barely believe my eyes. Your beauty is but an extension of that power. Very, very, impressive."

With a sigh of exasperation Merika retorted, "Save it, Tudor, I am not buying." The more time she spent encircled within the confines of his arms, the more she knew this was not where she wanted to be. She might have to be cordial to him, but she didn't have to like him, or cater to his ego. She tried to be polite, but the sudden distaste she felt for him made it difficult. There was something very wrong about the vibes she was getting from him, and it was beginning to scare her. He was acting much too possessive, and sure of himself for her peace of mind.

"So who says I am selling." Tudor purred, as he pulled Merika closer, to rest a cheek against the side of her head. "You are so light and fragile. It makes a man feel so very powerful."

The dance came to an end, and Merika stepped back to drop a small curtsy. Tudor bowed, then offered her his arm, as if to escort her from the floor. She realized what she was about to do was rude, but didn't care by this point. She needed to get away from him. She turned away from him and flashed a great smile of invitation at Daffyd, knowing he would catch the hint, and not misinterpret her meaning. He caught the unspoken message, and quickly rushed to her aide.

"I believe this is my dance, am I right?" Daffyd asked Merika.

"As rain, Daffyd," Merika purred, as she took his hand, and allowed him to waltz off with her.

Taking one look at the besotted look on Daffyd's face made her feel guilty, and it must have shown on her, because he tossed her a lopsided grin as he replied.

"The look is for effect, so Tudor doesn't get the wrong impression. A man would have to be blind, as well as stupid, not to realize that you needed help. Tudor had no intention of letting you walk away from him. I am so pleased you chose me to play the role of knight gallant."

"Daffyd, I am honored you came to my rescue. You are like a brother, always there to rescue me when needed," Merika confessed.

"You could do me the honor of allowing me a few illusions, fleeting though they may be." Daffyd teased.

Merika sparkled as she smiled up at him, and he gave a mock groan as he continued to tease. "Oh yes, keep it up, I love this. I feel like the most sought after man at the party. What do you think my prospects are going to be after this?"

Merika threw her head back a bit, and laughed in response as she replied, "Some girl is going to be so lucky to be your choice for wife. I hope she is wise enough to realize it."

"If she doesn't, I am sure that you will point it out to her for me,"

Daffyd continued.

"You can count on it." This time their laughter was shared, nor did it go unnoticed amidst the crowd, although the general consensus was, that due to their massive difference of power levels, they would be ill matched. They were content to consider themselves good friends, something that made Daffyd suddenly appear much more desirable to the other young ladies.

Tyrus stood beside his brother, as he watched Merika with ill concealed admiration. She didn't act the part of the belle of the ball, nor was she, but she did not lack for partners. Her grace and beauty made her popular, and the flashing diamonds in her hair proclaimed her position. She seemed to have it all, but she did not abuse the advantage it gave her. In fact, he had to wonder if she found the attention irritating.

"Merika cuts a fine figure." Rodan spoke, as she flashed by them, encircled in the arms of a middle-aged man.

It looked as if the man Merika was dancing with was trying to tell her something, and she was ignoring what he was saying. So typical, Tyrus thought. She was good at that.

"If I remember correctly, I did mention that Merika would fall on her feet like any other decent cat," Tyrus stated.

"Merika has been remarkable. Tudor took to the floor with her earlier in the evening." Rodan informed Tyrus.

"Really?" How did that go?" Tyrus asked.

"To be honest, I have a suspicion that he was not as pleased with the results as he could have been. You know how Tudor feels about himself, and how irresistible he thinks he is to women." Rodan snickered.

"So?" Tyrus pressed.

"So Merika seemed not so impressed. He still looks as if he is trying to figure out what went wrong." Rodan grinned, as he looked over to where Tudor was standing. That man was watching as Merika danced, and he was wearing a frown.

Tyrus gave a bark of laughter, then in a bit of curiosity, asked. "So, who has she seemed to really take a shine to so far?"

"Daffyd," Rodan remarked.

"He is too weak for her, it would never mesh." Tyrus decided.

"It took everyone a whole half a minute to figure that one out. It has made him an icon amongst the other females though." Rodan pointed out.

"How has he taken to that idea?" Tyrus wondered.

"He seems to like it actually." Rodan chuckled.

"Good for him. Personally, I always thought icons were overrated." Tyrus sniffed.

"How would you know?" Rodan teased.

"From watching people like our new Alpha Prime," Tyrus answered.

"I don't know about that, I think Merika seems to be able to handle it well enough," Rodan hummed thoughtfully.

"Unless she is being pressed to do something she doesn't want to do. Watch. Tudor has decided to move in for the kill. Which reminds me. How are you making out with your efforts with Serena, my smitten baby brother?" Tyrus teased.

"You can call me smitten, when all we do is stand here and talk about Merika? From what I see, that is the pot calling the kettle black if I ever heard of it." Rodan teased back.

"The girl intrigues me, but not to the point of lunacy. Now back to Serena." Tyrus informed Rodan.

"Have you ever heard the word spurned? It seems like the more I try, the more ground I lose." Rodan admitted.

"Maybe you are going about it the wrong way." Tyrus suggested.

"Perhaps. It is a thought. Maybe I should speak to someone who knows more about women." Rodan considered.

"I would be more than happy to offer my vast well of experiences." Tyrus offered.

"I was thinking of someone with a less bigoted opinion of the weaker sex. I want to marry the girl, not drive her off." Rodan confessed.

"You think I cannot be rational when it comes to women?" Rodan sounded offended.

"You are smart brother, no doubt about it. But when it comes to women, you are operating with shutters. I honestly doubt if you have the experience you pretend to have. Your mother sure left a poor impression on you. If she wanted you to be single and bitter for the rest of your life, she has been more successful," Rodan stated.

As Rodan and Tyrus concentrated on their conversation, and ignored everything else that was going on around them, the air seemed to suddenly crackle, and Rodan's eyes rounded. "What was that?"

Tyrus grinned in amusement and replied, "That is Merika."

Rodan turned to watch, as Tudor took Merika into his arms, against her will, and began to waltz off with her. She had been forced to abandon the young man who had just offered to partner her for this dance and Merika did not looked very pleased about leaving him behind. Tudor, Rodan thought, should have known better.

Tudor had made several errors, in Merika's eyes. He had physically pushed the young man who had just asked for this dance from her. He had not asked her if the interruption was ill timed, or whether she even wanted to dance with him again. Worse, he showed no signs of conscience about what he had done.

Now, Tudor was holding her too tightly, and too close and Merika resented it. She was not feeling comfortable with his actions, or in his presence, and she hated the way he was looking at her. He made her feel like a possession. She did not feel as if he respected her, and knew that life with him would be one of being controlled. She was not going to let that happen, no matter how sure he was of himself. She wanted a man who felt empathy with those who surrounded him, and would love her for herself. She didn't want someone who wanted her for what she looked like, or for her talents. She was not someone to show off some man's finer points. She had been raised to think that a woman stood at her man's side, as a cherished partner. Tudor, she was sure, was too much of a bully to understand what she would be talking about, if she ever tried to explain it. The way he was acting towards her at this moment, she was afraid he might try to force the issue with her.

Tudor was having trouble believing the subtle messages he was getting from Merika. She acted as if she wasn't attracted to him! It was ludicrous! All women loved him and wanted him. They thought he was one of the most handsome men in the valley. There had to be something wrong with her, although she looked normal enough. He gave it a moment more thought, then decided that she had to be normal, otherwise she would not be the Alpha Prime. So what was wrong with her? Maybe she was not reading him right? Maybe he needed to be more direct.

One minute, Tudor seemed to be giving Merika the impression that he was having trouble figuring out whatever it was that he was thinking about her, as they waltzed. The next minute, his eyes darkened, as he stopped halfway through a turn to suddenly pull her tightly against him, and he kissed her. Merika, could not have been more shocked. She had expected him to do something. But not this!

There was something about Merika that made Tudor feel strong and very masculine. She was so petite and feminine. His mouth closed over hers and, he felt the softness of her lips, smelled the clean sweetness that clung to her, and tasted her. She inflamed him, and he cupped the back of her head with a hand as he pulled her closer with an arm.

This was not going to happen! Merika was not going to allow Tudor dominate her like this! How dare he think she could be manipulated in such a primitive way? The air crackled around them, and she squirmed for release.

"Damn," Tyrus muttered, as he raced towards the dance floor. Rodan was hot on his heels. Kodac also ran to intercept what could become a catastrophe. Surely Tudor knew better than to try to force his attention on a woman who wanted nothing to do with him, especially one with the power potential that Merika had shown.

Tudor stepped back as he felt a burning shock of sheer electricity shoot through him, and he looked into the fair face of the woman he had just kissed. There was no sign of passion in those blue diamond eyes; there was sheer fury. He backed away from her, sensing further danger, and he could tell that danger was real.

A fine bolt of lightning shot from a clear sky to land before him, sending him flying. The guests who surrounded them gasped and screamed. Merika walked up to Tudor, to loom over him, as she snarled. "If you ever try to touch me again, I will bury you in a red ant hill, right up to your neck. Also, in case you doubt whether or not I could overcome your power, let me assure you...I. Can. Do. It. Even with you being an Alpha male."

Suddenly Merika didn't seem so desirable to Tudor and he snipped back at her. "After showing us your true self, who would want you?"

Rodan arrived on the scene first, and replied. "I would, if I had not chosen another."

Other voices followed, affirming Rodan's words, and Tudor no longer felt so popular or righteous. Kodac, to set the mood back to the way it had been before this incident, ordered the band to play, and Rodan turned to the first female that came near, and whisked her off, to resume the dancing. That left Tyrus to see to a still steaming Merika, and she was livid.

"Merika?" Tyrus bowed before her as he motioned for Tudor to leave. "Would you honor me with this dance?"

Tyrus' voice washed over Merika like cool water, his tone soothing and somehow familiar. Despite that, it took her a few moments before she could place him. "Of course," her voice returned, sounding collected. She stepped into the circle of his arms, and they took their place in amongst the other dancers.

Safe. That was the word that resounded through Merika's mind, as she relaxed in Tyrus' arms, and she allowed him to take the lead. Here she felt oddly at home, though she knew next to nothing about the man who was holding her. She remembered Tara saying that no woman need fear unwanted attention from him, and that thought helped to anchor her, despite an inner voice that told her that Tara was wrong.

"He attacked me!" Merika stuttered and would have buried her face into Tyrus' strong shoulder, that was mere inches from her nose, but he held her away, so she wouldn't get too close.

"Everyone saw what happened, Merika. You can be assured, Tudor will be taken to task over his actions. He should have known better. It is over now and you are safe." Tyrus spoke to calm her.

"Yes. Safe." Merika repeated, sounding distant, and without warning, she collapsed.

"Damn," Tyrus muttered, as he caught the fainting Merika in his arms. As he swung her up, to cradle her against him, he caught Rodan's eye, and sent him a quick message. "Get Serena and Sephra. Merika is going to need them.

Twice, Tyrus and Rodan exchanged the burden of Merika's weight as they carried her to Sephra's home. They moment they arrived, Tyrus dumped her onto the bed in Serena's room. Serena had gotten the message from Kodac, and had run ahead, to show him the way, as well as pull back the blankets for him so he could lay Merika down.

"That dress must weigh half a ton," Tyrus growled, as he shook his arms to get the blood circulating in them again.

Sephra rushed into the room, took one look at Merika's pale form lying prone on the bed, and snapped out one order at the hovering men. "OUT!" She then motioned to Serena to help her strip Merika.

Kodac had remained outside of the house. He had soon been approached by a concerned and contrite Tudor, one who was concerned about the harm he had done.

"I never meant for her to get hurt!" Tudor exclaimed.

"Your action didn't help the situation. But, you had to have known that Merika has been running on empty for a long time already, it was all over her personal signature for anyone to read, if they wanted to. What were you thinking? You are an Alpha, you know better than to push someone when they are in that condition." Kodac berated Tudor.

Tyrus walked out of the house to join them, and frowned at Tudor, as he snarled. "What are you doing here?"

"I came to help if I could," Tudor admitted.

"I would think you have helped enough," Tyrus stated. "Couldn't you sense her agitation? She all but ran from you after that first dance. That alone should have told you something."

"I need a wife. She was perfect," Tudor defended his actions to Tyrus, as he wouldn't have done with Kodac. To him, Tyrus was no more than another suitor, competition for the hand of the woman he wanted for his own.

"There are over four thousand other perfect women out there, any one of them would have been more than pleased to have your notice," Tyrus continued.

"Yes, for a while, but not on a permanent basis." Tudor answered.

Rodan, having joined the trio earlier, piped up. "It can be difficult to be an Alpha male, especially one who is considered handsome and virile. I understand that probably better than anyone. The popularity goes to your head and you think you can get any female you decide you want. Most of the time the woman you want, the one that really means something, is not the kind to just look at what is on the surface. You have to work to get that kind of woman. You have to show you are more than a pretty face, and a physically fit body. They want to know that you will love and appreciate them, as much as you do yourself, and that you will be consistent."

"Rodan knows what he is talking about." Tyrus pointed out. "He has found such a woman, now he needs to prove his sincerity and worth to her. I am not sure quite how he is going to accomplish that yet, but he has been trying."

"I will figure it out. Serena is worth it. You will find, Tudor, that there are many women like her out there. You just have to take a few moments to pick the one out who will suit you." Rodan replied.

"Easier said than done," Tudor muttered.

"And all the better for the challenge." Rodan admitted.

"I suggest you give Merika a wide berth. At least until she is better able to deal with everything she is facing. That could take years, especially for her to accept that you are sincere in your regrets about how you pressured her. Either way, I doubt if she will ever accept you as a mate." Kodac explained, then turned, as Tyrus started to leave, to address his son. "Where do you think you are going?"

"I am no longer needed, so I am going back to my job in the forest." Tyrus answered.

"You are not finished here. We may still need you to form a focus, in case things go wrong." Kodac reminded Tyrus.

"I have more important things to do than being put into the role of a babysitter. You seem to think my work in the forest has less than no value." Tyrus objected.

"No, Tyrus, I just believe a life is more important than finding items that can wait." Kodac replied.

Sephra stepped into the circle of men and, looking to Tyrus, she spoke, showing that she had heard every word. "You are needed. Merika is bleeding from her nose, and is responding to nothing I can do to make it stop."

"Damn," Tyrus swore, and he turned away, though every line of his body showed how affected he was by this news. He didn't want to care, not like this, but he was finding out the hard way that keeping his feelings separated from what was happening with Merika was more than he could do.

Tudor watched Tyrus with interest, and suddenly knew why Merika hadn't responded to his advances. Tyrus! It had been Tyrus, who had come to her rescue, and it had been Tyrus who had taken her into his arms to help soothe her nerves. The man was in love with her! Why did he hesitate? He knew he wouldn't have, if he was in the same position, even now he wouldn't have, he would have gone to her, shielded her, loved her. This wasn't his woman though; she belonged to another man, and would have nothing to do with anyone else. He wasn't about to tell anyone that though. Let them find it out for themselves.

"Tyrus," His father's voice whipped through him. "Do you go to her aid or not?"

"Are you sure this is absolutely necessary?" Tyrus wondered.

"If I were not, I would not ask. If you feel you would rather not, then I suggest release your tie to her, so someone else can help her. There are any number of others who would." Kodac reminded Tyrus.

"I will see to it." Tyrus growled, as he turned back to the house and slammed through the door.

Tudor turned to his host, to let him know what he was dealing with, even as he admitted to his confusion. "He loves her. Why does he fight it so hard, or is the feeling not returned?"

"Tyrus and women are not an easy subject, and I mean not any woman. So, it will not be easy for him to accept what he is feeling. If you wonder if he knows the feeling for what it is, I would have to say, I think he suspects it. Does she love him? I have my doubts, as this is only the second time she has met him. Love can be a strange thing. Even if she recognized the attraction for what it is, she could refrain from acting on it, because of his attitude." Kodac admitted.

"Merika seemed to welcome his help on the floor," Tudor pointed out.

"A stick to a drowning man. She is going to need a lot of time to get through this, and he is going to be pricklier than a hedge hog." Kodac replied.

"You sound like you are expecting to enjoy this." Tudor teased Kodac.

"That, my young man, we have yet to find out. Now, I suggest you go back to the party and look for your own bride. If anyone asks, Merika is all right, and she rests. And no, we have no idea for how long. If it takes too long, I will take a hand in the matter myself." Kodac informed Tudor.

Kodac turned to Rodan, and smiled at his son's expression, as he asked. "What?"

"You are up to something dad, spill the beans." Rodan pushed.

"Our guest of a few moments ago was more perceptive than he believes. I am going to enjoy this, as long as I can put it together." Kodac replied.

"I thought only women tried to pair off couples." Rodan chuckled.

"Right, and if I believed that, you would have me attempting to swallow a raft of other things. Also, as I remember, you have your own problem when it comes to the weaker sex." Kodac pointed out.

"Weaker alright. These women have us jumping through hoops," Rodan retorted.

"You are learning son. Now, I better go see to Tyrus. By now, he will have exhausted all he knows about how to help, and he will find himself coming up short." Kodac replied.

Tyrus had done better than Kodac thought he was capable of. He had stopped Merika's nose from bleeding, though that took constant contact to maintain, and he was sitting on the side of her bed while he held her hand to do that. Merika herself seemed oblivious to it all. She lay beneath the covers, with the blankets pulled up to her jaw, and a peaceful look on her face. Sephra and Serena stood nearby as observers.

"So what do you think, Sephra?" Kodac asked.

"It is going to take a lot more than Tyrus holding her hand to bring Merika around." Sephra replied.

"What is your recommendation?" Kodac asked.

"Both Tyrus and you know what is needed. The question is, will he do it?" Sephra asked.

"And both father and you know the answer to that. I refuse to compromise either of us in such a manner. It would neither be fair nor right." Tyrus answered.

"You know the risks if you don't." Sephra argued back.

"Do you have any idea what you are asking?" Tyrus replied.

"I know," Sephra assured Tyrus.

"I am only human," Tyrus answered on a groan.

"How hard can it be, she is comatose," Serena pointed out. "Surely you aren't the type to take advantage of an unresponsive woman."

As the conversation progressed, Sephra pulled Serena out of the room, telling her it was past time she was asleep. Serena would have loved to argue the point, but she knew better than to try with her mother. If Merika hadn't collapsed, they would have still been outside dancing. Besides, the conversation was just beginning to get interesting.

"Bothersome female," came Tyrus's most common response.

Kodac shot back at Tyrus. "I told you before. If you do not want to take responsibility for Merika's recovery, all you need to do is let go of your link with her. There are any numbers of Alphas outside who will be glad to step into your place."

"I will not do that. Merika is my problem, and I am not releasing her, at least not yet. She isn't stable enough." Tyrus answered.

"Then you know what your responsibilities are." Kodac stated.

Kodac watched as a haunted look crossed his son's face, and heard Tyrus give a sigh and mutter, "Damn."

Kodac hid the grin that threatened to cross his face. To be fair, he could almost feel for his eldest son, holding someone you were attracted to in your arms, when you were both naked, to make sure that the maximum efficiency of your powers were transferred to regulate a problem could be hell. But, it had to be done, for more than one reason, as far as he was concerned. He was Tyrus' father, and he wanted his son to find a good partner in life. This wasn't the way it usually happened, but it would bring these two people closer. He wanted someone who would make his boy happy, and he happened to think that Merika would fit the bill. He also wanted someone for his son who could make him a father, which would make him a grandfather, while he was still young enough to enjoy the sight and sounds of children racing around, was that too much for a father to ask of his son?

"Alright, but it is being done under duress," Tyrus finally caved in and agreed, not knowing the direction Kodac's thoughts had taken. There was no other option to Merika's problem that he could think of at this time, and he knew it.

"If it will make you feel any better, I doubt if Merika would like the idea either," Kodac pointed out.

"That would be a sure bet," Tyrus mumbled drily.

Tyrus shrugged out of his clothes, and with a groan of resignation, he slipped under the covers to take Merika into his arms. She was equally naked and, as Tyrus molded his body to hers, Kodac shut the power in the room off and grinned to himself as he did.

CHAPTER X

In the dead of the night, Tyrus felt as if he was lost. He was surrounded by the warmth and scent of the woman his inner senses told him he wanted for his own, but he refused to act on. Every time he moved, he could feel the smooth softness of Merika against him and he felt the burn of her touch to his soul. He suppressed a shudder, as her hair brushed against him, as it caressed his skin with its satiny softness. He told himself that he was only making the both of them more comfortable, as he fitted her back against his chest and wrapped his body around hers. It wasn't long before his hands were running over her pliant body as he dozed. When he realized what he was doing, he tried to control his actions by crossing his arms around the front of her chest, and sighed as his forearms pressed against breasts that were fuller than he had expected. He gave an involuntary sigh of bliss, and followed it up with a groan of frustration; he was definitely going to go to hell in a hand basket for this. How did he let his father talk him into doing something so asinine? It wasn't bad enough that he couldn't control his roaming hands, but there was another part of him that was demanding he take action as well, and the effort it took to say no, was killing him.

With an involuntary whimper, Tyrus nuzzled the back of Merika's neck, resisting an urge to lick and kiss her skin above where her blood surged in her neck. His mind took in everything and, it seemed, pooled everything into a very full and painful arousal. Sharing a bed with her had been no more than what he had expected, and everything he had feared. Nor was there a thing he could do about it. Not unless he wanted to possess her as she slept. That was something he refused to do, he might not be feeling strong when it came to resisting temptation at the moment, but he had more honor in his soul than that. Eventually, he was sure, the gods would take pity on him and let him sleep.

For the state of his sanity, they had to.

It took a few hours, but eventually, Tyrus did sleep, unfortunately it was to wake to even greater pain. He thought that it had been in his dreams that his fingers had been busy, as they caressed Merika's breasts, his teeth were nibbling on an earlobe, as he moved to lick and nuzzle at her neck and worse, he woke to find his body draped over hers. He could only pray that she was unaware of anything he had been doing, as she seemed to be fast asleep. It was the only redeeming feature in his mind.

"Damn," Tyrus swore, as he slowly pulled himself from Merika's body, so he could retake control of his faculties. This was worse than he had feared; he was never going to be free from this woman. Then again, if he was to be honest, did he want to be?

There was no question in Tyrus's mind, he needed space and time to think things through. Someplace where Merika's presence would not influence his decision. He padded into the washroom where he showered and dressed. When he returned to look at her again, she appeared wane and her breathing was shallow. He heaved a sigh as he recognized signs of her regressing. Well, he reasoned, it would hardly be helpful if he let himself go hungry. By now, he presumed, she had gotten past the most critical point, and he should be able to leave her alone for a while. His brief attempt to escape was preempted by the arrival of Sephra and his father entering the room. They were both bearing trays filled with food, and looks of recrimination.

"Where do you think you are going?" Kodac greeted Tyrus.

"I had planned to get something to eat. Merika probably isn't in a state to eat, but I am starved." Tyrus growled.

"Merika will be as well, although feeding her will be a little more difficult. She is going to need some nourishment if anyone expects her to get better." Sephra replied.

"Of course, and I am the Patsy who is expected to be instrumental in accomplishing this I presume?" Tyrus's voice was dry with sarcasm.

"Who better than the one who will not release her mind," Kodac returned.

"I would think, under the circumstances, that you would consider that tie bloody convenient." Tyrus snapped.

Sephra uncovered a few of the dishes, as she intervened. "I hope this will help your mood, come and eat while it is still hot. Then you can help me spoon some broth into Merika. It is the best we can hope to do for her at this time."

Tyrus and Kodac exchanged hostile looks, as they sat to eat their meal while Sephra went to see to Merika, whom she managed to rouse enough to help into the washroom. Before the men finished eating, she had her patient bathed, and tucked back into bed. She propped Merika up with pillows and covered her bed with a sheet, so she couldn't choke when she tried to eat, or get the bedding wet or dirty, if some of the food spilled. While she waited for the men to finish eating, she watched Merika for signs of danger, in case there had been more to her collapse than what they had thought. It seemed, however, that this was not the case.

"I might be able to do this on my own," Sephra decided. "Merika is in better shape than I could have hoped. She has a strong metabolism, it bodes well for the future."

"Good, I assume then that I can go." Tyrus replied.

"Not quite yet. Tyrus, she is still very weak. Surely you must feel it. You are an Alpha, and should be sensitive to these things," Sephra spoke, as she focused his attention on Merika.

Tyrus just sighed, as he ran his hand through his hair. He did feel it, but foremost in his mind was the need to get far away from

Merika. He knew all he really had to do to break free was to release his hold on her, but he found himself unable to do that. She was too much a part of him already and every time he saw her, that point was driven ever closer home to him. He had barely tolerated the sight of her in the arms of each man she had waltzed with, despite knowing that none of them meant anything to her. It was no different when she hadn't been on the dance floor, because he had noticed each of the people she talked with, and he felt jealous. What made it worse was that they had been free to enjoy her company, without feeling the pressing need he did for her.

A NEED FOR HER! WHERE DID THAT COME FROM?

The thought that flowed through Tyrus' mind struck a chord. He did need her. Deep in the recesses of his mind and heart, lived the knowledge that he could not let Merika go, because he feared to lose a part of himself. She was that one element he feared he could not live without. A part of his soul had recognized her importance in his life the moment it had touched her essence, and now it was up to him to accept it. He was, for the first time in his life, in love. The discovery was enough to make him panic. It didn't help knowing, that at the moment, that the woman he was beginning to love was dependent on him for her very existence, and it grounded him.

After he was no longer needed to boost her energy level to sustain her life, Tyrus decided, he was going to take the time to think things through, and deal with his newfound feelings. After all, there were still his experiences with his mother that he had yet to come to terms with. There was no question in his mind that Merika was nothing like his mother. When he was satisfied with all the conclusions he suspected he might come up with, he would come for her, and no one would question the focus of his intentions.

Kodac could only sense the turmoil deep within his son. He had no way of knowing the cause, though he considered the reason simple to imagine. Being certain of anything with Tyrus was never an easy matter; his mind twisted and turned in ways that sometimes had no rhyme or reason. This was probably one of those times.

"You are right, and I can feel it. The tie I refuse to let go of, often tells me more than I want to know. I cannot release her though, not yet. Not unless I know she is capable of standing on her own," Tyrus admitted. He didn't say anything about the rest of the thoughts he was having. Those, he was barely able to admit to himself, never mind anyone else.

"Well, that is your decision, you know the cost," Kodac stated.

"Unfortunately, I am too well aware of what I am doing. I know it has its ups and downs," Tyrus added

A whimper of distress escaped from Merika, as she moved, and a tear escaped from the corner of an eye, to run down her cheek.

"Does she wake?" Tyrus asked.

"If she does, it will be only for a moment, she is very weak." Sephra reminded Tyrus.

"Then it is time we resumed her treatment, before she begins to lose ground again," Tyrus stated.

Between Sephra and Tyrus, Merika was fed, and he once more took her into his arms, so he could hold her close. This time, he elected to sit in an easy chair, with her on his lap, while she lay draped across his chest. As soon as they appeared to be comfortable, Sephra left, promising to send Serena in later with a lunch. Kodac elected to linger, and when they were alone he spoke, as he picked up a blanket to cover the young couple.

"You find it much easier now that you are both clothed, don't you Tyrus?" Kodac chuckled.

"What do you think? You are a man. You were once young. If they would have tossed you naked into a bed with a naked woman what would you have done?"

"You mean what did I do? I was much younger than you, she was beautiful and, we thought, in need of help as much as Merika. I was also quite drunk. You were the result. It is something no one knows, and I would not have told you this much, if circumstances would have been any different than they are. After it was over, I was ashamed of my actions, my weakness. When I was told of your conception, I refused to marry your mother. By that time, she had told everyone how she had trapped me into a position where I had no choice but to accept her as my wife. She had not left anything out, and I had learned a hard lesson. You were the only thing good that came out of it, and that poisonous witch took you from the valley, to raise you away from my influence. I had no choice but to let you go. I had responsibilities and it was impossible to follow you, even if my father would have let me. That is the way it was. I am not asking for absolution, I am just letting you know that I understand what you are going through. I want you to know that you are stronger than I was, and I am proud of you. I always have been," Kodac told Tyrus.

"Father, I will tell you something you may or may not suspect. If I would have been thrown into a bed naked, with a naked woman, ten years ago, and drunk as you are telling me you were, I would not have lasted five minutes. I would have done no different than you. So, I believe you should stop short of painting my portrait with a halo. Even now, I am sitting here rather than laying on the bed, because it is almost beyond my strength and control not to bury myself in her comatose body. I am not feeling so proud of myself."

"Well, either way, I am proud you are my son. Now rest and allow your strength to help Merika get better." Kodac replied.

"I am not so sure I will be able to rest." Tyrus confessed.

"If you want, I will help." Kodak offered.

"Considering your pressures for me to take Merika to wife, perhaps we should just let things run their course," Tyrus answered.

"Well, just so you know, the offer is there and there is no malicious intent implied." Kodac replied.

"I know." Tyrus answered.

Kodac walked to the door and watched Tyrus for a moment. The boy needed some help, for he was sharing enough strength with Merika to make any man feel tired, and this was being done, after he had spent a fitful night of sleep. Kodac thought about it, and decided that if he could feel the draw, she must have been seriously deleted. The last thing he needed was for Tyrus to get sick as well. With that thought in mind, Kodac put Tyrus to sleep, then sent a strong charge into the comatose bodies that were wrapped so tightly together before him. He estimated that he probably had saved them about a week of recovery time by doing so, and it had cost him next to nothing of his own energy, as the onus was still on Tyrus, who was still strong and young.

Four hours later, Serena entered the room with Tara, and they were both bearing trays.

"See? What did I tell you? Safe as a babe in its mother's arms. That man has ice in his veins." Tara stated.

"Tara, if you are going to be ignorant and demeaning, you can leave," Serena replied.

"Well, I am still having a difficult time believing she rejected Tudor. That man is hot." Tara sniffed.

"It was obviously not meant to be. Besides, Tudor has moved on," Serena pointed out.

"Yes, I have noticed. Tell me, how did he ever manage to talk Kathleen into a dress?" Tara questioned.

"I have no idea, but it looks good on her, and they seem happy, so let it be," Serena ordered.

The girls talked, as they set up the table, then Serena woke Tyrus, who, in turn woke Merika, as he rose to carry her to the table.

"Where am I? What happened? Tyrus, put me down, I can walk you know," Merika objected, the moment she realized where she was, and who was holding her.

Tyrus's lips twitched, as he set Merika onto her feet, so she could toddle to the table to stand beside her friends.

"Mother says the two of you are supposed to sit and eat every last bite, no arguments," Serena ordered.

Merika took stalk of her surroundings, her arraignment, and her company then spoke. "What happened? The last I remember, I was at the banquet."

"You passed out, Merika. Tyrus caught you as you fell and brought you here. Do you remember anything about it?" Tara asked.

"Not much. Just the confrontation with Tudor." Merika admitted.

"Right now, Tudor is feeling very guilty and responsible for the state you are in. He is looking for a way to make up for his actions. He never meant for things to go so far." Serena let Merika know.

Merika nodded, as she used the table and chair as a crutch, while she lowered herself into the seat. "Every bone in my body hurts." She whimpered.

"You panicked and over reacted a little." Tara snickered.

Tyrus growled at Tara for that comment. "How would you know? You were half the clearing away."

"Everyone knows. Tudor can get any female he wants without resorting to violence, just look at the man," Tara remarked, with an accompanying sniff.

"Tudor was out of order. Merika acted in self-defense. If you have trouble believing me, just ask anyone else who saw what happened. Either way, I suggest you get your facts straight before opening your mouth." Tyrus' tone was less than cordial, reflecting the contempt he felt for her. In many ways, she reminded him of his mother, which accounted for the major part of his animosity. The only difference he could see was that his mother knew what she was doing. Tara, in his estimation, was too stupid to know the difference. Lord, but he hated ignorance.

Tara just gave a shrug of indifference, as she filled them in on a piece of news she was sure none of them knew about. "No matter what he has done, he now has a new love interest. Anyone remember Kathleen?"

"Kathleen, as of the would never be caught dead in a dress, Kathleen?" Tyrus questioned.

"That is the one. Well, you should see her now. She could use a few finishing touches, and I doubt if she knows much when it comes to housekeeping, but Tudor doesn't seem to mind." Tara gossiped.

"Things like that can be learned, and Tudor has a mother and three sisters to help teach her. I see no problems there. As I remember, the female members of that family know more about humility than their men." Tyrus stated.

"I doubt there is much more room for arrogance in that family than the men exhibit," Serena added.

Merika ignored it all as she concentrated on eating what had been put in front of her, her hands were shaking violently, and her concentration was centered on holding on to the spoon as she moved it up and down. About three quarters of the way through her bowl of broth, she laid her spoon down on the table, stood, and refusing all help, she made her way over to the washroom, where she emptied her stomach, her bladder then almost had to crawl to the bed. When she got to the side of the bed, no one would listen to her whispered protests for independence. Tyrus lifted her off her hands and knees, placed her on the bed and covered her up. She whimpered, as she settled into the warmth of the covers, dug her face into the softness of the pillows, wound her arms around one, and cried.

"I know baby," the male voice she was used to hearing crooned into her mind. "I know. You hurt, but you knew, power has its price. Things will get better, but you need to rest more first."

"I am so alone. Never leave me." Merika's inner voice cried.

"Rest my sweet, rest. With sleep will come peace and healing. Let your body do what it must. You must not fight it," the male voice whispered gently.

"Merika?" Sephra's voice filtered through her consciousness.

"Please, Sephra," Merika moaned, "I am so tired."

"I know, Merika, I know. But you need to fight, and to do this, you must eat something, anything, and you have to find a way to keep it down." Sephra softly advised, before looking at Tyrus in question, to hear his thoughts about their patient.

"I know it looks bad, but Merika is in better shape than you think. Sleep is what she needs the most."

"Maybe so, but she still needs some sort of nourishment to sustain her." Sephra insisted.

Tyrus sighed, then picked Merika off the bed, as he sat down to prop her up against his chest, so Sephra could spoon some broth into her, so she didn't choke her while doing it.

When they were finished, he settled her back down on the bed, tucked her in, and left the room. "It is time she was left to do some of this on her own. It will make her stronger for having to do so."

Kodac met Tyrus at the door, as he arrived to check on Merika's progress. "Where do you think you are going?"

"Merika needs to do the rest of this on her own. If she continues to use me as a prop, she will lose the independent confidence that makes her such a strong talent. I am going back into the forest." Tyrus insisted.

"We are not that short of wood." Kodac objected.

"I want to get this task over with. We cannot remain here forever, and our time is growing short. We will soon be needed elsewhere," Tyrus pointed out.

"You feel this?" Kodac wondered.

"I feel something father, but whatever it is, it is not in the Valley. There is something coming, but it is wrong for this world, it does not belong." Tyrus admitted.

"I am feeling the same thing and, the sensations seem to emanate from the portal," Kodac agreed.

"Another lost member of the Valley?" Sephra asked. It wasn't the impression she had been getting. Lost members of the valley were usually easier to discern.

"No. Not this time. This could be trouble. We have had few instances of breaches from outsiders, but it has happened. It has never turned out for the good though." Kodac answered.

"What happened the last time?" Sephra wondered.

"That was almost two hundred years ago. It turned out to be a young couple that was running away to get married. No one ever figured out how they managed to get through the portal, but they did. Before they were removed, ten people died." Kodac recalled.

"Why?" Tyrus asked.

"Because son, as you are aware, in human nature it is well known that what cannot be understood or explained must be destroyed. Our powers have no rhyme or reason, they just are. It is not something we can take lightly, nor is it something others can accept. It is the main reason we put a block on the entrance to the valley. It protects people on both sides."

Tyrus and Kodac walked, as they spoke and as they reached the trail entrance they stopped to say their farewells. "Watch over her father."

"Troublesome female, have you ever noticed it?" Kodac teased.

"Right from the start." Tyrus confessed.

"She needs a husband." Kodac pointed out.

"You tried to get her one, remember?" Tyrus reminded Kodac.

"Still am." Kodac replied.

"You are trying in all the wrong places. I am not ready for a wife.

I might never be." Tyrus warned.

"Not even if you love her?" Kodac asked.

"Especially if I love her. Father, never hope for more than there is or more than I can give." Tyrus replied.

"If you cannot accept her for your own son, you must let her go," Kodac pushed.

"First, she needs to quit hurting so much. I can feel the pain so strong in her. I have to wonder at times whether it is pity I feel rather than anything else," Tyrus admitted.

Tyrus turned and left then, and Kodac watched, until he lost sight of him. "Go then my son, and figure out what it is you want and feel. When you know, come back, you will probably find her waiting for you."

CHAPTER XI

"Rodan, Merika." Tudor greeted the couple, as they met next to a miniature waterfall just inside the perimeter of the forest.

Merika had been sitting on a rock near the pond where cascading waters had formed over the years, soaking up the peace and tranquility of the atmosphere. That was where Rodan had run across her by accident. He had been about to approach her with a question, when Tudor had walked up to her. Tudor was holding Kathleen's hand, and they were both smiling happily.

"Tudor, Kathleen." They greeted in union before Rodan added.

"I have found other interests, more attuned to my nature."

"So we see, I had heard you found a new love interest," Merika teased lightly

"What I have found is a potential wife. What we need, are witnesses to our vows. First and foremost, I would like to apologize to Merika for my actions at the ball a couple of days ago. I had no right doing what I did. I learned a valuable lesson that night. The reaction I was looking for from you cannot be forced. I was looking at you for all the wrong reasons. If I had seen Kathleen earlier, I would have known that. In fact, I doubt if I would have cared about your powers at all." Tudor admitted.

"So, what we would like to know, is whether you would consent to witness our vows?" Kathleen inserted.

"Of course, any time you want. When would you like to do this?" Merika asked.

"Now," Tudor stated.

"But how about blood tests, waiting periods, licenses, preparations?" Merika wondered.

Rodan laughed aloud and explained. "This is not the outside world. Here, we are free to live our lives in our own fashion. We have no government or religion, there is no one who hovers over our choices in life, or dictates what we can do. We have our rules, as any people should, to make sure we don't abuse our powers, but that is a matter of common sense. As far as marriage vows, those too are simple, but binding. They are a lifetime commitment."

"And you wish to do this now?" Merika asked.

"If you are receptive to our request." Tudor answered.

"Well, if it is what you want and you are sure about this, why not," Merika responded.

"Kathleen," Tudor turned to take her hands in his. "You are sure you want me?"

"From the moment I saw you. You are sure you feel the same way?" Kathleen asked.

"More than ever," Tudor admitted, before he continued.

"Look into my eyes, let our powers merge. Kathleen, you are my love. I promise you all that I am and will be for all my life. Heart and mind, body and soul."

"I am yours until death tears us apart. Heart and mind, body and soul," Kathleen responded.

Together, as one, they finished. "We are, with these pledges, bonded as one."

Their lips merged, they shimmered as one, and disappeared. Merika looked at Rodan and asked one word. "How?"

"The power of binding. It is possible, and I bet no one will find that couple for a while, unless they want to be found. Every man has a secret place where he cannot be traced, and it is usually there that he takes his bride, until they are ready to rejoin the world. That can take anything from a day to a week. Longer than that is considered more than a little indulgent." Rodan admitted.

"Outside of the Valley, what they are doing, it is called a honeymoon." Merika replied.

"I know. There are times when I wonder if I will ever get to the point of achieving mine." Rodan admitted.

"Not making any progress with Serena?" Merika teased.

"I am at a loss what to do or think. At first, I thought my attentions would be welcomed by her. Now, I am not so sure." Rodan admitted.

"No, Rodan. At first, Serena looked at you with eyes that were filled with the dreams of a child. She was in awe of your reputation. That fades very fast when a woman gets to meet the real man behind the legend. Serena understood that, but you continued to see no further than the hero worship in her eyes when she first saw you. Hero worship can fade fast. It won't keep a woman like Serena at your feet for long. If you want her, you are going to have to show her that you see her for who she is. You may even have to reach beyond who you believe you are. It can be scary doing things like that." Merika admitted.

"I had thought I had done everything I could think of to attract Serena's attention and keep it." Rodan replied.

"Oh, you caught her attention all right. She then looked at you as a man and found you wanting. She now sees you as someone who is vain, someone with little or no practical purpose." Merika informed Rodan, in a blunt fashion. She figured it was something he would be able to work on.

"How did she come up with something like that?" Rodan wanted to know.

"You pose and primp, you surround yourself with people who flatter you and look no further than the surface. You know you are no more impressed with them than Serena is with your actions. She has led a functional life, she knows what she is looking for." Merika noted.

"As you seem to know so much about this, how about letting me in on the secret of how to win my heart's desire," Rodan probed.

"No secret. Serena is looking for a practical, functional man. One who is not afraid to get his hands dirty, one who is not afraid to stand up for what he believes in, even when others oppose his views. She wants a man who isn't afraid to let those about him know that his affections and regards are the property of another. She wants to know that the man she loves will be happy with that choice." Merika shared.

"So what does she want me to do, that would make her believe in my sincerity?" Rodan wondered.

"That question is answered simply enough. If you truly want to be that man, Rodan, you will have to convince her that you are sincere. If you can do that, while giving her reason to believe that you have a practical purpose for living, she will come around quickly enough." Merika assured him.

"Easier said than done. What would you have me do to prove all this to her?" Rodan looked for details.

"To start with? Think over what I have told you. It is not that hard to figure out. I do know one thing, you will not do it by surrounding yourself with a bevy of besotted females. You are going to have to work for her regard. Now, it is your turn to give me a little advice. Considering how popular this place seems to be, how does anyone manage to get a little solitude out here?"

Merika wanted to know.

"That depends how good you are with taking directions and returning by the same trails." Rodan admitted.

"I have yet to become lost, once I have traveled over an area. I seem to have been blessed with a good sense of direction." Merika stated.

"Are you sure you want to be alone?" Rodan asked.

"For a while. When I am ready to rejoin the crowds, I will know how to get back." Merika assured Rodan.

"Very well, but remember, there can be danger in being alone at times, exercise caution. Now, if you go in that direction and follow that trail there, you should be safe enough." Rodan directed.

"Much obliged." Merika answered.

"I cannot promise you that you will not run into anyone else, but I know of no one who has gone in that direction today." Rodan admitted.

With a nod, Merika headed off in the designated direction, intent on seeking the privacy she thought she craved.

Almost an hour later, Merika almost rammed into Tyrus, as she was descending a steep bank. He dodged her, as she rushed down the trail, no longer in complete control of the speed of her decline, and his arm snaked out to halt her motion. Moments later, he was busy lecturing her, as he steadied her, before he released her.

"Has no one ever told you not to run when you are going downhill because it might be dangerous?"

"I had never meant to run, but the path got so steep, there was no way to stop my feet from moving faster." Merika admitted, as she added. "Thank you for the rescue."

"Well, next time, try to be more careful. What are you doing out here anyway? I would have thought that you had plenty of men back in the clearing worshipping at your feet." Tyrus sniffed.

"Do not even think to go there, Tyrus, because I can be just as nasty as you can. Besides, I have as much right to be walking in the woods as anyone else. Even you. Fancy that!" Merika retorted.

Tyrus looked at Merika in surprise, blinked a few times as her words sunk in, then threw back his head and laughed aloud. This woman was incredible! Here she was, probably lost in the middle of the forest, no food, no water, no fear of her surroundings, and she was tossing out subconscious and vocal challenges like candy to anyone willing to take her up on them. Unbelievable!

Merika frowned as Tyrus laughed at her, then stuck her pert little nose in the air, as she pushed past him and snipped. "Miserable excuse for a human being."

She had not made a half a dozen more steps when she lost her footing and landed flat on her backside. Tyrus laughed all the harder, as he stepped up to her side and offered her a helping hand up. She slapped his hand aside, as she got up on her own and brushed the leaves and loose dirt from her skirt. Tyrus just shook his head in continued amusement then spoke.

"Come on Merika, it is obviously time for a break, and not only just for you. Would you join me for a light lunch? I am willing to bet you are thirsty and hungry, and if you had thought to bring supplies with you on your hike, I would be surprised."

Merika tossed Tyrus a look of annoyance. The man was right, she had not given food much of a thought, though she had not ignored it at all. She had packed an apple and a bottle of water. Unfortunately, she had left both by the waterfall. She was getting hungry and she had to admit, she was very thirsty. Nor was she stupid enough to ignore the warning signs that accompanied the signals that told her that she was not yet up to strength.

"I forgot my lunch by the waterfall when I was talking to your brother." Merika admitted.

"Rodan sought you out for advice?" Tyrus sounded surprised.

"Do not sound so surprised. I am not a total moron, you know." Merika defended herself.

"Never said you were." Tyrus commented as he lifted her down to the bottom area of the path. He then pulled a blanket from a basket, in an area that had been cleared, by the side of the walk. He spread it out, lowered himself onto his knees and pulled out a cloth sack filled with food.

Merika watched Tyrus in silence, as he pulled a few vegetables, meats, breads, cheese, fruits and water bottles from within the confines of the sack. She then remembered Tara's description of the man behind the mask. With a smile, she sunk to her knees, and proceeded to make herself comfortable, as she reached for a bottle of water that she cooled with a thought.

"I am more thirst than hungry, and I thank you for your offer to share. I really had no intention of making what was supposed to be an hour outing into a day long hike." Merika admitted.

"I assume Rodan had more than a little to do with that." Tyrus noted.

"He is totally baffled by Serena's continued immunity to him." Merika explained.

"I gather that Serena is not making things easy for him. Good for her. I daresay, he will appreciate her more, if he has to fight for her." Tyrus' voice sounded amused and he chuckled. "What is she looking for?"

"I told Rodan that she is looking for someone with more depth of character than he has been prepared to show her. Though not quite in those words." Merika admitted.

"Rodan has plenty of depth. I am surprised that Serena has not seen that for herself." Tyrus noted.

"She has, but she is being careful. One can never be too sure of these things. It is something that he will have to convince her of." Merika pointed out.

"So, what other pearls of wisdom did you bless him with?" Tyrus wondered.

"Not much to be honest. Just those few tidbits of advice, as well as advising him not to be afraid to show her that he isn't afraid get his hands dirty. I then wished him luck." Merika continued.

"You sent him off to work and wished him luck?" Tyrus almost laughed aloud at the sight his mind conjured out of Merika's words. "There had to be more to it then that."

"If there was, it was nothing I could have said. I am afraid he will have to fumble his way through, just like anyone else. If he wants her bad enough, he will find a way to get her. If he has any Instincts, and the brains to go along with them, it should not be too hard. Serena is over the moon for him." Merika confided.

"Then why the games?" Tyrus asked.

"No games. Serena just needs reassurance. A woman needs to know her feelings are returned, so she knows she is not barking up the wrong tree." Merika replied.

"Seems much the same as a man to me, only more complicated." Tyrus added.

"You really think so?" Merika wondered.

"If it has anything to do with a female, yes. Now lets get onto things that matter. You may have noticed that I pack a heavy lunch sack. The reasons are simple. I never know how long I will be gone, whether I will end up alone or find some starved out creature lost in the forest. So feel free to indulge," Tyrus offered to share.

"Very well. As one starved out creature to another," Merika teased, as she picked up a knife and quirked an eyebrow at him. "Do you trust me enough to allow me to make you a sandwich?"

"Why not." Tyrus shot back, as he reclined onto his elbow. "You have been cooking for everyone for weeks now, and I have not heard of a single casualty yet."

"That was Angela's doing, mainly. I have been little more than glorified kitchen help." Merika answered.

"That is not quite the way I keep hearing it. Half the men in the Valley are in love with your culinary skills as much as anything else. It is rare that a man finds a woman who can cook as well as she looks, especially when she is a famed beauty." Tyrus noted.

"I am not a famed beauty. There are any amounts of women out there that look better than I. Nor are they any less of a cook. It was just easier to let another take the load and not have the responsibility." Merika informed Tyrus.

"Modest too. As for not being a famed beauty, I remember hearing plenty about you in the outside world. You were also a known enigma. Now, in my experience, that would be a story that would need researching. How did all that come about without anyone suspecting you have great power?" Tyrus wondered.

"Everyone expects a person, in the position I used to hold in the outside world, to have great talent, nor is it something reserved to people from the Valley. To say the least, power goes hand in hand with that kind of notoriety. It is a place everyone looks but no one expects to find anything out of the ordinary. A child progeny growing ever older, it happens all the time." Merika remarked with a shrug.

"Sounds like you are trying to hide something," Tyrus pointed out.

"More like not quite ready to share?" Merika remarked.

"Must have been horrendous. How could your mother have done something like that to you?" Tyrus wanted to know.

"It was not like that, and as far as my mother goes, I could not have asked for a more loving, caring and nurturing parent." Merika defended her mother.

It was the beginning of a three-hour walk down memory lane for the both of them. Merika spoke of times spent with her mother, as they had formed a firm and lasting bond. It was time spent in different kitchens, where Merika had learned the trade from her mother, as she had made her living. She had wanted more than she had, for her daughter, so she had sent her to the best of schools, and encouraged her blossoming talent. It had paid off in spades, as Merika had grown, matured and evolved.

Merika continued to push, to bring Tyrus out of his shell, but didn't meet with much success. Tyrus refused to offer much in return for her efforts. His youth had been a nightmare of neglect and abuse. It was not something he wanted to share with anyone. It was something he had fought even as a child, and had risen above. It had taken a great amount of effort, and even greater resolve, but he had done it. To spite his mother, he had thwarted every evil manipulative plan she had groomed him to undertake. His greatest pleasure had been to see her in her grave. To him, it meant she was no longer alive to torment him, or anyone else. He then went to search for his father. That was when he had found himself drawn to the Valley. He had lived in his father's house from that point on.

Tyrus watched Merika in silence, as she spoke of her mother, her face glowing, her eyes sparkling, her every fiber radiating happiness. It was something, he realized, that she would someday pass on to her own children, perhaps, if he was lucky, their children. The more he saw of her and heard from her, the more he wanted, and needed her in his life. She made him feel as if there was still something worthwhile in the world.

A sudden sense of time having passed brought Merika up short and she looked up at the patches of sky that she could see through the towering trees.

"Look at where the sun is! I have to get back to the homestead." Merika jumped to her feet, as she started to head off down the path, speaking as she left. "Thank you for the lunch and the company, I really enjoyed myself."

"Wait, give me a moment, and I will escort you through the woods, so you will be safe and won't get lost." Tyrus offered.

"Not to worry, I never get lost. I do appreciate the offer though." Merika assured Tyrus.

"You might as well accept the offer, Merika, as even if I were to leave you go on your own, I would not be satisfied unless I followed you to the edge of the woods. There is more danger in these forests than two or four legged ones. Some people believe them haunted, others think the very trees live, or something lives within them." Tyrus told her.

"Like Sprites, Elves and Fairies, etc. Things like that only live in our imaginations and if people were to see you escorting me to safety they would begin to wonder if you were developing social graces. You do have a reputation to live up to you know." Merika teased.

Tyrus laughed again astounded at how often he had done so while in Merika's company. Laughter had not played much of a part in his life; that it did so now, only seemed more meaningful. He was in the midst of digesting all of this, when Merika shimmered and disappeared, leaving him with a brief mental message.

"You need not worry about my safety, Tyrus, I can take care of myself. I have returned to the kitchen where I shall make a picnic lunch for tomorrow. It is only fair that I return the favor of sharing your fare today. Assuming, of course, that you want to meet me again tomorrow." Merika offered.

Back in the forest, Tyrus smiled wider, as he replied. "Nothing would give me greater pleasure. Same place, same time?"

"It is as good a place and time as any," came Merika's reply, followed by silence.

Kodac had felt a change in Tyrus, during the time he had spent with Merika, and he could have danced with happiness. He was so pleased. He had never felt his eldest son happy before, and to do so now was not only telling, but monumental. Earlier in the day, Rodan had come to him, to tell him that he had sent Merika into the same area that Tyrus was known to be in, as he scouted the forest for trees to harvest. Kodac had estimated that his son's greatest burst of pleasure, had come at about the same time that Merika would have crossed his path.

Another burst, this time of amusement, had coincided with Merika's sudden reappearance at the homestead. Nor did it have anything to do with the fact that she had left him. Kodac decided it probably was connected to the way she had left, which was something he was going to have to talk to her about later. She should be well aware of the dangers that were involved in executing such a spell, and she was not yet fully recovered from her last power drain. This was no time for grandstanding. While he was at it, he was going to talk to his son about exercising a little control over her actions as well, as Tyrus stood a better chance of succeeding at that than anyone else in the Valley.

A message burst into Kodac's mind, as Tyrus defended himself from his father's blame. "To control actions such as Merika just did, would take a warning of intent that she was about to do something. I not only did not know she was going to transport, I had no way to knowing she could."

"Stay out of my mind son," was the reply Kodac sent back, noting that a few months ago, Tyrus would not have been able to read him at all. It just proved to him what he had known the first time their minds had touched, Tyrus was just beginning to develop the finer points of his powers and they were proving to be stronger than any Valley Alpha in over a hundred and fifty years.

Tyrus was, in Kodac's mind, a son to be proud of, not that he was any less proud of Rodan. It was just that their talents ran in different directions, just as their techniques did, and both had a good grasp on results. They did tend to be a little dense when it came to things that affected them personally, but he assumed that would change.

In the matter of Tyrus and Merika, it seemed Rodan had came across the right way to get them together. He led them to each other, and left them alone for nature take its course.

CHAPTER XII

The next day started off with next to perfect weather, the sky was blue without a cloud to mar its perfection, the wind a mere whisper. There was just a hint of dew on the grass, to forecast the upcoming season, and the scent of late blossoms remaining in the air.

Merika woke early and went to the kitchen, where she spent the next couple of hours putting together a special picnic lunch. It was not that the slight meal took much effort to prepare, but the time it took to bake and cool the treat she had made enough to transport, ate up most of the morning. She was determined to prove that she was capable of great feats in the kitchen, if for no other reason than to prove that she could.

Things were not so simple for Tyrus. The breaching of the portal was not such a simple thing. Whomever had come through had weapons, and there were signs of them having been used. That made whoever welded them dangerous. That also left him to find the intruders. He had spent hours exchanging information with Kodac, and verifying it, before he realized that it was the middle of the day, and he had forgotten about his meeting with Merika. When he checked with Rodan on her, he was told that she had left well before noon to take a walk in the woods. He knew where he would find her.

There were four of them, dressed in jeans and jackets. Three men and a woman, and they were all armed. Merika watched them from the shadows, afraid to move, in case she was discovered. She knew she would be in trouble if they saw her, knew they had no business in the Valley, it was written all over them. They had no discernable natural powers. The weapons, however, made them something to be feared and respected.

"This place gives me the creeps," the woman complained, as she stepped over a protruding root.

"Shut up, Nancy," one of the men growled back. "It is your fault we are here."

"Where is here anyway?"

"By the looks of it, nowhere. We are going to be lost in this miserable tree ridden landscape forever, and no one will ever realize we were here." Another man complained.

"I am starved." Nancy whimpered.

"We all are, so shut up about it. You're only making things worse," the man who looked like the leader ordered.

"I am so hungry I swear I can almost smell food. Good food." Nancy continued, as she ignored the other man's order.

"Wishful thinking sis, but then you always did aim for the best." One of the men who shared Nancy's coloring spoke.

"Why settle for less if you can afford better." Nancy smiled up at him looking smug.

"You stupid cow, you are broke, remember. It is why we are here, dressed like gorilla solders and running from the law. This is your fault." The leader spoke loudly.

"Enough, Eduard, she had no way of knowing that stock broker was crooked, he had a good reputation and came well recommended. You would have done the same." Nancy's brother replied.

"I would never have given him access to the whole bank role. I am not that stupid," the leader snarled back.

"Well, I would have never entertained the idea of robbing a

bloody bank." Nancy returned.

"You fell in with the idea quickly enough when it was suggested." Eduard commented.

"Like I really had a choice?" Came back Nancy's sarcastic reply.

The man berating Nancy replied back. "Give me that, 'I was just a poor defenseless female line', one more time and I will put a round of bullets through you myself. You are anything but a low class slut." Eduard continued.

"You wish. I do what I have to, to survive, Eduard, and I could care less what it takes to accomplish it." Nancy defended herself.

"I swear I can smell chicken," another man noted, as he lifted his nose to sniff at the air.

As the group of intruders prowled through the forest, Tyrus reached out to contact Merika with a warning.

"Merika," her guardian's voice sounded in her mind, and she tried not to move, as her attention shifted. "You are in danger, Merika."

"I ascertained that much on my own. As luck would have it, they have not noticed me." Merika responded.

"We are coming for you. When we get close, we will ask you to act in certain ways. Do you think you can do this?" The male voice in her mind asked.

"I have been known to be able to act out a part, remember?" Merika replied.

"I remember but this is not a stage or screen set, and the bullets in those sub machines are real." The male voice warned.

"I held on to the roles I did because I could make the storyline look real. Oh, just so you know, these outsiders are superstitious." Merika informed the others.

"I know, but I would not count on that slowing down their trigger fingers. What did you think? That you could say boo, and they will drop their guns and run? What if they are trigger happy, and you get in the road?" The male voice asked.

"How would you know about their trigger fingers?" Merika returned with equal sarcasm.

"I know. I have felt these people roaming through the woods for hours. These people are more apt to spook and shoot than run. You must get to know the difference." The male voice advised.

"There is someone close by," another voice sounded aloud. "Look at what I found."

"I heard that," the male voice sounded in Merika's head. "Just what did they find?"

"Lunch," came Merika's reply. "Fried chicken, potato salad, bottles of water, raw vegetable pieces with a dip and peach cream pie."

"As long as it is not a member of the population, the rest is expendable." Came back the reply.

Merika just chuckled as she answered. "At least none of it will go to waste."

Tyrus had, in the meantime, withdrawn from her mind, and turned his thoughts inward. "Peach cream pie. Damn."

Soon after, both his brother and his father joined Tyrus, and they were ready for a fight if it came to that.

"Ready?" Tyrus asked, the moment they finished gathering.

"So, what do we do?" Rodan asked.

"We bring the forest to life son. That is how it is done. After the intruders are taken care of, we will have to strengthen the portal, and in case either of you thinks this is going to be easy, I will give you fair warning now. Remember how weak Merika was, after the storm? All three of us could feel like that before this is over." Kodac warned.

"All of us?" Rodan asked.

"All of us. Now, tell Merika not to be scared, nothing will hurt her. I would also suggest that she not move." Kodac informed Tyrus.

Tyrus took a second to send Merika the message, then turned his full attention to his father.

"She is not always the easiest to give orders to, but she will take direction if left with no other choice."

"Typical female. Under different circumstances, I would probably allow her to help, but not this time." Kodac replied.

"Her? Help?" Tyrus snorted in disbelief.

"She is the female Alpha Prime, son. She does have the power needed if called upon. But first, she needs to finish resting and healing." Kodac reminded Tyrus.

"Well, here is hoping she does as she was told. Bothersome woman." Tyrus commented, after making sure she understood what was expected from her.

Kodac couldn't help but smile, as he took note of the softer tone Tyrus used to spout off his favorite saying in relation to women in general.

"The focus is mine, neither of you have the training, the

knowledge, the maturity or the strength to do this yet. By the time we are finished, however, you will both know the secrets of the portal sentries. Now, merge." Kodac ordered, as he caught the combined efforts of his sons, and expanded it outwards to link with the land. He poured his essence into the spell, until he felt as one with the ground and trees, and could see all within them.

"Did you see that?" One of the three men pointed at a tree that had seemed to move.

"Trees only move when you have been smoking up, Tim, or have you been indulging in something even more toxic?" Eduard asked.

"I haven't had enough of anything to make trees move. Nor do I have any to share, if that is what you are asking." Tim replied.

"Trees that move are not going to affect these characters," Merika sent her information to the focus. "They are not only armed, but high. We are going to have to find a different way to get their guns away from them."

"They are all on drugs?" Kodac asked.

"I don't know if they all are, but two are for sure. Kodac, they are going to find me here, I am too close. Do I dare even try to move?" Merika wondered.

"No, but if you are located you must act something out to try to save yourself." Kodac dissolved the focus and turned to Tyrus. "Go to her. I believe you were going to meet for a picnic anyway? We need a way to disarm them without anyone getting hurt. Then, we need to get them out of the valley, so we can reset the portal. Merika cannot be allowed to transport right now, make sure she knows."

"She knows, or she wouldn't still be there." Tyrus stated.

"Look at what I have here," The man that had been called Tim earlier crowed as he found Merika's picnic stash.

"Food and it is still warm. That means there has to be someone close by." The leader spoke.

It was then that Merika decided she had no choice but to act. It was time to wander into their lives. What she would do when she got there, she had no idea, but she would think of something.

"Are you lost or something?" Merika spoke, as she approached the group from off to the side.

The four members of the group jumped almost as a unit, and the sound of guns being armed reverberated though the air.

Merika jumped in response, and gasped as four sets of hostile eyes focused on her. When they noted her period dress, and the fact that she had no weapon, they relaxed their stance.

"Who are you?" Eduard asked.

"Tanya Wade. Why?" Merika answered.

"The Tanya Wade?" Nancy spoke as she moved forward. "You shooting a movie?"

"A movie?" Merika knew the way she said that made her sound like a stupid parrot, but the idea had such potential that she could find no way of stopping herself from aping the words. At the same time she sent Kodac a mental message. "Come here on horses, dressed as Knights Templar, and be prepared to play the parts of a troop of actors on break."

"Well, everyone knows you have taken a leave of absence." Nancy interrupted Merika's mental conversation.

"There are several sets being prepared at the moment. The part of this film about, is being shot from here, and is the least expensive. You must be from one of the other sets, because of the military set up." Merika swung back into her role.

"Do you know where they are shooting?" Tim asked.

"Sure, about four miles from here. Just follow that track. It will lead you straight to their camp." Merika pointed at a trail that was sure to lead them directly to the portal. If they travelled the whole four miles, they would leave the valley, and the danger would be over.

The sound of horses approaching from a distance, heralded the arrival of Kodac and his party, and Merika turned her attention to their entrance. "Here comes more members of the cast to join us, we are supposed to congregate here for a bit of a lunch, and to wait for the rest of the crew."

"Crew?" Eduard asked. He didn't want to be caught in the middle of a bunch of actors. He just wanted to get out of here.

"Yes, we will eat, while we practice our lines and have a little rehearsal. Later, we will start shooting the forest scenes, before moving on. Would you like to join us for a small lunch?"

"I think we should move on." One of the men spoke.

Another disagreed. "The least we can do is have a bite or two. I am not sure about you, but I could eat a horse."

Moving to set up a new scene, Merika went to pullout a light blanket she had brought, followed by the food from the large wicker basket. She had no sooner finished setting out the plastic cups, when her backups arrived.

"Might as well eat while it is still a little warm." Merika delivered her line, not trusting herself to look up. She was afraid that if she did she would start to shake.

"Visitors from another set?" Kodac motioned with his chin at the intruders.

"I assume so," Merika answered.

"We took a wrong turn somewhere. Tanya has directed us to the proper set." Tim replied.

"They might want to grab a piece of chicken and a drink before they leave though." Merika informed the others.

"Food!" Rodan made a show of bowing over Merika's hand, after he dismounted, "My lady, you know the way to a man's heart. We pray you will find it in your heart to share your meager fare with us poor travelers. In return, we promise to serve and protect your honor with our very lives."

"Sir knight, your chivalry gives me heart, and I would be pleased to share all that I own," Merika answered, sounding as if she was reciting lines.

"Man, talk about an offer!" One of the strangers commented.

Everyone broke into laughter, as they sat on the blanket, and Merika defended the comment. "No self respecting knight would take advantage of any member of the weaker sex."

Removing his helm he had on, Tyrus tossed it aside and commented, as he helped himself to a piece of chicken and potato salad. "I, for one, do not adhere to the myth of the weaker sex. Most women I know are infinitely stronger than the members of the male persuasion."

"That is because you allow it." Merika replied, oblivious to a swift gasp from Nancy.

"You! I lost every cent I had because of you. You took advantage of me, then left me." Nancy screeched, as she pointed an accusing finger at Tyrus.

"As I remember, I told you to get out of the stock market because you tended to gamble with long shots. I figured you were going to lose everything you had on that gamble you were about to invest in. You told me to mind my own business. As far as taking advantage of you otherwise, I never touched you." Tyrus denied.

"You did!" Nancy whined, as she glanced at one of the other men. She then tossed Merika a hostile glance, when Merika laughed aloud about that accusation and brushed it aside.

"You really cannot expect anyone to believe that about my fellow actor, at least not here."

"Why not?" Nancy asked. She didn't understand any of this, and she could tell none of her companions could either. What was going on?

"He has no interest in women in a carnal sense. I was told by a reliable source that he was the safest man in the Valley for any female to be with. He is gay, someone you can be friends with and not have to worry about being pressured by."

The whole assembly went silent, as everyone stared at Merika in shock. Tyrus looked as if he had just been delivered a shock, when everyone looked at him in question. There was a period of awkwardness, where no one said anything, then one of the strangers stood.

"I think we will have to go now, especially if we want to appear in any of the shots. If we miss the light we won't get a part and there is no money in that."

Taking the major part of the meal with them, the group left. When they were out of sight, Rodan rolled over laughing. "Gay? Who thought that up? Never mind, it worked like a charm. Is there any chicken left?"

Kodac had more important matters on his mind, and he let them know it. "Where did you send them, Merika?"

"About a half a mile outside of the entrance to the portal. I assume that is all right?" Merika answered.

"Then the next job is up to us. First, I suggest we take Merika back to the homestead." Kodac spoke, taking note of the black looks Tyrus was giving her. "We will clean up here, then I will take her back. You two can stay and finish off that peach pie, while I take care of the rest. Oh, and Rodan, if I were you I would not push things too far."

"Point taken." Rodan replied with a big grin. The humor of the situation was still causing his eyes to sparkle bright. "And yes, we will make short work of the pie while you are gone."

"Tyrus, track them. Make sure they actually leave. I want no loose ends, and remember to reserve as much of your power as possible. You are going to need it all for the portal." Kodac ordered.

Kodac looked at Merika as she finished gathering whatever was left, as she collected the garbage their meal had created. When she was finished, he held out his hand for the basket, as Rodan pulled her to her feet.

"Time to go Merika. Sephra will be waiting for us." Kodac ordered.

"Who will bring you back to the homestead? You mentioned that the three of you would be tired beyond previous experience." Merika wondered.

"Merika, Sephra has nine sons and a spouse. We will be taken care of. I realize you care, but leave it go. Your powers have more limitations than your intentions, and you are not near as strong as you think. You have done well, but some of what you have done with your power needs to be guided by someone who knows what he or she is doing. With this in mind, please do not do something we may all live to regret." Kodac tried to reason with her.

"I thought I was helping." Merika replied.

"You have, but like a child, you need time to develop. Do nothing this time, rest, heal, and leave us do our job, as you do yours." Kodac ordered.

"Have I done that badly?" Merika asked.

"No, but you need to be warned. You are impulsive, young, and inexperienced. You have been in danger for most of the time you have been here. I want to see you live, love, marry and have children. Promise me that you will not use your powers, until I tell you it is safe," Kodac requested a little cooperation from her.

"But..." Merika began.

"Promise me, Merika." Kodac insisted.

With a sigh, Merika agreed. There had been little beyond what she had done in the kitchen that she could claim as a controlled issue of talent. She did know, however, that if Kodac thought that what they were about to do would tax the combined strength of the three major valley male primes, it was something that was beyond her capabilities. She figured that if she understood that much, it meant she was beginning to recognize her limits.

CHAPTER XIII

Kodac didn't waste any more time than he had to after returning Merika to Sephra's homestead. The first thing he did was send out a general notice to the Alphas who were still in the area to report to him immediately. He knew there were at least fourteen that were still in the vicinity, and he was even happier when another answered his call. He hadn't known that Darnell was close by, and he considered that a stroke of good fortune.

"Darnell, your arrival is most opportune. We need as many Alphas as we can get to form a circle," Kodac greeted his friend, as Darnell rode up to join the group of men surrounding Kodac.

"I heard your call from twenty miles away, and transported those who had come with me here immediately. I am at your service." Darnell replied.

Kodac didn't care that Darnell could be serious competition for Tyrus' suit for Merika, not at the moment. The safety of their world and his people were primary, and took precedence over his son's love life. Darnell was an Alpha Prime, nearly as powerful as Tyrus, and he would be able to take some of the strain off of them in the meld. The problem posed by the unstable portal was looming before him like something he had no control over, and he hated that type of scenario. He liked things in his world to run smoothly. It made life easier. Darnell's appearance gave him an edge on that.

"I will take you up on your offer. Evan has sent his sons to gather the horses, and we will ride to tend to the rift the moment they get here," Kodac informed Darnell.

"Do I have time to water and rest my horse for a few moments before we leave? We have been riding since daybreak, and were ready to stop for a rest when we received your call. I didn't give anyone a chance to do that, and they could use a few moments before we go on." Darnell admitted.

Evan was quick to step in with a solution to that problem, as he replied. "I told Daffyd to bring extra horses with him from the barns, in case they were needed. Your steed needs rest and care. Your men can see to that, while Sephra shows your sister where they can set up their tents and takes her to the house to settle her in with the other girls."

"We appreciate that. Celia hadn't been travelling well and a good rest will see her back to normal within a few days," Darnell answered.

It didn't take long for Darnell to dismount, while he told his men what was expected of them. He then helped Celia down from her horse, and sent her off with Sephra, along with his gratitude. By the time he was finished seeing to these things, it was time to mount up on a fresh animal and ride again.

The Alphas who had gathered to accompany Kodac and Darnell followed suit, and they galloped off together as a unit. It wasn't long before Darnell and Kodac were leading the pack of men into the forest, and despite the danger of their horses tripping over roots or downed trees, they continued to spur their mounts onwards. They needed to get to the portal fast, and they all knew it.

"Will there be anyone else besides us available to shore up the portal?" Darnell asked.

"Tyrus and Rodan should be waiting for us at the portal entrance by the time we arrive. They will both be happy to see you. They are expecting to be thoroughly exhausted when this is over. Your presence means that is less likely to happen, or at the very least, they won't be as affected by the task." Kodac admitted.

"Glad to be of assistance. I will be happy to see Tyrus. It has been a while," Darnell stated.

"He will be just as pleased by your presence," Kodac informed Darnell. He knew the two young men were friends, and had spent quite a lot of time together. They knew each other well and, Tyrus especially, would be relieved to know that there would be no less than four Alpha Primes there to make up the focus that was needed to stabilize the portal. He hoped that, as they all liked and respected each other, it would mean that they would be able to work well together.

"Tyrus and I have worked together in the past, but not on anything like this. This is more than most Alpha Primes would want to tackle without proper backup." Darnell stated. He knew that if there would have been no other choice, Kodac would have addressed the problem on his own, but he would have paid a high price for doing so. Shoring up an established portal that was in danger of collapsing took considerably more power to do than creating one, which also took a lot of power.

"I wasn't aware that Tyrus and you had merged forces before. That will make the job go much smoother," Kodac replied.

"I have never worked with Rodan, but I will assume he operates much the same as his brother," Darnell added.

"You would be wrong there. The concept of their doing so is logical to assume, but it isn't the way things are. Rodan only has three-quarters of the strength Tyrus has, and it shows at times like this. That is why I will connect with Rodan and you, while Tyrus completes the focus from the other side, by linking to Rodan and you. We will supply the ground that provides protection for you and Rodan, so that you are not affected as strongly by the shoring. Between the three of us, we should be able to easily compensate for any shortcomings my younger son has," Kodac planned, as they rode.

"You realize that Tyrus is the type to shield us if anything happens that could cause us harm? It is the one thing I noticed about him, he tackles the problems he takes on with the idea that he needs to protect everyone," Darnell passed on his observation.

"I noticed. He will also come out of this weak and grouchy as a bear. Tyrus does not make a good patient, but that isn't my concern. Sephra will have to deal with him when this is over, and I am sure she will know how to handle the situation." Kodac snickered.

"You are bad," Darnell replied with a grin, as they arrived at their destination.

"And proud of it," Kodac confirmed, as he reigned in his horse hard, to make it come to a fast stop and quickly dismounted. He didn't bother with hobbling the animal. He knew that when he wanted him later he would be able to recapture him easily. All he would have to do is send out a summoning, and his ride would return. It wouldn't take much power, and he was certain he would be in a lot better shape than his sons.

Rodan and Tyrus were already on the scene when the rest of the men who were to make up the circle of power entered the entrance area. They had spent their time preparing for the merge and exchange of power that would be needed to stabilize the portal, so people who didn't belong in the valley would no longer be able to cross over. It wasn't going to be done in the same way that Evan and his sons had tried, when they intended to bind Merika. They were going to have to anchor their power to the Earth, to give their work the extra strength it would need to be successful. The Earth element held a greater power than fire.

"It is about time that you got here," Tyrus joked, as his smile widened, when he saw Darnell ride into the area beside Kodac.

He then added. "Darnell, you don't know how welcome you are. I feel like I am receiving gifts, and it isn't even Christmas yet. Your arrival is well timed."

"I am not attracted enough to you to be considered a present, Christmas or otherwise, but I am always happy to see a friend. I heard you needed someone to show you how things like this are done, and offered my services," Darnell teased back.

"I will accept any help I can get, this is not going to be easy," Tyrus admitted.

As Darnell and Tyrus reconnected, and Tyrus introduced Darnell to Rodan, Kodac set up the outer power ring. He placed each of the male alphas next to the one he thought they would mesh with the best, and began to set things into motion.

The moment Rodan, Tyrus and Darnell felt Kodac reach out towards the portal with his power, they took their places. He pointed to the places where he wanted them to stand and then finished creating the connection needed to heal the tear in the frame of the portal.

Kodac first checked on the area that shone around the outside of the doorway, to find the darkness that would tell him where the crack was located. When he was finished doing that, he turned, to listen to the music of the matrix of the build that had made up the portal in the beginning, to see how badly it had been affected. He found the sounds discordant, which meant that the one problem was creating the other. He hummed lowly, as he pulled the outside power base into the inner circle, and focused the strength of the merge created by the lesser Alphas, to aim it towards the portal itself.

The reaction of the entrance to their world was immediate and strong, as it flashed a bright golden light at them. Tyrus was the one that formed the shield, as Darnell had predicted he would, to keep the others safe, while Kodac moved in to repair the rift. This was going to take time.

Kodac slowly ran his hands above the outside frame of the portal, as he continued to hum, and powered what seemed to be a never-ending supply of energy into the matrix of the doorway. It seemed to be able to need more than he had expected, but that was not the major problem; keeping it stable was. While Kodac worked, Tyrus kept them safe, and Darnell formed the base that kept them bonded. Rodan continued to feed them energy and power from the link with the outside circle, as well as the Earth.

The moment Kodac felt the rift close and snap into place once more, he pulled back. The disconnection from the power source was something the portal didn't seem to like, and it flashed out strongly in protest, as it tried to latch on to them. Tyrus, once more, stepped in to shield the focus from the attack, even though he knew it might harm him.

Both Rodan and Kodac acted, as they returned to the merge to pull Tyrus away from the hold that the portal had on him. What they found, was that Tyrus was able to hold things into place on his own, but he couldn't hold it all. That would come with the building of his talent, which was still happening. As Darnell moved back in to help them, the sound of a snap came from Tyrus and they were all thrown back, away from the opening of the portal.

The portal had rejected the presence of the Alpha Primes, as it couldn't control them. Now that it was stable, it shone steadily from the inside area that faced the valley, while the other side showed no signs of its existence. Kodac tested the strength of their work, and smiled. They were successful. The portal was fully repaired, and back to the way it had been when it was new.

"It is done," Kodac announced, and then turned to look at his sons, who were lying prone on the forest floor. They were exhausted, but they were still in good shape. Now, it was going to be a matter of keeping them quiet while they healed, which was going to take a while. How long it would be before they were back on their feet, he didn't know, but he knew it wouldn't be quickly enough for them to ride to the homestead where help awaited them. They were going to have to carry them home.

Kodac ran testing hands over his sons' comatose forms, to see what damage, if any, they might have sustained. He was pleased to note that outside of their state of extreme exhaustion, they appeared to have gotten away with few, if any, lasting effects. No matter, the lingering effects of this day were going to last for a while.

"I told you Tyrus would use his strength and power to shield us if things got dangerous," Darnell spoke directly to Kodac.

"He isn't nearly as bad as Rodan. Rodan tried to move to give him backup, but he doesn't have the willpower to fight that Tyrus has. That eldest son of mine is very stubborn, and he won't give in during a fight. He is going to be a very strong Alpha Prime when he is finished developing." Kodac informed Darnel. There was a sense of pride in his voice that was very pronounced, even through his own exhaustion. Darnell, he noted, seemed barely winded, something he planned on asking him about later.

Darnell answered Kodac's question, without being asked.

"Tyrus took the hit. Rodan was on his right side and got the largest backlash from the matrix grid. He has sustained the greatest shock to his system. He will probably bounce back quickly, for he is young and resilient, but it will take a few days at the very least. I will have this registered for future reference, so those who follow in our footsteps know what needs to be done if they are ever faced with this situation again."

Evan didn't need to be told what had to be done, or that the task of the outside power ring was finished. He dissolved the base that existed between the lesser Alphas, and ordered everyone involved back into action. They needed to collect their horses, and then figure out how to transport Tyrus and Rodan back to the homestead, so Sephra could see to them. They were going to have to move the two comatose men carefully through the forest, so no more harm came to them. He smiled inwardly, as he thought of what his wife was apt to do to make sure these two men behave while they recuperated, and figured that Merika and Serena would probably feature in that part of their healing. It would be interesting to see how that worked out.

CHAPTER XIV

"Serena, you will tend to Rodan," Sephra ordered, as she walked out of the room she had designated as the recovery room. "Merika will see to Tyrus."

"But mom..." Serena sounded her reluctance, while Merika just looked shocked.

"Do not, 'but mom' me, my daughter. Neither of these men have enough strength left to tie their shoes at the moment, nor will they have for the next three days. Kodac is not in much better shape, and I am willing to bet that none of them are going to be good patients. To further complicate matters, Tara has gone into labor. I am going to be busy there."

"What are we supposed to do? I have never taken care of anyone sick before." Merika admitted. She had been with her mother during her last days, but this wasn't the same thing.

"They are not sick, they are exhausted. Keep them quiet, fed, watered, and, most of all clean. If they need to use the facilities, help them anyway you can." Sephra ordered.

"That could prove awkward." Merika replied drily.

"Neither of these men will do anything to compromise your modesty. Knowing men as I do, I think they will be more embarrassed than either of you would be. You will learn, men are like that, they have their pride at a time like this." Sephra informed Merika and Serena.

"Where do we sleep?" Serena asked.

"Close enough to hear if they need anything," Came the response, then Sephra left to tend to a loud Tara.

"Good thing it is nighttime," Merika replied. "I am not sure about Rodan, but Tyrus is not going to be an easy patient at all. Grouchy old bear."

Serena giggled, then, looking mischievous, replied, "I think I know how to get them to behave."

"Without repercussions?" Merika asked, sounding dubious.

"So what are they going to do about anything in their condition?" Serena replied, with a wink.

"We only have a few days, Serena." Merika warned.

"Maybe so, but even after, they will not be in a position to retaliate, not without some serious backlash from trying to do so." Serena grinned, as she tossed Merika a devilish look.

"Alright, count me in, where do we start?" Merika agreed.

"First we make sure they are not going anywhere. We take their clothing." Serena began to lay out her plans.

"Then?" Merika pushed. She had her doubts if this was going to work, no matter what Serena thought. Then again, what did she know?

"We tie them to the beds of course, with just enough line to allow them to get to the washroom." Serena continued.

"Something tells me we are going to live to regret this." Merika warned.

"So what can they do to us?" Serena repeated with a snicker.

"We are playing with fire." Merika answered.

"Feels good to me. Come on, Merika, tell me you are braver than you look." Serena teased.

"This is Tyrus we are talking about. Everyone walks around him as if they are traveling on eggshells. Giving him a taste of his own medicine might feel good in the short run, but my mother always told me not to go courting trouble." Merika remembered that piece of advice. She had always found that it paid to follow it in the past.

"So, we are not courting trouble, we are jumping in with both feet. So, are you game, or are you chicken?" Serena wanted to know.

"Let me sleep on it, white feathers and all," Merika answered.

Rodan was the first to get restless, and the first to make trouble. Serena hadn't needed to sleep on it to make up her mind that she was going to go ahead with her little plan.

"Where are my clothes?" Rodan bellowed from his bed.

As Serena and Merika were sharing a bed in the next room, Rodan's yell of outrage woke them simultaneously. They exchanged a sleepy glance, then Serena broke into a giggle, before getting up to tend to her patient.

"Do you need something, Rodan?" Serena asked, in her sweetest voice.

"Nothing you can help with." Rodan growled back.

"Need to use the necessary, do you?" Serena continued to taunt, with a purr to her voice.

"Get out!" Rodan roared.

"Sorry no can do. I have my orders. As for helping you walk to the little boys room, you do realize that it is within my power, don't you!" Serena continued to push her luck.

"How about some clothing?" Rodan spoke slowly, and he

sounded dangerously close to blowing.

"You are dressed appropriately, for a male in bed. Nor are you going to be allowed to leave the room for several days, so get used to the idea." Serena sniffed.

"I am not walking around in front of you wearing nothing but my shorts." Rodan insisted.

"Rodan, I have nine brothers. I can guarantee you, I will not be shocked by the sight of a man in shorts." Serena assured him.

Tyrus, having been woken up by the fuss, drawled, "I bet I could shock you."

"You, I have nothing to worry about, Merika is your nurse." Serena informed Tyrus.

"That should prove interesting, I would think her more in line for getting help than giving it. But sure, I am positive I can shock her too." Tyrus assured Serena.

"Naughty boys," Serena chided them. Then warned. "You can either make this easy on us, so we can make your convalescence pleasant for you, or we can make your time here a living nightmare. Now, Rodan, I believe you need a hand to cross the room?" Serena offered.

Rodan grumbled, but chose to allow her to help without incident. When it was Tyrus's turn he made no fuss at all, but Merika got the feeling this was just like the calm before the storm. There was going to be a price to pay for what Serena did, and they would both pay it in the end, whether she had been a part of it or not.

The next morning, Merika and Serena served breakfast to Tyrus and Rodan in bed, cleaned up, and then helped them as they could, before leaving them to rest. When they returned with a light lunch for the men, it was to find them prepared. They were sitting up and talking with their father. Merika was quick to offer to get a meal for Kodac as well. Before long, all three men were fed, and Kodac had helped his sons use the washroom as best as he could, rather than trouble the women. When they were alone again, Kodac quizzed his sons.

"You both seem very cooperative all of a sudden, why?"

"Serena had a bit of a talk with Rodan last night. Now, we are not quite sure, but I think she threatened us. Merika, I think we can handle, but Serena, she is dangerous." Tyrus explained.

"Serena?" Kodac smiled. "Why should she scare you, when Merika is the one with all the power?"

"Merika may have the power, but Serena, growing up with nine brothers, will know more ways of getting even than Merika will ever begin to imagine." Rodan replied.

"You are sure this is the woman you want to marry?" Kodac wondered.

"Damn right. Our sons will have no idea what is coming at them." Rodan chuckled.

"And you Tyrus?" Kodac asked.

"Me? I guess I will do my best to welcome Serena into the family, even if she is a clothes thief. After all, it won't be me who is living with her," Tyrus admitted.

"That is not what I was asking and you know it." Kodac responded with a frown.

"There is nothing more for me to add father, and that is just the way it is," Tyrus insisted.

Kodac sighed in disappointment, then made his way back to his room to rest. His sons were not the only ones who had been weakened by the meld, nor was he as young as he once was.

"So, now what do you have in mind?" Tyrus addressed his brother, as he settled back into his bed.

"Brother, now I plan to throw every sneaky, underhanded trick I know out to lure Serena into my web. By the time I have finished with her, she will be happy she is mine." Rodan declared.

"That is your ultimate goal, but where are you going to start? Besides how will you know whether she is caught, or if you are?" Tyrus wanted to know.

"As long as we are together in the same bed, the rest is immaterial." Rodan answered as logically as he could.

"Never quite thought of it that way." Tyrus admitted.

"Somehow, I am not surprised brother. When it comes to women you always did tend to cut off your nose to spite your face." Rodan replied.

"Entirely justified I assure you, and if you knew more about my history, you would agree." Tyrus insisted.

"So what are you going to do about Merika?" Rodan asked.

"Not a thing." Tyrus answered.

"You realize you could lose her?" Rodan warned.

"Maybe, I could care less. I mean, sure, she is good company, fun to be with, a great cook, and she is beautiful to look at. But she is not mine to lose. She is her own person." Tyrus pointed out.

"Maybe, but she could be more, she could be yours to love, too." Rodan pushed.

"Leave it go. The last thing I need is you, as well as Kodac, on my back. If you can think of nothing else to talk about, just go to sleep." Tyrus grouched. He was not about to talk to his younger brother about his non-existent love life. It wasn't his business. They didn't even need to know that he was working on it, in his own way. No one needed to know that, not even Merika. He would let everyone know what he decided, when the time came to announce his decision.

"Sounds like a plan. I am beat anyway." Rodan chuckled.

As the men spoke in their room, Serena decided to take Merika to task, as they cleaned in the kitchen. "I notice you are not putting the effort into Tyrus that I seem to have to with Rodan. What is with that?"

"Tyrus is stronger. I noticed, he is quite capable of independent movement. Personally, I think Sephra overstated the extent of their exhaustion," Merika noted.

"So, what are you going to do about it?" Serena asked.

"What I have to. I bring Tyrus his food as he needs it, but the rest is up to him." Merika answered with a careless shrug.

"He treated you better when you were down." Serena reminded Merika.

"He doesn't need me, Serena, and I am not about to force my services on him." Merika insisted.

"He needs you, Merika, he just doesn't want to acknowledge it." Serena pointed out.

"Then that is his problem, isn't it." Merika shrugged a shoulder then, looking out into a flawless day, announced. "I think I am going to go out for a bit of a walk."

"Alone?" Serena asked.

"Sephra forbid that for now. Rayjan is taking me to the waterfall pond. He says it has become a common meeting ground for anyone during their breaks." Merika informed Serena.

"You are not on break, neither of us are." Serena reminded Merika.

"You might not be, but I definitely am. Tyrus won't even notice I am gone." Merika reminded Serena.

"Mother is not going to be pleased." Serena warned Merika.

"Why not? Rayjan is one of her favorite sons." Merika replied.

"He is not much of a match for you." Serena noted.

"We know, but I am helping him catch the eye of another." Merika told Serena.

"I thought you said that jealousy was a poor base to use for a relationship." Serena answered, as she jumped to her own conclusions for why Merika was helping Rayjan.

"So who said we were trying to make anyone jealous? He needs an introduction, I know her, end of story." Merika informed Serena.

"Is she really suited to him?" Serena wanted to know. After all, this was one of her brothers that they were talking about, and she wanted to see them happy.

"I doubt if I will know until I see them together. He seems to be attracted to her though." Merika pointed out.

"That is not much to go by. A woman my brother finds attractive that he has never met. Could be one of a thousand." Serena admitted.

"Well, I know neither of them well enough to make a judgment, but I will learn." Merika declared.

Rayjan walked through the kitchen door and tossed his sister a smile. "Checking up on me little sister?"

"What kind of sister would I be, if I cared less whether you were happy or not with your choice of a wife?" Serena asked.

"Truth of the matter sister, I am not so sure she is right for me myself. I just would like to meet her at this time, to see if there is something there." Rayjan admitted.

"And if you find nothing?" Serena wanted to know.

"Then there are a half a dozen others that will show promise I am sure. Either way, I could use a wife. So Merika," Rayjan offered her his arm, "shall we be on our way?"

Merika just laughed up at Rayjan, as she took his offered arm and replied. "Lead on, you Casanova."

Several hours later, Merika chuckled as she watched Rayjan. He had obviously decided that the girl that he had thought so desirable earlier in the day, no longer held the same attraction. Now, he was trying to find a way to get away from her, without hurting her feelings.

Merika's musings were interrupted by a voice off to her side, and she looked up into the face of a very handsome man.

"What are you doing out here all by yourself?"

"I was enjoying myself." Merika admitted

"Mind if I join you?" The stranger asked.

Merika shrugged a shoulder, and he sat beside her. "My name is Darnell."

"I am Merika." She replied.

The man was pure power, and every fiber of his being telegraphed the fact. Merika took in his dark hair, blue eyes and chiseled appearance and smiled. For some reason, she felt impressed.

"I heard about you at Kodac's gathering." Darnell admitted.

"You almost missed it." Merika teased.

"Just as well. I am not very comfortable in large crowds." Darnell responded.

Merika just tossed him an amazed look, and replied. "Why in Heaven's name not?"

Darnell shrugged a shoulder as he answered. "I know what you are thinking. I have been told the same thing over and over, but truth of the matter is that I am just not used to being a part of a crowd. It is a little hard on my sister though. She is beautiful, talented, powerful, but lonesome. I had hoped to get an invitation from Kodac to introduce her around after we arrived. Now I hear that the three Alpha male primes are indisposed. Which means that she may not get another chance to meet members of her own talent range for a few more years. As the female Alpha prime, you can act in his place in such an instance, so I am asking if you would honor her with an invitation to join the company here."

"I had not realized that everyone here had been invited." Merika responded.

"Most have not, it was only Kodac's banquet that held that distinction, but that is over, and we did not wish to seem to presume." Darnell explained.

"I can see no reason why you should feel that way, you are just as welcome as anyone else, and that includes your sister. Please feel free to pass on my invitation." Merika spoke openly.

"Her name is Celia, and she can cook and help out. She will be happy to do what she can as will I." Darnell offered.

Merika was surprised, when Darnell took her hand in his, and shook it. He was genuine! His hands were calloused and strong, his features weather checked, and although he was just as handsome as Rodan, albeit in a dark way, he was not so puffed up with conceit that he had to work to get past it. They spent the rest of the afternoon talking and exchanging stories, as they got to know each other, then Merika had to run, to get the evening meal for Tyrus.

"Where have you been all afternoon?" Serena hissed.

"I told you were I was going. Why? Was I missed?" Merika wondered.

"Not really, and you were right about Tyrus, he is in much better shape than Rodan. So, meet anyone interesting?" Serena wanted to know the details of Merika's afternoon. She had been cooped up all day, and hadn't even had a chance to leave the building. It wasn't fair.

"Some guy named Darnell. Do you know him?" Merika wondered.

"Yes, as a matter of fact. I know his sister better though. Both are hard working members of the community, although Celia tends to be pushy. Her talents run into cooking and she can probably teach both you and Angela something about culinary arts." Serena informed Merika.

"Sounds interesting." Merika admitted.

"Darnell is downright dreamy. Talk about your tall, dark and handsome. I cannot for a moment understand how he managed to escape the same trap as Tudor, where his conceit is bigger than he is. He gives everyone the impression that he believes he is not quite up to standard. Women just stand and gape at him, and powerful! Wow! He could give both Tyrus and Rodan a run for their money, if he put his mind to it. He would never win in a real contest of course, but it would still be a close call. Thinking of him for yourself, Merika?" Serena wanted to know.

Serena had still been talking about Darnell when she entered the room where Rodan and Tyrus rested, and she finished as she placed the tray over Rodan's lap. Rodan fairly jumped at the subject.

"So who is Merika looking twice in the direction of, do we know this person?"

"Darnell is here. He is such a dream." Serena stated.

The two men exchanged glances, and Rodan narrowed his eyes, as he noted Serena's reaction to Darnell, as he addressed her. "I gather you are impressed by this man."

"Who could help but to be? He is all I have ever been told to look for in a man. Strong. Industrious. Presentable. Modest. Considerate." Serena listed off Darnell's stellar attributes.

"When are they going to announce his canonization?" Tyrus's voice was dry with bridled sarcasm.

"Oh he has his faults, but he at least acknowledges that he has some. Merika has invited both him and his sister to stay for a few days." Serena informed Tyrus and Rodan.

"Break out the balloons and strike up the band. What is his sister like?" Tyrus pretended interest in Celia.

"Celia is more outgoing, but seldom gets a chance to leave home long enough to attract someone who would appreciate her." Serena admitted.

Darnell thinks the same thing. He is afraid that if she doesn't find someone for her own soon, she will either be stuck in an arranged marriage, or she will never wed at all. Actually, I was astounded when he told me that. I was of the impression that arranged marriages were no longer practiced." Merika spoke, as she expressed her surprise.

"They usually aren't, but you do still hear of them in remote circles. Darnell's family would fall into that category." Rodan informed Merika.

"Despite their power and talent level?" Merika asked.

"Theirs is a very secluded homestead. It is not so surprising that they are often forgotten and overlooked, despite their strengths." Rodan explained further. He didn't say any more about them than he felt was absolutely necessary, because, as far as he was concerned, Darnell's sudden appearance was somewhat of a complication. Darnell was serious competition, for both him and Tyrus, when it came to women like Merika and Serena. He was powerful and handsome. He wasn't conceited, like Tudor. He was a hard worker, a family man, the type that women looked for. Would he cause trouble for Tyrus or him? It was hard to say, especially if Tyrus continued to act as he had when it came to Merika.

"By the way, Sephra was here earlier. She wants to talk to the two of you. Something about neglect." Rodan informed Merika and Serena.

Merika looked at Serena in innocence and asked. "Have you been neglecting poor Rodan?"

"Not that I am aware of, but you have left Tyrus alone, so you could spend a whole afternoon with Darnell. Who do you think most likely to be on my mom's derelict duty list?" Serena asked.

"Tyrus is quite able to use his own motor skills, so I can think of no reason he would need me to act as a a crutch." Merika sniffed.

"Men need more care than us poor females, Merika, you should know that." Serena spoke with exaggerated care.

"That is right, Merika," Rodan teased, as he forked some peas into his mouth. "We need that extra TLC, to make up for all the other times we have missed out on it. Tyrus was diligent in his care of you when you were weak and overtaxed."

"I was almost comatose when he did care for me. He looks far from suffering to me. Personally, I would be surprised not to hear that he no longer needed to be babysat at all." Merika declared.

"I agree, I am quite capable of taking care of myself. I am smart enough to know when I have overtaxed my system and when I should be quiet and rest." Tyrus spoke with a haughty demeanor.

"Low blow brother," Rodan chuckled. "Merika is missing the experience we have both benefited from. I would say that she owes you a picnic lunch or two yet."

"I showed up for that lunch, though I am not adverse to granting that request. I used to enjoy my time with Tyrus, such as it was." Merika admitted freely.

"Really?" Rodan hummed as he teased. "The hand that tamed the savage beast?"

"More like, afraid to get saddled with playing nurse again." Tyrus stated.

"Well, Serena, what say we go find your mother and see what she wants?" Merika suggested.

"If we wait five minutes they will be finished eating, and we can take their trays with us." Serena pointed out.

"Point taken. Then we can go to the kitchen to meet Celia. So who do you think would be a good match for her?" Merika considered.

"Rayjan, maybe even Daffyd." Serena replied. She considered Celia a good enough catch to offer her brothers for the task.

"Always trying to pass off one of your brothers to some poor unsuspecting female. You should be ashamed of yourself." Merika teased.

"Probably Daffyd, when I think of it. Last time I saw Rayjan, he was quite taken with a little blonde." Serena continued, as she ignored Merika's teasing remark.

"You would do something like that to your own brothers?" Tyrus added from his bed.

Serena grinned and answered back. "In a heartbeat. What are sisters for? Besides, it is not as if I am hoisting off a hostile termagant onto anyone. Both Celia and Adela are quite affable, and both bring a good amount of talent with them. They will make good sound matches, well balanced and full of potential. Besides, they seem happy together, and if it is meant to be, it will. Not all women are like Tyrus's mother you know. In fact, few really are."

"What do you know about my mother?" Tyrus snarled.

"Enough to know that she left you scarred and bitter. Consider yourself lucky to be rid of her, and move on to better things. I know I would never allow anyone like that ruin my life and future." Serena returned.

Merika said nothing, but looked interested. One look at the sudden darkness in Tyrus's face was enough to warn everyone that they had touched upon a subject best left alone.

"Take the rest away." Tyrus growled, as he shoved the remainder of his meal away, and Merika moved quickly to catch the tray and contents, as it threatened to fall off the bed.

"No reason to take out your nastiness on Merika, Tyrus." Serena snapped at him as she picked up Rodan's empty tray.

"Get out," was all Tyrus hissed, before sinking back under the covers, and turning away from them.

The two girls just exchanged a look and left.

"Wow, talk about hitting a raw nerve." Serena was not sure whether to allow the building giggle escape or not. She did know, however, that whatever it was that bothered Tyrus about his mother was something that was not going to heal any time soon.

"Tyrus never talks about his mother, beyond the few references we all hear about her being a piece of work. We spent hours sharing memories of our youth, he never once spoke of her." Merika informed Serena.

"So which do we do first? Greet Celia, or go to see my mother?" Serena asked, as she decided to dismiss the matter of Tyrus' mother from her thoughts. Tyrus, from what she could tell, was the only one who could deal with that part of his past. Anyone else who tried to help would only end up hurt.

"Get rid of the load, and see which one crosses our paths first." Merika suggested.

As it turned out, Sephra was already in the kitchen area, familiarizing Celia with the facility, much as the others had done with Merika. So, it was a matter of being able to kill two birds with one stone for Serena and Merika.

"Of course, there is no longer the need for the mountains of food that were consumed through the past few weeks. Most of the people, who were here, have left to return to their own homes.

But, we still go through great amounts of supplies." Sephra told Celia.

"Wherever I can be of service, feel free to ask." Celia offered.

"Darnell says you are a good cook," Merika spoke.

"I am a functional cook. I have seen your work, and while I can make everything I have seen, I do not have the style you do to make them look fancy like you do." Celia admitted.

"That just takes a little practice and imagination, you can learn both. I will show you what I mean when we work together if you really want to know," Merika showed she was willing to work with Celia.

"Tomorrow then," Celia agreed.

"Now, I believe I told your patients I wanted to have a word with the two of you." Sephra turned to address Serena and Merika.

"They seem fine to me," Merika spoke, and Sephra snapped back.

"Did I ask? You left Tyrus alone, except to feed him, all day. Is that what you had been told to do?" Sephra asked Merika.

"Tyrus is quite capable of walking to the commode on his own, and he does not need me to sleep. Remembering my own convalescence, because of the same reasons, I found I gained ground faster when I forced myself to move on my own." Merika defended her choice.

"Sound thinking on his part, but not yours. I presume you enjoyed your afternoon out?" Sephra asked.

"Immensely. I started out with Rayjan and ended up with Darnell." Merika responded. She knew this wasn't the end of the Tyrus situation, Sephra had as much as insinuated that, but maybe she could somehow derail the rest of what she was going to say about the matter with another subject, at some point.

"Darnell is quite impressed with you. Do you intend to spend tomorrow with him as well?" Sephra asked. She sounded deceptively interested. She knew what was on Merika's mind, and she wasn't about to let her get away with it. That young lady was playing with the wrong kind of fire.

"Maybe," Merika answered vaguely. Her friendship with Darnell wasn't anyone else's business but hers. They got along great, and she was more than happy to get the chance to spend some time with a man who wasn't so prickly all the time. She also enjoyed her time with Tyrus, but it could be tense at times. He was moodier than she wanted to deal with, especially now.

"To what end are you interested in Darnell?" Sephra wanted to know.

"According to Serena, he could use a wife. We picked out a possibility and I am going to introduce them. The rest is up to them. If it works out, fine. If not, well, we tried. I don't have any nefarious intensions where he is concerned." Merika replied.

"You are matchmaking? You cannot even find a husband for yourself." Sephra sniffed.

"Ask me if I am worried," Merika answered carelessly, although she sounded miffed. Sephra had no cause to take her to task over Tyrus, and she didn't care what anyone thought about her spending the afternoon with Darnell. The time they had spent together had been perfectly innocent and she had nothing to be ashamed of.

Sephra just shook her head, and then turned her attention to her daughter. "You have at least been more vigilant."

"Rodan seemed to need the care more." Serena admitted.

"He did, he does, and he will continue to. He does not have the power to bounce back as quickly as Kodac and Tyrus have. He also hopes to help out with more of the finishing touches in the houses. I want you to do whatever it takes to keep him away from there. I am willing to bet you have more success with him than you did with getting Merika to do what she was supposed to," Sephra added.

"He is easier to intimidate. Is that all you wanted to talk about?" Serena wanted to know.

"Only one more thing. As you mentioned the idea of matchmaking for Darnell, who have you chosen for him?" Sephra asked.

"Adela. He is so reserved and shy. She will bring him out of his shell." Serena gave Sephra a name and a reason.

"So would Merika." Sephra pointed out.

Serena leaned over to whisper in her mother's ear, "I have other plans for Merika."

"Well, I have other plans for Adela. She is for Rayjan and the match has already been made. Who do you think would suit Celia?" Sephra asked.

"Daffyd." Serena admitted.

"You may have something there. Whose idea was that one?" Sephra wanted to know.

"Good question. At first, when I suggested it to Merika as a possibility, she was not at all surprised." Serena informed Sephra.

"The connection stuck in my mind the moment Darnell told me about her. I like Daffyd; he deserves a really nice wife. Celia sounds like she might fit the bill, and the more I hear about her the better I like the idea." Merika admitted. "I really like Daffyd a lot."

"What do you think of Celia with Tyrus?" Sephra seeded the thought.

"Tyrus is so volatile I am not sure if he would be good for any female in his state." Serena stated.

"The right woman could snap him right out of those moods." Sephra noted.

"I have reason to believe he is not interested in women, so I think this conversation is silly." Merika pointed out.

"I cannot believe you said that." Sephra spoke to Merika. She wasn't sure what Merika meant, but something about the way she said it made her wonder. Was she talking about Tyrus' phobia about his mother, or something entirely different?

"There are times I have trouble believing it myself, but I have my reasons." Merika replied.

"Then you must know or suspect something that has eluded the rest of us." Sephra answered.

Merika shrugged a shoulder, as Serena stifled a yawn, which caused Sephra to scoot them both off to bed, after telling them that they were to be up early to serve Tyrus and Rodan their meals in their room once more.

CHAPTER XV

The next morning seemed to be the beginning of several different surprises for Merika. First, she gave a soft little knock on the convalescent room door before walking in, to find Rodan and Serena locked in a kiss. Neither seemed to be aware that anyone else was in the room, and neither should have been where they were, dressed as they were.

"Serena!" Merika's voice was an echo of the shock she was feeling.

Both Rodan and Serena were in his bed, under the covers, and both were clad, as they had slept. Rodan was in his shorts and Serena in a linen shift.

Serena gave a gasp as she raised her eyes to look into her friend's face, and then jumped up from the bed. She got tangled in the sheets, and while she attempted to pull down her nightgown, she yanked painfully on her hair when it caught under Rodan's shoulder.

"It is not what it looks like." Serena was quick to go on the defense.

"Of course it was," Rodan chuckled.

Both Merika and Serena turned and glared at Rodan, while Merika asked. "You care to tell me just what you think it looked like?"

"It looked like we were kissing in my bed." Rodan smiled as he stretched to fold his arms behind his head.

"You are no help at all," Serena snapped, then turned to Merika to explain. Rodan needed a drink water, and then he needed to use the washroom. I stuck around, so I could help him back to the bed when he was finished, and fell asleep on the bed."

"I rolled her over and just crawled in beside her. Serena sleeps like a log," Rodan informed Merika, as he smiled smugly, while adding his part.

"How about Tyrus? He isn't in that bad a shape that he couldn't have helped Rodan," Merika stated, as she looked at Tyrus' bed for the first time since she walked into the room. It was empty.

"Tyrus left sometime during the night, in case, you didn't even think to check. I have no idea where he went to, if you remember he was in a bit of a state last night." Rodan reminded Merika.

"Well, either way, Serena you have a patient to see to, I am going to help with breakfast. Tyrus, if I am not mistaken, is no longer a factor." Merika decided.

Merika and Serena left, but before they went very far, Merika stopped Serena. "Your secret is safe with me, Serena, I will never tell your mother."

"I am not so sure mother would understand. I was so tired, and Rodan was taking forever in the washroom," Serena tried to explain.

"Devastating devil though, right?" Merika teased.

Serena just grinned and replied. "And he is all mine, another secret for you to keep. He is taking shape quite well."

Daffyd joined Merika and Serena, as they walked towards the kitchens and teased. "You are late girls, mom is not going to be pleased."

"We lost a patient." Merika thought to use Tyrus's truancy to their advantage. "Tyrus went AWOL during the night. We looked for him, but I think he is off pouting somewhere."

"Well, I have a different message to give you, Merika. Darnell says he will meet you by the falls, same place as yesterday." Daffyd replied.

Merika gave a pleased smile, and hooked her hand through Daffyd's arm, and drew him along with her. "Come along, handsome, we will make you something special for breakfast. She tossed Serena a wink and together they moved on.

Celia turned to face the trio, as they made their noisy way into the room and forgot all about the hot pan of buns she had just pulled out of the oven as her eyes met Daffyd's. He stopped cold in mid sentence, as his eyes took in the exquisite beauty before him and he looked into the deep blue of her eyes. Merika was quick to grab some kitchen mitts and relieve Celia of the hot pan.

"Daffyd, Celia. Celia, my brother Daffyd," Serena introduced the couple, then pushed her brother towards Celia. He jerked forward but remained tongue-tied.

"Get out of here, the two of you, you are creating a traffic jam. Daffyd take Celia to see the water fall. Tell Darnell, I will meet him there as soon as I am able." Merika added.

With something to do, the couple left, hand in hand and Merika made quick work of finishing off the jobs Celia had taken on for herself to do, while Serena saw to gathering food for a breakfast meal. Angela showed up, and shooed the both of them off.

"Celia is just as productive in the kitchen as you are Merika, the rest is up to me. As you said before, this is my kitchen, at least until someone better suited comes along. From what I just witnessed, that just could be Celia. Good thing we hit it off right away."

Serena went off to see to Rodan, while Merika made her way to the waterfall to meet with Darnell.

"I cannot thank you enough. Celia is happier than I have seen her since she was a child. I could hardly believe my ears, when Daffyd asked me for permission to take her for his wife. She just arrived last night. Who would have thought anything like that could happen so fast?" Darnell greeted Merika.

"All it takes is the right people to meet. In the outside world, things would have never moved so fast, but I am finding that people in the Valley seem to just know when they have met their match." Merika pointed out.

"True, but until you do, there is always a chance that the right one could be overlooked. Then, there is the enjoyment to be had in the cultural interchange and the general search in the first place." Darnell replied.

"I think I know what you mean. Where I grew up, we call it dating. It was something there was little or no time for in my life." Merika admitted.

"Or in mine. We missed a lot. Chances are, the right one passed us by without us knowing about it. I cannot afford to send signals that might not be understood anymore, not at my age. So I am going to ask you outright what it is that you feel for me?" Darnell wanted to know.

"I just met you, Darnell, what am I supposed to think? I enjoy your company and I like being with you." Merika admitted.

"I think being raised in the outside world has robbed you of the trust your instincts deserve, and as I am not receiving any signals from you because of it I am going to kiss you to test the waters." Darnell warned Merika, before he acted.

"Not a good idea," was as far as Merika got, as Darnell's lips met hers. This time she allowed it to happen. Unfortunately, she found the exchange did nothing to excite her. Sure, being kissed by him was pleasurable and even comfortable. But it was like kissing an old friend, or worse yet, a brother.

Merika pulled out of Darnell's embrace and shook her head. "It is no use, Darnell. I will never be able to think of you as anything more than a good friend and pleasant companion."

"I had hoped for more as liking a life mate is important, and I do like you, but you are right about what there is between us. We don't feel anything more than a mutual bond of friendship. Trying to force anything more out of this relationship would be doomed to failure. It might even destroy what we have. That would be tragic." Darnell agreed.

Sephra wandered into the area Darnell and Merika were in. There was a young girl by her side, one she wanted Darnell to meet. The young woman had honey colored hair, which hung in sheaths down her back, and framed a heart shaped face. A pair of green eyes sparkled with intelligence and her full and inviting lips smiled in greeting, as they stopped to join them.

"Have you seen Tyrus today, Merika, we are looking for him." Sephra asked.

"No, in fact, Rodan told Serena and I that he had left sometime during the night." Merika admitted. There was no reason to hide the fact that she was ignoring him, not now, he was gone, and it had been done under his own steam.

"Well he might be gone, but he still needs to eat. Could you try to help us track him down?" Sephra asked.

"I will see if he is in the woods." Merika offered.

Merika shimmered out, then back in a few minutes later. "His usual spot is deserted."

"I saw Tyrus early this morning. He was headed for the high falls. Why?" Darnell pointed to a path that led up an incline.

"Did he have a sack or package with him?" Sephra wondered.

"No, nothing. I never gave it a thought. The path is easy, though seldom traveled. I thought he might be looking for a little solitude. Tyrus is like that," Darnell answered, giving the impression that he knew Tyrus well enough to make a remark like that about him.

"Well, that answers that question. Darnell, would you take care of Lida while Merika and I pack a lunch for Tyrus? He is pushing his limits and hasn't eaten. Merika has been given the task of taking care of him during his convalescence, and has been remiss in her duties." Sephra informed him.

"My pleasure," Darnell purred, as he offered his arm to Lida, and she blushed profusely.

Sephra and Merika walked away, and Sephra spoke. "I could have told the two of you that you were wrong for one another."

"I believe we knew that right from the start, but he said he had to try, and I could see no harm in a kiss. Not one that only confirmed what we already knew." Merika confessed.

"I know you mean well, Merika, but a strong Alpha Prime like Darnell could make you to lose control of your senses. Especially when he is as desperate to make a match as Darnell is." Sephra informed her.

"Are you sure Lida is going to be safe?" Merika worried.

"After dealing with you, I believe Darnell will be a little more careful. It is a good thing you are such a strong person." Sephra replied.

"How is Serena making out?" Merika asked.

"She has Rodan sitting outside in the sun. The fresh air will do him good." Sephra noted.

"So what do you suggest I take for Tyrus?" Merika wondered.

"Nothing too heavy, yet it will have to be nourishing. What do you have available?" Sephra asked.

"Some light meat rolls, a hearty soup, some fresh fruit, a sweet desert to boost his energy. Too much and it will make him uncomfortable." Merika considered his condition, as she named the things she figured he would be still able to stomach at this time.

"A bottle of red wine might not be out of order, to help his digestion and boost his metabolism. Most people overlook the medicinal quality of a good wine. You are as much to blame as anyone. It is more than flavoring you know." Merika pointed out.

"I know and I understand, but back to the lunch, your choices sound good. I will leave you put it together and then you can take it up to him." Sephra agreed.

Merika sighed, as she watched Sephra head off to see to something else, then returned to the kitchen to put the meal together. An hour and a half later Merika dropped the basket full of food beside Tyrus and he growled at her.

"Do you realize I came up here to get away from you?"

"Do you realize you have had nothing to eat all day, and because of your pigheaded ideas, I had to traipse half way up a mountain to feed you?" Merika snipped back. If he was going to be nasty, she decided she could give back as much as he gave.

"No one asked you to." Tyrus grouched.

"No. They ordered me to." Merika replied, as she sunk down to her knees and unpacked the meal.

"You could have told them to jump into a lake. I would have." Tyrus stated.

"Probably, but then I would have had to deal with you catching cold as well." Merika teased, as she handed him the bottle of wine and opener. "Pop the cork. Sephra says it is for medicinal purposes."

Tyrus frowned, as he joined Merika by the spread and popped the cork. "I guess, I should be gracious and say how hungry I am, and that I appreciate your efforts."

"Not expected, that would not be your style at all. Just shut your mouth and eat." Merika ordered.

"One is not conducive to the other," Tyrus couldn't resist the temptation to tease.

"You know what I mean," Merika replied, as she stifled a small giggle.

Together, Tyrus and Merika worked their way through the light lunch, before settling down beside each other to watch the waterfall in a companionable silence. Before either realized anything had changed between them, Tyrus looked down at Merika and noticed she was leaning against his shoulder, she was fast asleep. He shifted slightly, until his arm encircled her shoulders, and wound the blanket about the both of them to ward off the chill of the encroaching late afternoon breeze. He smiled, as he watched her in her sleep. Her eyelashes formed dark crescents against her pale cheeks, and he could tell she was still not finished healing and now neither was he. They made quite a pair. He heaved a heavy sigh, dropped a soft kiss on her forehead and, resting his cheek against the top of her head, he also fell asleep.

Tyrus woke with a jolt, as Merika opened her eyes and gave a cry of alarm. "Just what time is it anyway?"

Tyrus looked around, noting the rising sun and knew something was wrong. They should not have slept as they did, not solidly throughout the night. "Damn," he swore under his breath. "This could have serious repercussions. What was in the wine?"

"What do you mean? Merika snapped as they scrambled to their feet.

"Where did the wine come from?" Tyrus wanted to know.

"Sephra, she went somewhere and came back with the bottle. She said it would be good for our digestion." Merika explained.

"Something tells me I am going to have a little talk with my father and his partner in crime. In the meantime, I think we need to get back to our proper places, before we are missed. Just leave everything as it is. We can meet later and compare notes about our experiences over lunch. No more food or drinks that you or I have not prepared ourselves from now on. This is the cruelest thing they could have done." Tyrus spoke angrily. He couldn't believe Sephra and his father would do something like that to them. He had trusted them, Merika had trusted them, and they had betrayed the both of them. He was going to have words with them over this.

Merika transported herself straight to her bed, where she quickly prepared herself for what remained of her sleep time and crashed.

Tyrus went straight to his father, where he immediately went on the attack. "That was a dirty trick father, I hope you are proud of yourself."

"That depends," Kodac's response was thick with sleepiness, as he was still abed and not quite awake yet. He was conscious enough to know what Tyrus was talking about, and his response, as he asked. "Did it work?"

"Did we almost freeze sleeping off a bottle of drug laced wine? The answer to that is yes, and we will consider ourselves lucky if we have managed to escape without catching a cold. How could you?" Tyrus came close to yelling at his father for the first time since they had met. He was livid, and not sure what he was going to do about this. It was one thing for Sephra and him to plot to bring Merika and him together. It was another for them to drug them. This he was not about to take lying down.

"Well, neither of you were doing so well on your own," Kodac informed Tyrus.

"With your experience in the past, I would have thought you would have known better." Tyrus shot back.

"Merika is not the same as your mother." Kodak replied.

"Thank heaven for that. You will, father, never try anything like this again. Am I making myself clear? Leave us be, we will work this out on our own. If we are meant to be a couple, it will happen." Tyrus stated.

"So where is our maiden fair?" Kodac wanted to know. He knew he made it sound as if he was pushing the matter aside, but that wasn't really the way it was. He was concerned, but probably for all the wrong reasons, especially as far as his son was concerned. Tyrus wouldn't understand at the moment, not in the mood he was in. Hell, probably not in any of his moods. His son was such a moody character, he was apt to go back into the forest now and brood again, as he had been earlier. What was he going to do about him?

"Merika is probably in her own bed by now, and with luck she is sleeping. She is no more pleased about what you and Sephra tried to pull off than I am." Tyrus warned Kodac.

"So what can either of you do about it? You were both given a little push, to see if you would come together. It is done all the time. It either works, or not. Only the couple involved can determine the outcome. The rest can only hope. Rant and rave all you want son, it is all the good it will do you." Kodac informed Tyrus.

"So you refuse to leave us be? Can we at least trust either of you not to drug us again? That was a low blow, father." Tyrus stated.

"Tyrus, I do not need to do anything. Whatever happens from now on, the two of you will do it on your own, without any help from me. But, don't try to tell me there is no attraction between the two of you. Merika is an innocent in love and desire, but you know how it can burn. I have seen it in your eyes every time you look at her. It has been that way from the first moment you laid eyes on her, and it eats at your guts even as you try to deny it." Kodac pointed out the truth to his son, as he saw it.

"Leave me be," Tyrus enunciated in his anger.

"Go to bed, Tyrus. Sleep. I told you. It is not I, but you, who will determine your future. I am going back to sleep." Kodac decided.

Tyrus stormed out of his father's room, out of the building, and across the clearing. But the time he had reached his room, he had reasoned out his father's wisdom, if not his right. What he had said was true. He would be the master of his own fate, no matter who tried to lead him in another direction. He thought of Merika, as she had looked in his arms, so trusting and innocent and he sighed, as he swore.

"Damn."

His father knew and understood him too well. He would try to sleep now, but he doubted if he could.

"Still in a foul mood?" Rodan spoke as he watched Tyrus enter the room they shared through sleep-blurred eyes.

"No, just frustrated. Father and Sephra drugged our wine, and we slept most of the night away," Tyrus explained.

"Is that all? You should hear about the trouble that I am courting." Rodan replied proudly.

"I know what you are after, but at least you are doing it of your own free will." Tyrus complained.

"Face it brother, so will you. It is beyond our power to prevent ourselves from doing so. I am willing to my fate with a smile. You, on the other hand, will fight it right to the bitter end. That is what you have done all your life. You know no other way." Rodan pointed out what he thought was the obvious.

"You think you know our fates?" Tyrus asked.

"Our fates are simple. Like all men of our kind, we will love, marry, lead and protect our people. We will raise our families, and when it is all over, we will die. My future is with Serena. I will win her love and hand. It might not be easy, she seeks to remake me without knowing that I am already the man she seeks. Merika is another matter. She does not realize that you are her life. She will learn it quickly enough though, for when you decided that it is time for you to claim her, there will be no question in anyone's mind that your decision has been made.

"You are so sure Merika is the one I seek?" Tyrus sounded in surprise.

"To everyone, but you brother, the answer to that is obvious. Find a way to deal with your feelings for her, or live with the consequences." Rodan advised. He wasn't about to fight about this with Tyrus, or talk the matter to death. What needed to be done would either happen naturally, or not at all. The choice was up to Tyrus.

CHAPTER XVI

It was nearly time for her meeting, and Merika was feeling ill at ease again. There was a feeling around the upper falls that told her something about them had changed. There was someone strange around who had not been invited. She stood by the side of the path that led to the clearing, and reached out to test the atmosphere for malice. She found nothing to give any impression of ill intent, though there was a person she didn't know in attendance.

"You might as well join me, Merika." A male voice called out to her from inside the clearing.

"Who are you?" Merika asked. She wasn't about to walk into an area without knowing something about what she was getting herself into, not when she didn't know anything about this person.

"Rafik. I am Tyrus' half brother, and I have come to visit him." He replied openly.

"Tyrus never mentioned any other brother than Rodan." Merika stated.

"Doesn't mean I don't exist. Tyrus never mentioned a brother named Rodan to me. How do I know he exists? It isn't that I don't think that Rodan isn't real, it just serves as an example of what a checkered past our family history has. When I last touched base with Tyrus, he was thoroughly fed up with the general rat race in the outside word. He had decided to go to find his natural father, in hopes that this world was more grounded. How did he make out?" Rafik asked, sounding as if he actually cared.

"You will have to ask him to find that out." Merika answered.

"Fair enough." Rafik replied.

"Tell me, how did you know my name?" Merika wanted to know.

Rafik shrugged a shoulder and replied. "How does anyone in our family know anything? We just do. Oh, and if you see a strange looking guy coming up the path to join us shortly, don't be scared. That will be Rhys, he is a friend."

"Another stray of the community coming home?" Merika asked.

"Rhys would fit in anywhere, the louse. Powerful here. Powerful in the outside world as well, he could almost rival Tyrus for strength, and I bet they get along just fine when they meet." Rafik gave a long sigh and added. "He is going to really like you."

"You know that the same way you know my name, I suppose?" Merika commented drily.

"No, all I need to do is see you to know. With Rhys it is simpler, he tends to appreciate the finer things in life and you definitely fit the bill. Unless I miss my guess, you will like him as well." Rafik stated.

Merika was still not impressed. She had had her fill of men wanting her for her beauty or power. Up to this point she had refused to move forward, while Rafik continued to be vague, as far as she was concerned. Standing in the shadows and waiting for one of them to bridge the gap was getting her nowhere. She took a firmer grip on the basket that she held and stepped out into the full sunlight of the clearing. It was warm and welcoming, and she turned her face up to catch the full effect of it on her skin.

"Here, let me take that for you," The man that had introduced himself as Rafik, spoke, as he rose to take the loaded basket from Merika. He was surprised how heavy it was, and that she showed no effects from carrying it up the mountain trail. "I shall assume you had a date with my brother for lunch, and that is why you brought the picnic."

"Tyrus can be easy to be with. There is no serious pressures, and he can be pleasant, if not pushed." Merika compared the two men. Both were handsome in a dark way. She was willing to bet Tyrus tended to be darker, in personality, as well as coloring and it showed. Rafik had a more open look to him, although his dark eyes had shadows in them that defied exploration. They didn't have the same snap to them that dared you to even try. Tyrus's did though.

Rafik smiled at Merika's frank scrutiny. He liked her honest and uninhibited inspection, especially as it seemed it was more for character than looks. When it came to physique, he knew he could hold his own against most men, after all, he was a well-endowed man in his prime, and he looked the part. He missed the edge of danger to him that Tyrus had that, for some crazy reason, it seemed to attract the ladies. Women seemed to feel that Tyrus needed nurturing. But, the snarls and snaps that he was apt to greet them with soon put them off. He wondered why Tyrus' usual attitude wasn't working with this woman, for it was obvious by the way she talked that they were friends.

Returning Merika's scrutiny with looks of definite appreciation, Rafik wondered just how close Tyrus and her had gotten, and whether he stood a chance with her. He decided it would be a waste of time to pursue that, in the end. When Rhys arrived, he doubted if either of them would soon exist for her. Rhys went through women like a hot blade through warm butter. Then again, perhaps she was not attracted to that type, unlikely as that thought might be. As he finished considering all these things, he spread his senses out once more, then noted.

"Tyrus and his father are heading this way, I can feel them. You know, Merika, you surprise me. I can think of no one else who would describe my overly surly brother as pleasant and easy. He must be slipping."

"I know he snarls and snaps, but it is just meant to keep people at a distance. I can both understand and relate to that. I understand a good part of his problem stems from the relationship he shared with his mother." Merika stated.

"Our mother was a sadistic, manipulating, self serving bitch of the first order." The light in Rafik's eyes snapped in sudden ill-disguised humor, making it obvious that both brothers shared the same opinion of their mother. "She made our lives hell. I doubt if there was a man on the face of the planet she did not use, or try to. Tyrus and I had different fathers. But, the one thing in common we shared, was our hatred for our mother. Tyrus bore the brunt of my father's hatred, so he had it doubly hard. He was older than I was and his father was not around to shield him. So, he was easy prey for their games when we were growing up. He has been so angry and bitter for so long, I doubted if he could have any kind of a real relationship with a female. I am glad you are here to prove me wrong."

"Oh, it is not like that between us." Merika laughed, perceiving Rafik's train of thought. "We are friends, buddies if that will make it any clearer. Tell me, how did you get to be so pleasant while Tyrus is so caustic? I know you said his father wasn't there to shield him, but that doesn't always mean much. You also mentioned that you both had trouble with your mother, and you both seem to have the same general opinion of her. So what made the difference?"

"I told you. He got the worst of it. I spent most of my time at boarding school, surrounded by friends and colleagues. I learned to bless every moment I was away from home." Rafik admitted.

"Why wasn't Tyrus sent away as well?" Merika wondered.

"Tyrus was a thorn in my father's side, one that father never learned to accept. Because of that, he was treated worse than a servant's child. All said and done, my father treated him in a way no one should be proud of. There was nothing anyone could do about it. Mother thought his actions were amusing, and encouraged it, while adding her own twist to the mixture. I was little more than a child, when Tyrus was subjected to the major abuse. He wasn't much older than I. My father pampered me. I was shallow, and more concerned with my own skin and having a good time, and still Tyrus stuck up for me. I avoided my mother like the plague, even in my youth. I sensed there was something about her that was not right." Rafik admitted. "It was later in life when I really found out what was going on, and I stayed away from home as much as possible. Our mother was getting worse, and her actions were beginning to include me, as well as Tyrus. My father had only so much control, she had him wound so tight around her little finger, he couldn't see the dangers she presented to his own child, never mind one that had been fathered by another man."

"Like most kids. I suppose you had little contact with Tyrus because of how he was viewed." Merika guessed.

"I worshipped the ground Tyrus walked on. He was the only one who could vex our mother and get away with it. He would just disappear and she would go on a rampage, trying to find him. To this day, I still wonder where he went, and how he got there." Rafik explained.

"So Tyrus virtually grew up as an abused child. No wonder he has a chip on his shoulder the size of Manhattan." Merika commented.

Rafik pulled a large blanket out of the basket, spread it on the ground and they settled on it, to start unpacking the rest of what she had brought, as he continued to talk.

"So what is your story? I got the impression that you were

another like us, raised in the outside world."

"I was, have you ever heard of Tanya Wade?" Merika asked.

"Hell yes, though I never had the privilege of meeting her. As small as this planet is reputed to be, it is still bigger than they claim." Rafik stated.

"I was never that accessible anyway. Few realize just how busy I was with my schedule and work load." Merika admitted.

"You are Tanya Wade!" He looked at Merika in surprise, then his face transformed as a big slow smile crossed it. "You are! The thought of meeting anyone like Tanya Wade, in a place like this, is so out of sync with what a person expects that you could have worn a neon sign, and I would have still not believed it possible."

"I know," Merika admitted, as she smiled back. "I love the anonymity."

"Somehow, you look different, dressed as you are." Rafik noted.

"I wore different styles in my roles, but you make me feel as if I should be surprised that anyone would be able to recognize me in decent clothing. My roles never ran into nudity or anything provocative. I wouldn't have allowed it." Merika stated.

"I watched every movie you ever made, and even some of your shows. I will be amongst the first to admit you were always fully dressed. But Lord, a man can always dream." Rafik ended on a wistful sigh.

"You are incorrigible." Merika laughed. "Something tells me you are a ladies man with a lot of experience."

"To the end." Rafik murmured in agreement, as he leaned forward on hands and knees to close the space between them. Only to be brought up short.

"Back off brother," Tyrus growled, as he preceded his father into the clearing.

Rafik smiled in amusement at his brother, then took a closer look at Kodac and commented. "I see you found what you were looking for. I am happy for you."

"What are you here for?" Tyrus refused to be sidetracked.

"Is that any way to greet a brother who has traveled half a world to be with you?" Rafik teased Tyrus.

"Out with it, Rafik." Tyrus ordered.

"Oh, all right. You never were much fun, not that I blame you much for that. Every time you looked happy, our mother found a way to destroy whatever made you feel that way. When she cared to notice at all, that is. But, she isn't here now, Tyrus, and I would say it looks like you have found all you ever missed. So why don't you just leave it go?" Rafik suggested.

"Somehow, I doubt if you traveled this far to share old memories brother," Tyrus stated bluntly.

"As usual, Tyrus, you are right. I need to talk with you, and, in this case probably your father as well. As he looks like an older version of you, I will assume Kodac is your father. Come and join us, Merika has packed a delicious looking lunch. It would be a shame to let it go to waste." Rafik invited.

Kodac gave Tyrus a light push on the shoulder, to press him onward, then made himself at home, next to Merika, who had been watching the encounter with interest.

"Did you hand-make this?" Kodac asked Merika.

Tyrus turned to his brother and explained. "Merika is one of our chief chefs."

Merika replied. "Both Angela and Celia helped, but yes the meal is essentially my doing."

"Sounds interesting, multitalented," was all that Rafik said, before adding. "In case no one else is aware of it, we are about to have company, others who are also sporting a hamper of food. One man called Rodan, and a woman called Serena."

"That is my younger son, and his soon to be wife. Well done." Kodac acknowledged.

"What would that make him to me?" Rafik wondered.

"The closest I can think of, would be stepbrother." Kodac replied.

"But for that you would have to adopt me." Rafik teased Kodac. "Looking at the way Tyrus acts around you, and how he is trying to shield you from me, I am thinking that would be a good thing. So, for the record, I am game if you are."

Kodac just laughed and shook his head, "I am to understand by your comment, that you think I have been good for Tyrus?"

"Tyrus looks at you with eyes that reflect love, affection and respect. He acts as if he thinks he might be needed to protect you. All this, when he knows I would never hurt anything of his." Rafik pointed out.

"Do you see Rafik as a threat, Tyrus?" Kodac asked.

"No. Rafik would never hurt anyone here, not even if he could." Tyrus confirmed. "Neither of us had an easy time of surviving our mother. We shielded each other the best we could."

Serena and Rodan entered the clearing soon after, and took their place in amongst the others. Serena added their food to the supplies Merika had brought earlier, then took her place by Rodan's side. She looked as if she was reluctant to leave him on his own, and he looked pleased about it.

Rafik smiled at Serena in admiration, as he teased them. "Are all the women extremely beautiful in your world, or have I lucked out in meeting two of the best first time around?"

Kodac answered. "You will find all our women are beautiful in various degrees. Now, I have a question for you. How could I have missed your coming through the portal?"

"Maybe because we didn't come through your portal." Rafik replied.

"We?" Tyrus was stunned. He couldn't begin to believe his brother had the power it took to open a new portal, never mind bring others through it with him undetected. His powers just didn't run that way, and he knew it.

"I come bearing news, and new friends for your world." Rafik stated. He sounded cryptic, and Tyrus was not in the mood for either mysteries or riddles.

"Like I said earlier brother, spit it out and get it over with."

"Alright. I found another portal that led to a world like this one, from a different area." Rafik informed them.

"Where, and when did you find that?" Kodac was more than just a little interested in this bit of information.

"I was skiing in the Canadian Rockies, when I got caught in an avalanche. As luck would have it, instead of being buried alive, I was knocked aside. When I came to, I found myself lying in the snow, near the entrance of an enormous cave. I followed an old path I found inside the tunnel and entered a beautiful valley. Eventually, I stumbled on people like us. Or maybe I should say they found me. There was no technology to speak of and it seemed like stepping through time into the past. They used horses and carriages and wore swords…"

"We get the picture brother. Get to the point." Tyrus interrupted, knowing that Rafik tended to get long winded, if left to do so.

"What I am telling you is important. These people are much more powerful than I am and they were just as curious about me as I was about them. Their women are drop dead gorgeous, just like here. There are a lot of parallels, and their world connects to this one, at least it does now," Rafik reported.

"You mentioned others that came with you. Am I right to assume that they have come to meet us, just as we would like to meet them?" Kodac enquired, as he ignored Tyrus. He was aware of the distrust his eldest son felt for the brother he had shared his youth with. He had heard Tyrus' reasons, and knew the truth of them. Despite the bad blood that existed between them, he also realized that the bond that had been forged out of mutual need and blood was strong there as well. They could be counted on to fight for each other, despite past betrayals.

"Yes." Rafik answered.

"How long were you with these people, Rafik?" Kodac asked.

"Almost two years, maybe a little longer. I left home right after Tyrus did. Mother was in a rare snit, and I didn't want to stick around. It used to get dangerous to be in the same space as her, when she was in a temper, especially when it got out of hand." Rafik explained.

"I remember that about her all too clearly." Tyrus backed up Rafik's statement. He then added, "She was in a rage when I left. She didn't like it that I was coming here to find my father."

"Yes, well, I wouldn't invite her to tea if I were you, because I doubt if anything has changed. She probably hasn't had a rational moment since," Rafik stated.

"No problem, and yes, things have changed there, although it is just hearsay on my part. Our mother had a stroke after you left, and she died." Tyrus replied. He didn't sound sorry or affected by their mother's death. To him, it was a relief. She could no longer hurt him where he was, and she always seemed to know when and how she would have the most effect.

"Now, I suggest you get back to the subject of the people you met through the portal, those that I assume you brought with you," Kodac pushed.

"Perhaps I could fill you in a little better." A new voice cut in, as seven people entered the clearing from what should have been a portion of the mountain they were resting on. "I am Rhys. I am a representative of my people. We bring you assurances of our peaceful intent."

Kodac stood up quickly, followed by the rest of those who had been sitting with him. He executed a perfect bow of greeting and replied. "In peace, we welcome you to our Valley. I am Kodac. These are my sons. Tyrus and Rodan. The women are Serena and Merika."

"As representatives of our people, I bring Kalla, Firth, Dara, Cormax, Meridor, and Derek. Some of our people, like those here, were raised in the outside world, then reintegrated into our society. We believe it is good to keep track of what is going on in the world, beyond the one we know."

"We do much the same. Come; join us for a light lunch. We need to talk and get to know one another." Kodac insisted.

Settling side-by-side, Kodac and Rhys motioned for their respective peoples to join them. Rodan and Serena sat together, as if afraid to expose one or the other to danger or exposure. It was a subtle, unconscious, message that spoke of possession, and it was understood and honored as such. Kalla and Firth followed their example. Everyone else spread out to sit indiscriminately. Each helped themselves to choice bits from the picnic offerings, and looked to their leaders to begin the meeting, while they enjoyed the food.

"Our Valleys are much the same, despite ours being nestled in the interior or a mountain range. We placed our portal deep inside of a cave, and only once has a stranger wandered into our Valley. That was young Rafik, and he came bearing news and information of another world like ours. He was not familiar with our way of life, so we knew he was from the outside world. We decided, as his powers mirrored ours, to study him for a while. In the beginning, we were inclined not to trust him. He knew too much about our ways of life, without having ever been to our world. We were not at all sure what to think." Rhys pointed out.

"I know the feeling intimately. We have been receiving refugees from the outside world for years. Most, who are drawn through the portal, to this world, was for them to be amongst their own people, whether they were born in the Valley or not. I noticed that it seems our peoples are attracted to one another, even in the outside world, almost as if we are not supposed to intermingle with those beyond the portals, though we can." Kodac shared his discoveries freely.

"Our people tend to stay home in the Valley, but occasionally, there are those who rebel. I find that phase changes with age. Those who leave, always return home." Rhys replied.

"Most of ours do as well, however, there is always the exception. But, no matter what, they usually always return to the Valley at some point." Kodac spoke as if in defense of his people. "Unless they die in the outside world."

"Yes," Rhys nodded. "That is too true, and people will be people. I created a portal to connect our two Valleys. With your permission, I will keep it open. Then again, to be honest, I will not be able to keep it open for long without the imprint of your power on it."

"I was beginning to wonder about the limits to your power. You have come into my Valley unheralded, creating your own doorway. What was I to think about that?" Kodak asked.

"My power is no more or less than yours. You have no fear there. As I can bar your way to my lands, you can bar mine. The people in this clearing have more power combined than half the combined forces of the rest of my Valley population, and yours for that matter, I would wager. It would benefit both of our worlds immensely if we joined forces as allies. I bet your people need an influx of new bloodlines every bit as much as mine do." Rhys added.

"We have been careful to make sure there is no inbreeding amongst the populace, but our population grows smaller, and our options diminish. In that way, I can see the benefits, and they go both ways, assuming you have the same problems we do. There is a lot to consider in this merger. We have only begun to think about all the pros and cons; you have had two years to think about it. You must allow that I need at least a little time to do the same." Kodac responded.

"That is why I have brought some of my people with me." Rhys admitted. "I thought that by meeting us in person, you would be better able to form an honest opinion. All we had to base ours on was Rafik, and he had no real working knowledge of your people or this valley. He knew about your valley, and your people. He has the same type of powers that we share, but it isn't the same as meeting those who come directly from the world he was talking about. What he told us was not a lot to base a decision on.

I am still not so sure I did the right thing, although just meeting you has alleviated a lot of my fears."

Merika watched, and listened to the meeting with interest. The two valley primes were evenly matched from what she could tell, and their minds worked much the same way, although Rhys was much younger. In fact, he seemed not much older than Tyrus.

Tyrus didn't appear to be pleased by any of it. A woman who was closest to Merika in power was closely watching him, and he was willing to bet she was the female Valley prime in their territory. There was no doubt she was beautiful, in a dark way, with long sheaths of chestnut hair, green eyes, a brilliant smile, and a curvaceous form made to bring pleasure to the right man. He was not that one though. He was more interested in a petite blonde who he thought could charm birds out of a tree. One with eyes so blue that they rivaled the sky, one who was looking at the foreign Valley Alpha Prime as if she had never seen a man before in her lifetime. He hated to admit it, but the look in Merika's eyes was irritating him. She wasn't supposed to look at others like that, only him.

"Hi, my name is Meridor," the brunette who had been watching Tyrus introduced herself, as she settled by his side, and he frowned.

"I am Tyrus." He knew better than to be rude at this time. His father was discussing a possible alliance that depended on them appearing to be friendly. But, what he was seeing, appeared to surpass that boundary. He looked at the invitation in Meridor's eyes, and decided that what she was offering would be friendlier than what he was willing to consider.

"My brother is speaking to your father, at least I assume he is your father. You look much like him. So, while they are busy, I thought we could get to know one another. What do you think?"

Meridor asked.

Meridor had followed Tyrus's gaze, and she inwardly grinned. She understood what was drawing him, and was sure she could distract him from his obsession with the other woman. At least, she hoped she could. She knew the woman was not near as interested in her brother as she appeared to be. It was the conversation going on that held her attention, though her brother was definitely worthy of the woman's attention if she was interested.

"Handsome, isn't he?" Meridor spoke with obvious pride in her brother.

"I suppose." Tyrus almost sounded dismissive, as if he didn't care.

"Rhys and I had different mothers, that is why we look so different from one another. From what Rafik told us, the two of you had the same mother, but you share you father's features and not his coloring. I can see a bit of you in Rodan. But you do not look at all alike at first glance. Are you related?" Meridor attempted to focus Tyrus' attention on her, by asking questions.

"Rodan is my brother," Tyrus stated.

"Strange, Rafik never mentioned him," Meridor noted.

"Rafik knows nothing of him, Rodan was raised in the Valley, Rafik was not, just as I was not." Tyrus informed Meridor.

"Do you ever miss your life outside the Valley?" Meridor wondered.

"No," Tyrus answered shortly.

"Why not?" Meridor wondered.

"I have my reasons. Most are based on the fact that those that are the most important to me live here." Tyrus stated.

"It would have noting to do with one beautiful Alpha Prime would it?" Rhys smiled at him, showing that he had noticed the two of them talking, and had heard them.

Both Tyrus and Merika gave Rhys stunned looks, and he smiled, as he added, "Well, you have to admit Merika is beautiful."

"Perhaps, but we are just friends." Tyrus replied, and Kodac could have wrung his son's neck for saying so.

Merika almost made Kodac groan as she added. "We are little more than acquaintances."

Rhys' smile widened, as he followed up on Meridor's comment. "There isn't an Alpha in our Valley who wouldn't be casting their attention on Merika in my homeland. Surely, she is not left on the sidelines here? It is unimaginable."

"There have been lots of men who have tried to catch Merika's interest, but so far..." Serena spoke up, leaving her comment open and accentuated with a slight shrug of her shoulder.

"I am just not ready to settle down yet, there is lots of time." Merika answered.

Rhys allowed his attention to linger on Serena and Rodan for a moment, then replied. "Sometimes it just takes the right man to cross your path to change your mind. Right, Serena?"

Serena blushed and smiled, as she gazed into Rodan's eyes and agreed. She did not tell Rhys that she had loved the legend, before she had met the man. Something's were just better left unsaid.

Meridor had no such qualms, as she purred, while looking at Tyrus. "Some women know a good thing when they see it, and have the good sense not to let it get away."

Tyrus frowned at Meridor. He wasn't interested in her at all, though he was not immune to her beauty. At the moment, however, her wiles were wasted on him. He noted the glint of speculation that shone in Rhys' eyes, as he looked at Merika, and it angered him. Angered him? Hell, he wanted to get up and beat the man to a pulp for looking at Merika the way he was. The glint in his eyes was more than interest, there was a hunger there. As Rhys' sister claimed she knew a good thing when she saw it, so did her brother. He would be damned if Rhys was getting Merika, not even if he had to marry her himself.

Cormax was the one who broke the sudden silence, as he spoke in snide tones that Tyrus recognized as similar to his own, spouting ideas he had often voiced himself.

"So, Merika, how much cruelty do you hide behind that stunning exterior?"

Merika turned guileless eyes on Cormax and replied. "I am exactly as represented, though I can change that at a whim if need be. In the outside world, I was an actress."

"Most women are, even in real life. It comes naturally to them, like breathing." Cormax stated.

"We are speaking of something altogether different. Nor are all females duplicitous. I have met men just as capable of the type of actions that you are insinuating are exclusively feminine traits." Merika argued.

Cormax grunted, it was a point he was not so sure he could successfully argue. He had been out in the world and his experiences were not the best.

Rhys watched Cormax, with a smug smile spread across his face. He knew his friend had just made himself look like a woman hater, and it would not set well with the young lady. He was also sure that his friend was attracted to Merika, or he would have never spoken to her in the first place. He was like that.

"So, whom do you belong to in this world?" Cormax changed the subject.

"Myself. I am not an inanimate object that I am to be counted as anybody's possession. Nor do I own anyone, for the same reason in reverse." Merika dismissed the question.

"Do you actually believe that pile of horse manure?!" Cormax was incredulous.

"Do you go out of your way to be objectionable or were you born ignorant?" Merika shot back.

"I am a realist, there is a difference." Cormax spat out angrily.

"I agree, but somehow I am surprised you would recognize it." Merika returned.

"Cruel, just like most women," Cormax pointed out.

"Why don't you just crawl back into whatever cave you slithered out of and leave me be?" Merika suggested. The last thing she needed in her life, was an overbearing boor to single her out to be his punching bag, which she felt was exactly what Cormax was doing.

"Like I said, cruel. You mock your beauty and gender. Probably vain as well. If not for that you would bring some poor, lonely, neglected male comfort and companionship." Cormax sniffed.

Rhys was enthralled with the picture of Merika in a temper, as well as Tyrus. True, Tyrus had seen her angry before, but not like this! She appeared to be lit from within. If it were possible, her eyes would have shot sparks, she was so inflamed. Did she really not like the man, or was there an attraction neither was aware of?

"Male chauvinist. I thought our world had run out of Neanderthals many millennium ago." Merika shot back.

"You think you are coming across any different?" Cormax hissed dangerously, as he leaned forward, as if to confront Merika.

"You are thoroughly objectionable." Merika sniffed, totally unaware of the trouble she was courting.

"I am right, whether you want to admit it or not," Cormax insisted.

"I refuse to listen to your drivel any further. This was supposed to be a friendly luncheon, so we could examine cultures. Not a battleground, though, for all I know, you don't realize that there is a difference. I am leaving." Merika announced.

"You can't just up and leave." Cormax reacted in surprise.

"Want to bet?" Merika shot them all a frown, as she shimmered out of the area.

A stunned look crossed over their faces, and Cormax asked. "Where did she go?"

Everyone shrugged their shoulders and Tyrus replied. "Merika can block almost any attempts anyone makes to trace her."

"Can you trace her?" Cormax asked.

"Usually." Tyrus admitted.

"So where is she?" Rhys asked curiously.

"Right now, I have no idea. Merika's block is tighter than usual, I can't get past them to see. I have never ever seen her this way. What did Cormax do to her?"

"Offended her, he is famous for that." Dara shot him a nasty look. "Cormax goes out of his way to insult everyone he can."

"Can I help it if Merika is unable to accept the truth?" Cormax stated.

"Sweep your own doorstep, you insufferable streak of misery." Dara shot back. "Cormax would be married by now, if he could say two cordial words to a female."

Tyrus suppressed the urge to laugh. Dara was giving him an impression of a slight pixie poking at a giant. She also fit the picture he had of a pixie very well, with her gamine looks and diminutive stature, and he could tell she had it bad for Cormax. That man needed someone to wake him up to what she was about, before he missed out on it.

"Come sit beside me, Dara, I promise not to overlook your obvious charms." Tyrus invited.

"Perhaps I will," Dara chirped, as she turned to Tyrus and flounced from Cormax's presence. He, in return, frowned at her retreating form.

Rhys watched it all unfold in perceptive silence. He could tell Dara was no more interested in Tyrus than he was in her, but the fact that she had stood up and flipped Cormax off, as she had made him finally take notice of her, well, it almost made him chuckle. He had always considered Cormax a blockhead. This just proved his point, but as far as Dara was concerned, it was past time he had a wake up call.

Cormax watched Dara as she sashayed over to Tyrus, and curled up on the ground beside him. Tyrus reached over to put an arm about her waist, as he drew her close to his side, and Cormax narrowed his eyes in warning. Tyrus took note of the gesture, lowered his lips to Dara's ear, and said something that made her throw back her head and burst out laughing. A mere heartbeat later, Cormax was crossing the distance between them to pull her away from Tyrus, and he was snarling and snapping at the both of them.

"You don't touch her, and you mind your place."

"Just what makes you think you have the right to tell anyone what to do? Especially me. I don't belong to you." Dara snarled back.

Cormax reacted by pulling Dara into his arms, as he looked into her eyes and growled back. "The hell you don't." They both disappeared together, and all attention turned to a grinning Rhys for an explanation.

Rhys looked at the enquiring faces around him, and calmly replied. "Something tells me we won't be seeing those two for a while. When we do, Cormax will be in a much improved mood. Nicely done, Tyrus, never thought of jealousy when it came to getting those two together, should have known Cormax was the possessive kind. So, how do we get Merika back now?"

"She will show up when she is ready, and there is nothing anyone can do about it. She is, after all Female Prime of the Valley." Kodac answered.

Rhys smiled wider and replied. "You are right on all counts, and in more ways than any of you seem to perceive, and don't ask me to explain. It is just a thought that popped into my mind, along with a feeling I had about her. It gets complicated sometimes, and you, Kodac, should have a good idea what I am talking about."

Kodac frowned, as he nodded in agreement. He did understand and yes, it could be very complicated. Sometimes, most times, there was just no explaining it. Though it made you wonder.

No one even noticed Kalla follow Merika. She materialized in a small clearing, where Merika used to meet Tyrus, and found her reclining on a log, propped up against a large tree trunk.

"Would you like some company for a while? I noticed your

reaction to Cormax, not that I blame you. A more opinionated, caustic excuse for a male I have never met. But he is gone now, and I thought you might need a friend to vent some spleen on."

"You think I am going to let someone like that bother me for long?" Merika gave a snort of disbelief, as she added. "Not likely."

"You are new to your life in the valley here, aren't you?" Kalla noted.

"I arrived only a few weeks ago. I have spent most of my time recovering from the transition between worlds. It has not been easy and I still have a difficult time believing this is happening to me. There was so much for me to accept, understand and learn. Then they act as if they expected me to choose a husband while I am doing this. Not happening." Merika stated.

"I understand perfectly." Kalla agreed.

"Do you?" Merika tossed her a skeptical glance.

"More than you know. Meridor might be our Female Prime, but she is no more powerful than I am. She is just a little, more, somehow." Kalla explained with a meaningful sigh.

"You look like you are comfortable in your world." Merika noted.

"You mean with Firth? He would be flattered that you had even noticed him, and yes, we are at that point in our lives when we are ready to make a commitment to each other," Kalla admitted.

"I didn't just notice him, Kalla, I noticed how well the two of you suit one another. It is the same as it is with Serena and Rodan." Merika explained.

"I noticed them as well, and I have eyes to see. Rodan is enough to make a girl drool, although I like my Firth better. Tyrus is another that could make a girl forget her place in a hurry, I wouldn't leave that sitting around unguarded for long if I were you. Did you see the look in Meridor's eyes when she saw him?" Kalla asked.

Merika smiled and shook her head. "Matchmaking, Kalla? Or do you just dislike Meridor that much? Tyrus and I will never be more than friends."

"Your friend caused a terrible row between Cormax and Dara after you left. Dara objected to the way Cormax had treated you, and he fought back. She retaliated by snuggling up to Tyrus, and Cormax got angry enough that he dragged her off."

"He won't hurt her will he?" Merika asked in concern.

"Heavens no, but I bet they are mated by now. Dara has always had a soft spot for Cormax, and he would never admit it, but he is crazy about her. She torments him in ways he didn't understand, but he will. She is no push over, even if she is super petite."

"So, what did you really come here for? More important, how did you find me? No one finds me when I don't want them to." Merika replied.

"I followed your trail. It is a gift I have that few know about. Rhys does, but then he seems to know about most things," Kalla explained.

"Just like Kodac, although even he can't trace my presence." Merika stated.

"Rhys seemed surprised you could disappear so quickly. He can usually track anyone, even me. By now, he will know where we are, although he might not know it is we, and not just I. If he believes I am alone, he will not understand why I went, or why I am staying away." Kalla added.

"It feels good to keep them guessing sometimes, doesn't it?" Merika smiled with a mischievous sparkle in her eyes.

"So true," Kalla giggled conspiratorially, then confided. "I had hoped that we could be friends, I haven't had a close friend since I was out in the world, and you know which one I am talking about. I also know that as long as Meridor is around that was not about to happen. She might want you as a friend, but only to her. She is very possessive about anything she thinks is hers."

"She is going to have fun with Tyrus then. He has little faith or trust in females, and is a thorough cynic. He isn't the owning kind." Merika explained.

"Yet, you call him your friend." Kalla sounded surprised.

"We accept each others boundaries and respect them." Merika replied, then leaned forward and confided. "Besides, I understand he really is not interested in women in the way everyone thinks."

Kalla's eyes grew round with surprise. "Tyrus? You can't be serious. That man just oozes with testosterone. Are you sure?"

Merika shrugged a shoulder and gave a nod. "I was quite surprised myself, though he can be as surly as Cormax when he has to deal with them in most cases."

"I don't think that makes him gay though. If that is all you have to go by, it isn't much." Kalla replied.

"Actually, I was told that by someone who has known him a lot longer than I have." Merika shrugged a shoulder, and leaned back against the tree again. "I just never thought it mattered. As someone who has no interest in women, I consider him safe."

"I can't believe you said that," Kalla admitted.

"It is so simple, everyone thinks there is more to the relationship than there is and leaves you alone to go your own way." Merika explained.

"And what do you want?" Kalla wondered, she had a feeling that Merika was fooling herself, but she wasn't about to argue the point.

"Good question. I know that in the outside world, I was sick and tired of acting. I enjoy my time in the kitchen, but it isn't the same here as it was on the other side. Everything is so different here. What do you want?" Merika asked, just to be fair.

"A simple life. Firth. I love him, it is that simple, and I believe he loves me. It won't be much longer before we marry. It just feels so right when we are together. Are you sure Tyrus is gay?" Kalla double-checked.

"If he isn't, I don't want to know about it. Why?" Merika wondered.

"Just thinking about Meridor. She is in for such a shock." Kalla replied with a wide grin.

Shortly after, Tyrus sent a message to Merika. "We are all going to the clearing, meet you there."

Merika turned her attention back to Kalla and asked. "They are returning to the homestead clearing, want to come meet more of us?"

"Sure, why not." Kalla agreed with a smile, and they both transferred out of the area to join the rest.

CHAPTER XVII

Kodac watched, as a new world seemed to unfold around him. He took the time to notice how Rodan and Serena spent more and more of their time together while they got to know each other. They didn't allow their time together to get in the way of connecting with their new friends either. They seemed to spend whole afternoons with each other, learning about the new world, as well as teaching the others about theirs. He was pleased to note that during it, their commitment towards each other never once wobbled. They were a couple, and everyone accepted them as one. The first part of his plans had worked out well.

The relationship between Tyrus and Merika was infinitely harder to read. Some days, they would ride off with Kalla and Firth, other days were spent with Meridor and Rhys, and it seemed as if they too were making the effort to learn all they could about the new Valley. It was not that simple though for Kodac to keep them together. By not being able to read Merika, he had to seek all his answers through his ties with Tyrus. It didn't take him long to find that their times spent with Kalla and Firth were much more enjoyable, and productive, than those spent with the other two valley Alphas. That, he realized could have many reasons, though the main one he attributed to the fact was that Rhys seemed more interested in Merika than anything else. Tyrus, it became evident, was jealous of the man. To make it more complicated, the green-eyed monster didn't settle on one thing for long, but on a variety of things.

Kodac could only second-guess by what he could see and hear. Merika was interested in both worlds and made no secret of it. She would listen to Rhys with rapt attention, when he talked to her, and that man seemed to never run out of things to say. He could just imagine how the focus of those flawless eyes was affecting Rhys. He wasn't that old that he couldn't remember how these things made a man feel. Meridor telegraphed frustration, which made her easier to read than anyone. She wasn't getting anywhere with Tyrus, and gave the impression that she was about to turn her attention onto someone else. Anyone else was his guess. That woman acted as if she was desperate to find a man. Tyrus tended to stick to Merika's side, especially when Rhys was around, although he made no move to claim her for himself. There were times when Tyrus couldn't be there to be with Rhys and Merika, something Kodac was trying to fix. The last thing they needed was for Tyrus to lose her, because he couldn't find time to press his own suit.

There were some days Kodac swore his son would drive him to drink. He was sure that with a little effort on his part, Tyrus could have Merika just as enthralled with him, as Serena was with Rodan. But that, he sarcastically thought to himself, would be too easy. No, he had to keep everyone guessing, had to play his stupid games, and in the meantime, the other man was gaining ground with the prize.

Kodac found that talking to Tyrus, about his lack of a relationship with Merika, was a total waste of time and energy. Tyrus would just smile, shrug a shoulder as if in disinterest, and tell him that things would all work out in the end. If he knew something, no one else did, because he wasn't sharing. This was driving him crazy! How could his son be so dense? Rhys was getting closer to Merika everyday they spent together, and this was happening more frequently.

Yes, Kodac heaved a great sigh of frustration. His matchmaking was going nowhere, and it was all Tyrus's fault. He couldn't really claim that Serena and Rodan was his doing, that had just sort of happened, and he was happy it had. Serena was a good choice for his younger son. They got along well together. Their powers matched, and she was a beautiful girl, inside and out. Yes, Rodan could have definitely chosen worse, he just wished they would take the final step and make it final.

Kodac watched as Merika left the kitchen with Rhys in tow. He was carrying another picnic hamper, and this time there was no Tyrus with them. That was not good. What was even worse, was that they seemed to be deep in a discussion about something, so much so that they were oblivious to everyone else around them, definitely not good. He wondered again where Tyrus was, and where they were headed. Maybe they were going to meet up somewhere, or not. This man was way too happy when he was around Merika, it was not a good sign, and he watched how Rhys bent a little closer, to hear what she was saying. He then threw back his head and laughed. Not good at all.

What made it worse, was the fact that he liked young Rhys. He was a good man, a strong leader. He knew what he was up to, where he was going, and how to get there. Where was his SON? What was Tyrus thinking? Letting those two go off without supervision! At this rate, Kodac decided, he was going to go gray worrying about all of it. Children could do that to a parent he had always heard, he had never believed it, until he met Tyrus.

Shaking his head again, Kodac shrugged off his feeling of inadequacy. Nothing had gone according to plan, just when he thought he had it all figured out. He had taken note of his eldest son's attraction to Merika from the first moment they had seen her, and he had approved. Tyrus, however, had immediately begun to erect obstacles. To make her more appealing, Kodac had tossed competition into the mix. He knew there was nothing more attractive to a man, than something another man wanted, especially when it remained elusive. Tyrus, he had been positive, would react in a predictable fashion. He hadn't.

First, there had been Tudor, to stir up Tyrus's possessiveness, for that was what he was feeling towards her. The reason he knew it was more, was because of the mental bond that he refused to sever. To Kodac, that spoke volumes, but it was time Tyrus pulled that bond tighter and claimed his prize. What he had done was not nearly enough to complete a formal bond. The result was that the connection was tenuous at best. Even Tudor, as unwelcome as he had been from Merika, could have severed it. Of course, Tyrus didn't know that, nor had he been about to tell him. But now maybe he should.

The problems Tudor had caused had made Merika suspicious, and Tyrus hostile to his manipulations, so Kodac tried to be a bit subtler. It had ended with Merika quickly befriending the new suitor. To end the problem this could have caused, Kodac had matched him and his sister with others, with the help of Sephra. What was it going to take to get Merika and Tyrus together? She was perfect for him. The knucklehead. He watched Rhys and Merika walk down a trail, and actually growled with frustration.

Walking through the clearing, as he checked on supplies and construction, Kodac noticed how the crowds had thinned out. This might not have been a true gathering, he thought to himself, but it had accomplished the same results. There had been many matches made over the last several weeks, and there would be many new births within the next year. One always followed the other. He just wanted to make sure that he was a grandfather to at least one, if not two, of those grandbabies. It was time.

A soft feminine voice slipped into his thoughts, and he recognized Kalla's touch. "You need not worry so much about Rodan and Serena, it won't be much longer until that match comes to a head and bears fruit. Not with the way they act when they are together. They get closer and closer every moment. If you find that you suddenly cannot reach them, you will know why."

"It is not so much Rodan and Serena that concern me, as Tyrus and Merika." Kodac confided. Of all the new people he had met from the alternate valley, Kalla was the one he felt he could trust the most. Though he was surprised that she had picked a mental link as a way to contact him.

"You shouldn't be surprised at this type of link either. It is my specialty, and very private. I was not aware that there was a special link between Tyrus and Merika though, that I should have caught right away." Kalla admitted.

"Tyrus fights the attraction, but uses the link when it is convenient. Merika denies it and keeps her shields up solid at most times. No one reads that girl." Kodac informed Kalla.

"That much I did notice. Rhys finds that fascinating, he has never met anyone quite like her." Kalla chuckled.

"He looks like he thinks he is in heaven." Kodac sighed.

"True, and Merika looks like an angel." Kalla sounded amused. "But she only thinks of him as another friend and acquaintance. "

"And just how do you know that?" Kodac wanted to know.

"Merika told me. Sometimes you just have to ask the right questions." Kalla grinned.

"Merika hasn't offered me much information." Kodac admitted.

"I am not surprised. Anyone can read the desperation that is coming from you in waves. But, when I think about that couple, I mean really concentrate on them, I can see what you are talking about." Kalla noted.

"Meaning?" Kodac fished for information.

"Well, there is a slight underlying tension between Tyrus and Merika, that could prove potentially interesting. If they were paired together in the right way that is." Kalla pointed out.

"I have tried everyway I know of, and even some I would normally have never tried." Kodac admitted.

"Men! Think they know everything. Sometimes these things take a woman's touch." Kalla stated.

"Sephra has also run out of ideas." Kodac mentioned, to show that this wasn't all his doing.

"And you have only one female in the whole valley with a functioning brain?" Kalla hummed.

"Well, it is good to note that the females from our sister Valley can be just as impertinent as our own," Kodac returned.

"Surely you have noted our similarities beforehand. It is the nature of our species." Kalla replied.

"So, do you have advice about how to get Tyrus and Merika together?" Kodac pressed.

"Leave them be for now. It probably is for the best, and I wouldn't worry too much about Rhys, although he could be a serious contender, if Merika was interested in him in that way." Kalla considered.

"Then what is your suggestion?" Kodac pushed.

"Focus on the ones you are sure of. For now, that is Serena and Rodan. The bond they share, their families will want to celebrate together. Plan for that moment, you might be surprised how others can be ensnared through their involvement. In the meantime, I will let you know if I see or hear anything new and interesting." Kalla spoke in the way of a fellow conspirator.

"I will look forward to hearing from you." Kodac replied, just before Kalla severed the link.

Kodac smiled, as the connection dissolved, and he stifled an urge to laugh out loud. If he had read all the nuances of the conversation right, and he was sure he had, he had just discovered a fellow conspirator. One he could trust. Ten minutes later, as he was halfway between two of the finished houses, completing his inspection, he came across Serena's father. He was directing the transference of the new owners' possessions.

"Just the man I want to talk to," Kodac greeted his host.

"Problems, Kodac?" Serena's father asked.

"Nothing that can't be easily solved. Is Sephra close by?" Kodac asked.

"She is inside, helping out." Came the answer.

"This is something best spoken of between just the three of us. In private." Kodac replied.

"That can be arranged." Kodac's host sounded both thoughtful and resigned. "I told Sephra to clear the house in a discrete manner so we may discuss our errant children."

"What makes you think that this is about them?" Kodac asked.

"Whom else could it be about, with the three of us in conference? Besides, both Sephra and I have been expecting a call from you for some time. None of us should be too surprised that it has happened." Kodac's host replied.

"Nothing much gets past the two of you, does it?" Kodac asked.

"With the number of children we have? If we were not so vigilant, we would have been sunk years ago." Kodac's host confessed.

Kodac nodded his understanding, adding. "I only had the one and it was all I could do to keep up. I would have never survived with more. I still can't seem to understand them very well, and they are men now."

"They are not that hard to figure." Kodac's host noted.

"So speaks the voice of experience." Kodac stated.

"You can't tell me that you are that old that you no longer remember what it is like to be a young man in love with a beautiful, amicable woman." Kodac's host snorted in disbelief.

"I knew Rodan was hooked on Serena the moment he saw her, but I hadn't expected it to get to this point this fast. I guess, I have been too focused on Tyrus." Kodac admitted.

"Not that I blame you for that one. Tyrus is a lot more complicated than anyone I ever met before. I am ashamed to admit that I am glad he isn't one of my sons." Evan added.

"You are entitled, but just so you know, I am proud he is mine." Kodac stated.

"You should be, he is a good man, just too damn complicated for my taste. I am also shallow enough to be glad that Serena chose Rodan rather than Tyrus, if she had to pick between the two of them." Evan continued.

"Rodan is the easier going of the two of them, that much is true. But he has his own thoughts on life as well, and not all of them are easy to live by either." Kodac stated.

"Well, we both know that power has its price. It is also well known your family has more than it's fair share of it. Despite that, I still would not consider changing places with you. Not for a second." Evan declared.

"That goes both ways, so it is well we are both happy with our lots in life. Ah, here is your lovely wife." Kodac replied, as Sephra approached them.

Sephra set down a tray filled with cups, coffee, utensils, sandwiches, and treats. And, at the enquiring look she got from the men, she explained.

"I am presupposing that this little talk is going to take some time. It sometimes pays to be prepared."

"I believe we are here to plan a marriage celebration." Kodac announced.

"I wondered when that was going to happen. Those two started becoming serious shortly after Rodan stole his first kiss. From there, it progressed to stealing moments alone, then hours. Much longer and everyone will wonder what is keeping them from just speaking their vows and getting it over with." Evan informed them.

"Then we are in accord on that front. The sooner their union happens, the better. I think we should press Merika back into service to begin baking. Without much doubt, Serena will want her to make the cakes, she does the best job. Merika will also have an idea of what she wants done and how. They have been as thick as thieves since they met." Sephra noted.

"Considering that they could soon become sisters by marriage," Kodac grinned. "I think that quite fortuitous.

"I wouldn't place bets on that if I were you. Young Rhys is apt to give everyone a run for their money. He seems quite taken with our Merika." Sephra pointed out.

Kodac's smile was quick to turn into a frown as he replied. "That is a young man with entirely too much time on his hands. And there is not a thing I can do about it."

"You are not the only one who would prefer to see Merika paired with Tyrus. A female Alpha Prime matched with the future Valley Male Prime would almost guarantee a secure future for all our people." Sephra declared.

"Neither of you two match making geniuses has discovered how to get them together yet, have you?" Evan pointed out.

"No, Evan, not yet." Sephra admitted with a sigh and Kodac added.

"It is hard to watch things unfold in such a painfully slow fashion when the end result seems so obvious. Anyone with half a brain can see they are well suited to one another." Kodac admitted.

"And if we push too hard, we will only succeed in driving them apart." Evan noted.

"We do have at least one person more than willing to help in the battle." Kodac informed Sephra and her husband.

"Who?" Sephra asked.

"Kalla." Kodac answered.

"You are sure of this?" Sephra wondered. She hadn't learned how to trust any of those who had come from the other side. Their loyalties were not here, they were where their homes were, and if it wasn't, then there was something wrong.

"As sure as I can be." Kodac replied.

"Well, if Kalla is in on this, you can be assured Firth will be as well. We may just be able to drive a wedge between Rhys and Merika yet." Sephra gave a mock sigh of relief. One, backing the enemy camp was suspicious, but if the couple that one belonged to backed up the other, than it just might work. It was worth a shot.

"But first, we must see to the celebration we need to throw for Serena and Rodan. Perhaps it will also serve for the other two as well, if we are lucky." Evan spoke wistfully. All he wanted was for everyone to go home, and for things on his homestead to return to normal. He didn't think that was too much to ask for.

CHAPTER XVIII

"Has anyone seen Merika today?" Tyrus asked, as he walked up to a group that consisted of Sephra, her husband, Kodac, Rodan and Serena.

Kodac looked at him, as if in total shock for a moment, then replied. "This morning. She was with Rhys and they had a food basket with them. I thought you had a way of knowing where she was at all times."

"She must have her blocks up tight. If I cannot locate her, then no one can." Tyrus replied.

Serena countered. "Kalla can most times. She says she has a very strong talent for finding people. I will ask her."

They all went silent for a few moments, while Serena made her connection and her enquiry. She then replied, "She knows she is with Rhys, but not their actual location. As far as she can tell, they are not in our Valley."

"Tyrus, I need to talk to you." Kodac's voice was tight and it snapped like a whip.

Tyrus's demeanor had turned cold, and his eyes lightened to an ice blue to match. His temper, Kodac could tell, was white hot, and when he answered, it was as if he was hissing.

"Is there any point?"

"That is up to you." Kodac snarled back. He decided this was not the time to back off. If he did, his son would probably pay the price. He wasn't about to fail him, not when he finally had a chance to show him how much he cared. He led his son to a quiet, secluded spot and began.

"I tried to warn you, but you wouldn't listen. Now you can just shut up and pay attention, while you pray it isn't too late for the two of you to still come together."

"She has the right to choose whoever she wants." Tyrus growled.

Tyrus' father snapped back. "Tyrus. This isn't a matter of may the best MAN win. Life doesn't operate that way, not when you are dealing with reality. Rhys might be a good man, but he isn't the right one for Merika, and you know this, as well as I do. So get off your high horse, and do something about it, while you still can, because I can promise you this, son, if you don't, Rhys will. He knows a good thing when he sees it, and don't think that mind link gives you the upper hand here, because he has the power to break it. If he manages to do that, it will be because you didn't care enough to stop him from doing so."

"Merika has a mind of her own, in case you haven't noticed, father. Even with that ever-present link, she has proved to be elusive. Has it ever occurred to anyone that she might not be interested in me?" Tyrus spoke the words that terrified him the most.

"So, then you are finally admitting that you care? Now that it could be too late?" Kodac asked.

"I never said I didn't care. Don't put words in my mouth. I wish I had never met the bothersome female." Tyrus yelled at Kodac.

Rhys and Merika had been walking into the clearing from a side path, as Tyrus spoke, and both stopped short, as they heard the final words that Tyrus said. Merika, feeling somehow that she had heard something that had not been meant for her ears, managed to retain her simile and teased.

"Which of many bothersome females would you be talking about, Tyrus?"

Kodac saw his son's face firm, the anger remained held tight within, deep in the recesses of his eyes, and he reached out a restraining hand to warn him as he quietly spoke. "Tyrus don't say anything you will regret."

Tyrus listened as much as he ever did at such a time, as he snarled. "You. I wish I had never met you."

"I see," The bright smile on Merika's face wavered for a moment, before she secured it, and turned to Kodac. "We spent a few hours looking at the scenery in Rhys' Valley, you would love the mountains. They are so regal and majestic."

Kodac took a look at the blinding smile, and the suspiciously over brightness of Merika's eyes, and replied. "I would love to hear about it, things have happened here while you were gone today as well, and I need to talk with you about them."

"Of course. I will just bid Rhys farewell, and be right with you, unless it concerns him as well." Merika answered.

"No, not really. It is to do with a celebration we are planning for Serena and Rodan. Rhys will be welcome to attend if he wishes, of course. It won't be for a while though. Maybe a week." Kodac informed them.

Rhys gave a pleased smile and replied. "So Serena and Rodan have decided to complete their union? I am happy for them and will make a point of trying to be there."

"You are welcome at any time." Kodac made a point of making sure that Rhys knew he was welcome. Despite all of his efforts, he figured he still sounded stiff, no matter how much he tried not to.

Merika offered Rhys her hand in farewell, and he used it to pull her into his arms to give her a quick kiss. She frowned at him, and squirmed for release. Giving him a quick rebuke as she did.

"That was uncalled for."

Rhys smiled at Merika, as he stole a quick glance at Tyrus, and replied, "But it was, oh so satisfying."

Tyrus, to all outward appearances, could not have cared less, but inside he was livid in a way that only an emotional pain could make a person. He hadn't liked how Rhys had taken advantage of the situation the way he had. To be fair to Merika, it didn't look as if she was any more pleased about Rhys' forward manner than he was. Nor did it look as if Merika was pleased with his forwardness, and that was a welcome piece of information. He was going to have to give her an apology. He owed her that much for treating her as he had. After all, it wasn't as if he owned her. That, he decided, was something he was going to have to work on changing, not that he thought that anyone could ever own another person. His father was right about what she meant to him, and he finally had to concede the point. Sometimes, things were hard for a man to swallow, and his father was just the type to crow about it.

"Merika," Tyrus's voice sounded contrite in the recess of her mind, and she tried to raise her shields to block him out.

Tyrus' voice still came through, though weak, and Merika knew that if she tried hard enough she could block him out completely, though she elected not to.

"Please don't, Merika. I didn't mean what I said, not the way I said it. You have no way of knowing what you do to me, and I have no hope of controlling my reactions, not anymore. I thought I could let you go, so you had a chance for a decent life with someone else. But I can't. Lord knows I have tried to do the right thing. Help me do the right thing." Tyrus pleaded.

The problem with Tyrus' words, were that although Merika felt them, and wanted to believe them, she was hurting too badly by the first ones she had heard from him earlier. How could she trust what he was saying now, when he had said what he had before, where she wasn't supposed to hear? Had they been the ones in his heart, as well as his mind? She needed time to settle down, so she could think clearly, because the pain she was feeling wasn't letting her do that now.

"Perhaps we should just to pretend it didn't happen, Tyrus. Sometimes friends can be cruel to one another without meaning to be. I need to work now, and think about this."

Merika turned to Kodac, dismissing both Rhys and Tyrus, as she focused her attention on the older man.

"So what have I missed that needs attention the moment I reappear?"

Tyrus and Rhys exchanged a look. Neither could believe that Merika had dismissed them both, as something insubstantial in her life, though Tyrus was the less surprised of the two. It was something he had learned to expect from her in the past. Rhys gave the matter some thought. He decided he had a lot to learn about Merika. She had made that much very clear. The conversation between Tyrus and her had not shed much more light on anything pertinent about her either.

Rhys gave no indication that he had heard their private exchange, yet he frowned in a thoughtful manner, as he tossed off a wave of farewell that included everyone. He could sense that something was going on, something he had missed. It was something to do with Tyrus and Merika. Just what that was though, he couldn't tell. Someone had sent Merika a message and she had answered. He knew it had been done on a very narrow band. Considering the power that took, and the people surrounding them, the connection could have come from anyone.

Kodac gathered Merika to his side by putting a fatherly arm

around her shoulders, as he drew her closer into the circle of his protection, and took the hamper from her hands, as he guided her to the kitchens. As he did, he began to talk.

"Rodan and Serena have decided it is time that they finalized their bond. Her family wants to hold a farewell celebration for them, before they leave the clearing. We were thinking you might have some special ideas for things like the cake."

"A wedding cake is way out of my league, Kodac. I mean, I can bake a cake, that is no problem, but the decorations are beyond me. I was an actress, my mother was the specialist." Merika was quick to make sure they recognized her limitations.

"We aren't asking for a miracle, Merika. It is just that you did so well with the banquet, we felt you would want to repeat your performance for Serena and Rodan. Nor will this celebration be near the size of the gathering. We are talking about a few hundred people, versus the thousands that attended the banquet."

"If what is expected from me is similar to the banquet, then yes, I would love to do this for Serena and Rodan. I presume this will be another rush job?" Merika asked, as she decided she would do whatever it took to make her friends happy.

"A week, maybe two, although I doubt that long. That part hasn't been decided, and it is up to the couple involved. After helping to set things back into order after this is over, we will be leaving Sephra's homestead."

"What about me? I can't stay here and take advantage of our hosts good will forever. Where am I to go?" Merika wondered, thinking there had to be some place in the world for her. She no longer wanted to go back to the world that she had known. She wasn't the same person she was when she lived there. She wasn't Tanya Wade any more. She was Merika. She no longer belonged in the world she knew."

"Your parents estates will be opened for you. We will help you settle in, and learn what you need to know, to run them on your own. But Merika, word of warning, like you with the banquet, there is only so much we can do with your estates." Kodac told her.

"I assume that what you are trying to tell me, is that they are extensive." Merika replied. It was no more than what she had expected.

"You will be expected to step into a pair of very large shoes. Both your parents, as you know were only children, and they were very powerful in their own rights. There were two estates, side by side, and you have the rights to both. It will be a lot of work for one person." Kodac warned.

"This is so much for me to catch up on, Kodac. Will I ever be able to fit in? Or will I be forever struggling with my short comings?" Merika sounded as if she was definitely in over her head. She wasn't afraid of having to work, but the future was looking dark, and very bleak.

"You are doing better than any of us could ever have hoped, Merika. I have come to love you like a daughter. You are a tribute to your parents. They would have been so very proud of you. I know I am." Kodac let her know how he felt.

For the first time since Kodac had met her, Merika gave a stuttering choke, as she turned to him and dug her face into his shoulder and burst into tears.

Startled by her actions, Kodac slowly enveloped Merika in his arms, and crooned in a comforting manner. "It is alright, we will be here for you."

"I never cry," Came Merika's tear filled response, muffled as it was by the materials beneath her face.

"Sometimes we need to, sometimes it is the only way we can get past things so we can move forward with our lives." Kodac admitted.

"I miss them. I miss them both. I know I never knew my father, but that doesn't make any difference. And my mother…" Merika gasped, as she caught her breath, and burst into another bout of fresh tears. "I miss her so much. My world is empty without her."

Tyrus gave a deep-throated growl, and within moments, he eased her out of his father's arms, to hold her tightly in his own. Just as quickly, Merika went from clutching at the material on the front of Kodac's shirt, to winding her arms around Tyrus's shoulders, as she continued to cry her heart out onto his chest. Tyrus made soft shushing sounds, as he ran soothing hands over her back and head. He kissed her forehead and temples, as he sought to comfort the hurt he had always felt had been there, just out of reach. He was visibly shaken by her breakdown, and most definitely out of his element. He was willing to try to help; it was the best he could offer.

"We are here for you Merika, you are not alone." Tyrus crooned, as he whisked them off to their meeting spot in the forest, so they could be alone.

Kodac turned to Sephra and her husband, and smiled. "Well, that was interesting. I wonder when we will see them again."

"I wouldn't get your hopes up too much," Evan replied. "People do things in times of extreme emotional stress that they normally wouldn't do. They are then embarrassed by their actions later, to the point where they not only revert to past behavior but even resort to more hurtful actins. This extreme situation falls right into that category. It will either work in our favor, or explode in our faces."

"Tyrus is more apt to explode than Merika in my estimation. Nor do I expect a miraculous transformation of their tenuous relationship. I do expect to see a slight lessening of tension between the two of them though." Kodac explained.

"I guess this will bring the plans for the celebration to a standstill for now." Sephra figured.

"I would be tempted to think so," Kodac conceded with a shrug. In his mind, he had seen forward movement in his eldest son's future, and that was all that mattered to him. He knew, at the same time, that what he was thinking could be little more than wishes blown into the wind.

CHAPTER XIX

Kodac continued to watch the troubled couple from a distance, as they returned some time later. He stretched out his senses to gather what bits of information he could from them, and frowned. He was not at all pleased with what he received. Their time together, such as it had been, had seemed to start off in a manner that he had thought full of promise, then must have rapidly deteriorated until they had parted.

He could tell that Tyrus was feeling hurt. His pain seemed nearly palpable, as he had walked away. Merika, looked as if she had lost her last friend. Had they quarreled? He stretched out with his powers again, to see what he could find out. He received no angry vibrations, just waves and waves of mental pain and confusion. Tyrus returned to his work in the forest, though he had very little left to do there. Merika disappeared into the buildings that housed the kitchen, to work her magic there.

"So." A vaguely familiar voice intruded on Kodac's thoughts. "You have managed to match one of your sons. But, the one you wanted settled in life the most has met with failure."

Kodac whirled about to see who addressed him, then broke out in pleased laughter. "As I live and breathe. Sheyleigh, I thought you were no more than a piece of history by now, and I am delighted. I remember telling Tyrus about you, not so long ago. I was sure that I would never see you again. I am glad to know I was wrong."

"You should have known I was still here, you silly boy." Sheyleigh teased. "I would have come back to haunt you. Especially after the clumsy job you have done trying to match that more than likely young couple.

"Sheyleigh, you haven't changed a bit," Kodac told her, with a touch of fondness.

"Are you sure about that?" Sheyleigh asked.

"Oh, I am sure, and I couldn't be more pleased." Kodac admitted.

"And that would be because?" Sheyleigh pressed. The idiot had made a mess and she wanted him to admit it.

"Because? Because, of all the people I know and can think of, you are the single most person I have ever met that can understand the mind of a woman." Kodac laughed at the thought.

"If you care to remember, you would realize that I also know the reasoning behind the actions of most young men as well. So tell me, what has these two children at loggerheads?" Sheyleigh wondered.

"That is a good question and I wish I had the answer," Kodac gave a frustrated sigh. "I am not sure what to think at the moment. A few hours ago I was sure an up and coming union would have been the results of their actions. With things the way they stand at the moment? I have severe doubts. Tyrus is in a state over something to do with Merika, and I can't begin to guess what that might be."

"Now that, I am not too surprised about. I can imagine that the two of them are very attracted to one another, and both are fighting it every inch of the way. For Tyrus, I think Merika is everything he has ever tried to avoid in the past. Talented. Beautiful. Famous. Powerful. Wealthy. Worldly. Innocent. Naïve. Lonesome. Hurt. Popular. Smart. Scared and so very, very lost. Someone he would want to shield, our poor knight-errant. She is a woman who has been bombarded by life altering changes every place she has turned since her mother's death. I doubt if she is comfortable with any of this yet. Face it, Kodac, the young woman must be reeling from all she has been forced to face since she got here. I am also willing to bet she is feeling manipulated every bit as much as Tyrus does, and I am sure he does. It is a state no one likes. And speaking of that young man, how is he holding up under all this pressure?" Sheyleigh wanted to know.

"Tyrus calls Merika a bother, and swears every time she throws him a curve. But I can tell he enjoys the challenge. When they are together, his signature is euphoric. When they are apart, he tunes in on her, seeking her out. When she exhibits signs of confusion, he is in her mind, trying to guide her. He comforts her. He supports her. He refused to release the mind meld that he formed with her when he tried to help her control her powers, from the beginning, when they first met. I told him he had to let her go, and he refused. Right now, his signature tells me that they have had some form of misunderstanding." Kodac told Sheyleigh.

"He is in love. It is a confusing time, for the both of them. Feelings are so much more sensitive during that time of our lives than at any other. How is Merika?" Sheyleigh wondered.

"She isn't a person I have had a lot of luck reading. Nor is this problem limited to just Tyrus and her. There is another man interested in her, and he is every bit as worthy as my son. I wish I could say otherwise, but unfortunately, that is not the case. Before Rhys came into the picture, Merika and Tyrus spent almost every afternoon that they could spare together. I thought that meant something. Now I am not so sure. Now, she spends her time with the both of them, whether as a couple or in a group. Nor can I tell if there is more to it than just friendship. Much as I think that she is perfect for my son, I don't want to force them into a relationship where they won't be happy." Kodac admitted.

"You think that is a possibility?" Sheyleigh asked.

"Anything is possible." Came Kodac's reply.

"True, although it is obvious that she enjoys Tyrus' company, from what you have told me. But what is feeding that feeling? If it is no more than a passing friendship, Tyrus could get hurt very badly, especially if Merika is anything like his mother. That was one female that did no one any good, especially not Tyrus. I never could understand what attracted you to her in the first place. The woman had no heart." Sheyleigh pointed out.

"What can I say, Sheyleigh. I was very young, foolish, rebellious and a little on the wild side. She was young and beautiful and certainly forbidden fruit. Need I say more?" Kodac made no excuses for his behavior, as he felt it wouldn't do any good, not with Sheyleigh. She knew too much about his past, and would have never let him get away with it.

"No, that would about do it. You were also more than a little drunk that night. Your friends were too. They thought the whole thing a great laugh. She was more than willing, for you were a giant step up the social ladder for her, especially with your power potential. Most people actually understood. Sometimes, it takes a little time for hot blood to cool when you are young." Sheyleigh responded.

"Getting back to the issue at hand, what would you do about Tyrus and Merika?" Kodac asked.

"I think I might start by asking that young lady just what her intentions are with my son. If you want, I will go with you to see for myself what she comes out with. Something tells me that should be very interesting." Sheyleigh offered.

"Great idea, although Tyrus would be mortified if he ever heard that I asked Merika such a question. But, we can talk, and you can tell me what you think." Kodac suggested.

Kodac and Sheyleigh walked in on Merika, as she was just putting the finishing touches on a huge batch of cakes. She frowned, as if in discontent, and Sheyleigh put a restraining hand on Kodac's arm, as she leaned closer to whisper in his ear.

"How can you miss the signals she is sending? She is hurting, lonely and downright miserable. I would wager she is in as much pain, if not even more so, than Tyrus. Something is definitely out of sync here."

Kodac nodded his agreement with Sheyleigh's observation, but wasn't about to take any of that up with Merika. The last thing she needed was his sympathy. That would only make matters worse than they were now.

"Merika," Kodac sounded jovial, as if he was in a teasing mood. "Merika, I would like you to meet an old, and very treasured friend of mine, Sheyleigh. Sheyleigh, this is the newest member of my people, Merika. She has been busily baking up enough food to feed the army who has been working and celebrating her arrival in the valley."

"Pleased to meet you, Merika." Sheyleigh welcomed her.

"I look forward to getting to know you," Merika replied.

Kodac didn't give either Sheyleigh or Merika much more time than being introduced, before he jumped back into the conversation, to get answers about how things were progressing. "Have you decided what you are going to do about the main cake, Merika? How you are going to decorate it?"

"I think so. I drew up a picture of what I want it to look like. I want everything to be perfect for Serena and Rodan. As far as the rest goes, I rather surprised even myself. The cake dough is ready to go into the ovens, so things can progress from there." Merika answered.

"I am sure that Serena and Rodan will be speechless, and if you are as happy as she is, well that would really make her day complete." Kodac declared.

"I will be. They deserve perfection." Merika replied.

"And how about you, Merika?" Kodac asked.

"Me?" Merika asked, sounding puzzled by the question.

"Yes, you. What do you want?" Kodac looked at Merika in a direct manner, and her eyes fell from his, as if not wanting to give anything away by look or manner.

"What I want is beyond my reach." Merika admitted.

"Really? And why is that?" Kodac wanted to know what Merika would come up with.

"Because my mother is dead." Merika responded, in a soft, sad voice.

"There is nothing anyone can do about that, and for that I am truly sorry. Nothing would have made me happier than to be reunited with my old friend either." Kodac admitted.

Merika gave a heavy sigh and replied. "I know."

"I would like to talk to you about Tyrus for a few moments though," Kodac approached the subject.

"Of course, is there a problem?" Merika wondered.

"Not that I am aware of, but he is not acting like himself and, as I noticed that you have been spending more and more time with him, I thought you might know the reasons." Kodac sounded hopeful.

"Well, I thought you would have been overjoyed with the time we spent with each other. You certainly pushed us at each other enough." Merika accused Kodac.

"I hope not to the point of error. At the risk of sounding like an over protective, or dramatic parent, I need to know what your intentions are towards my son?" Kodac asked.

"My intentions?" Merika gave a short sharp laugh. "Tyrus and I are friends. Nothing more. You see, Tara explained to me that Tyrus was the safest man in the Valley to be with, despite being the most difficult. I happen to agree with her opinion. He is safe to be with. I do not, however, find him to be particularly difficult now that I have gotten to know him. In fact, I find him quite relaxing to spend time with." Merika explained.

"Safe? Relaxing?" Kodac sounded his astonished disbelief. "I have heard many people describe my son in many ways, but these are words I have never heard anyone say in relation to Tyrus. Not in any context. Even I admit, he is difficult at best."

"First time I have ever heard that about Tyrus either." Sheyleigh spoke up for the first time since she entered the building. "I can't say I have ever met the man personally. I have heard a lot about him from people everywhere I have gone. From what I have learned about Tyrus, I would be willing to bet there is nothing safe about his true feelings about you. Nor are they in any way benign." Sheyleigh stepped forward, as she assumed control of the conversation. "I doubt if you would feel safe with him for long if he ever kissed you properly, even once. I am also willing to bet that is something he has never done."

"Why should he want to?" Merika wanted to know

"I can't believe you even felt you had to ask a silly question like that. Of all the men I have ever met, and I have met a lot of men young lady, Tyrus is one of the few I would describe as really hot. I might not have met him in person, but I have eyes. I would say even hotter than Rodan, in my estimation, and that is a man who has almost every girl in the Valley mooning over him. If you are any kind of a woman at all, I would be willing to wager any amount of money, that Tyrus could reduce you to a mindless, clinging vine with just one real kiss." Sheyleigh challenged Merika.

"What you seem to fail to understand," Merika argued in a reasonable tone of voice, "Is that our relationship is more of a meeting of the minds than a physical one. Tyrus is not interested in me in any other way. I understand this, and I accept it. In a way, I guess that would make me a safe bet for him as well." Merika explained.

"If you honestly believe any the garbage you spouted off, then you are delusional." Sheyleigh declared.

"Well, you can believe what you want," Merika sniffed. "Neither of us can stop you from building more into the relationship than what there is. We are comfortable around each other. Neither of us are interested in forming a deeper or more complex bond. I think anything more than what we have would make our friendship volatile and prone to breakdown."

"How about you and young Rhys? What are your feelings there? Do you view him in the same light too?" Kodac wondered.

"Heavens no. Rhys just wants a friend. He teaches me things about my powers and tells me things about his world. His is very fond of his home. It is nothing personal." Merika defended their friendship

"Well." Sheyleigh tossed Merika an incredulous frown. "I guess if we are entitled to our opinions, you are entitled to yours, young lady." Then, shaking her head in disbelief she spoke her thoughts aloud to herself. "Safe! I cannot believe that you actually believe that, even if you did say it for all to hear. More important, I wonder what Tyrus would say about it if he knew."

"What do you mean by that?" Merika asked.

"Tyrus is a virile young man, young lady. He is attractive and charming, when he wants to make the effort, which he has seemed to do with you. If what you are telling me is the truth, I can't think, for the life of me, why in Heaven's name would he make the effort to befriend you in the first place?" Sheyleigh pointed out.

"Why do you say that?" Merika asked.

"Use your head, Merika, think about it. You are a very beautiful, healthy female. Tyrus is the male equivalent. If that is not enough, along with the attraction there seems to be between the two of you, to create a heat wave, I am at a loss to know the reason why not. Unless, you are lacking, maybe that is what it is. Tyrus would definitely know an iceberg if he saw one." Sheyleigh baited Merika.

"Iceberg!" Merika was virtually speechless.

"Despite that, Tyrus must know enough about you to think that you are a worthwhile person. Maybe, that is why he has been so attentive. Maybe he believes he has to be nice to you, so you do not feel as if you are being driven from the valley. This is your home too, you know." Sheyleigh suggested.

"I am not an iceberg!" Merika couldn't help but comment. She couldn't believe that Sheyleigh had said that. She didn't fit that description at all; at least she didn't think she did. She objected aloud. "Nor does Tyrus see me as an object of pity. I resent the implications. That is downright insulting."

"Not trying to be, young lady. Just trying to reason things out. I figure that you have to be lacking somewhere, to have a man like Tyrus allow you to believe he has a benign character." Sheyleigh replied.

"There has never been anything but platonic friendliness between us. We are friends. It is a safe, comfortable, state of being. If more people would understand and accept the fact that a man and woman can stop at that, and quit trying to push us into a relationship neither of us are interested in, maybe things wouldn't get so complicated." Merika suggested.

"I am not pushing you at him, young lady." Sheyleigh sniffed. "I repeat, I am attempting to understand your relationship and reasoning. I am having a great degree of difficulty seeing the two of you as just pals. If you think it through in an impartial manner, you will see what I mean."

Merika tilted her head as she listened to Sheyleigh speak. The woman was making some degree of sense, though she wasn't so sure she wanted to hear much more at this time.

Sheyleigh could see Merika about to go stubborn, but pushed a little harder nonetheless. "Go to him. Ask him if he wants to be thought of as someone safe for you to hang around with. Especially in the way you are implying. Just see what he has to say about that!"

"Why should I want to do something like that?" Merika sounded mulish, even to herself and had the grace to blush.

Sheyleigh just pushed her more "To see if I am right or whether you are. That is why. The worse that can happen is that he confirms your misplaced comments and beliefs."

Sheyleigh gave that a few moments to sink in before pressing on. "I am also willing to bet that if you were to don an attractive gown and allow him to give you one proper kiss, that you would change your mind about him altogether."

"I can't believe I am even listening to you. This whole conversation is ridiculous. You are wrong." Merika clutched at her beliefs, desperate in her denial. In the meantime, a little voice inside her head told her Sheyleigh was right. She didn't want to hear that though, she didn't want to admit that she was living an illusion. So, she stubbornly added. "I don't believe that Tyrus is interested in kissing me either."

It was working, and Sheyleigh gave a smug smile of satisfaction, as she gave their discussion one last tweak. "Really? Prove it. Put on a gown that would make you look like a desirable woman. Go to him. Ask him. Tell him what you think, see how he reacts. One kiss, Merika, just one, that is all I am betting it takes. Have you got it in you? Or are you a coward? Have you got what it takes to fight for your man?"

Merika shrugged a shoulder in response, frowning, as she sought to make sense to the dare. And, she was sure, it was a dare. To her way of thinking, there was no question about that. Sheyleigh was nothing if not direct, maybe even too direct. There had to be more behind her suggestion than just a mere kiss. The thought that flowed through Merika's mind after, almost made her laugh. In her line of work in the outside world, people kissed one another all the time. It meant nothing. Her whole career had revolved around romance and heartbreak, and from what she had heard, there were lives in the everyday world that were not so very different. That was what soap operas were all about. Life, however, was not a show on television.

"Surely, Merika," Sheyleigh noted the determination that was building in Merika's eyes, and could have admired her for it, if it were not so misguided, and she purred in a suggestive tone. "Think. In that fertile mind of yours, you must have thought of how it would feel to be encased in those arms, pressed against that delightful male physique and have those lips touch yours. Think about it, Merika, they are probably the only soft part on that man."

Merika had listened to enough, more than enough. She turned eyes flashing with anger and lips lightly compressed, and although she sounded subdued, Kodac knew better.

"Was this what you wanted to talk to me about, Kodac?"

"Not at all, actually. The subject just sort of happened. I just wanted to know if everything was as it should be in the kitchens. Whether you have enough supplies and other items that you might need." It wasn't a total lie, he had wanted to cover this ground at some point, but as a diversionary tactic it was perfect, and the sudden confusion exhibited on Merika's face confirmed his suspicions that he was right on the mark with it.

This was a subject Merika felt confident in discussing. The kitchen had become her haven. Stocking the pantry was a much safer, more familiar subject, than her inner feelings for Tyrus. She looked at Kodac for a few moments, as her features retained their softness and smiled.

"You have provided all any chef could wish for. I think you deserve high praise, as does Sephra and her family, for having this dreamy kitchen. It is perfect for high volume culinary work."

Kodac was taken by surprise. No one had praised him to his face like that before, and it made him feel uncomfortable. To lay the unfamiliar feeling to rest, he pushed it aside with a shrug and careless, modest, comment.

"Mine is only a minor role in the major picture."

Merika was not about to let Kodac get away that easily, as she smiled at him and replied. "You are too modest. Are you not aware that without the things you supply, none of the things we create would exist?"

Feeling even more awkward, Kodac ordered. "Get out of here, Merika. I will have a couple of the women pull the cakes out of the ovens when they are done. I want you to join the other girls your age. Spend some time with Serena while the two of you are still single and without responsibilities. Let the others do some of this work. Besides, you are embarrassing me, and it is time for me to get back to work."

For the moment, the subject of Tyrus was firmly put into the back of her mind and forgotten. Merika turned and left the kitchens. Kodac had been right. She should be spending time with Serena before her marriage to Rodan. After all, who knew when they would have a chance to be together as friends again? Marriage was a whole new type of life. Merika gave a sigh of sadness. It was not that she begrudged Serena her future with Rodan, for Serena was too happy with the way her life was shaping up, to have Merika feel anything but happy for them. It was that she was going to miss her friend.

Kodac watched Merika leave, then turned to Sheyleigh with a growl. "If that stubborn boy of mine does not declare for her soon, I just might do it for myself. She has all the makings of an excellent wife, especially for an Alpha Prime."

"You are not serious! You and Merika?" Sheyleigh snorted.

"Of course not, but the thought makes me feel warm all over, and I would rather see that happen, than watch her walk into the sunset on Rhys' arm." Kodac admitted.

"I thought you said you liked Rhys?" Sheyleigh pointed out.

"I do. He is a man I can respect. But Merika is Tyrus'." Kodac declared.

"What if they decide otherwise?" Sheyleigh asked. She wanted to know how far Kodac was willing to push this obsession of his.

"Well, then that is another matter, isn't it?" Kodac admitted. There was only so far that he was willing to go in his interference. The young couple deserved the right to some freedom of choice.

"Well, I think we gave that young girl enough to think about, and from all I have heard about Tyrus, he probably thinks too much for his own good. Something tells me it would probably be a good idea if we quit pushing for a while. It might give the idea we fed Merika time to take root and sprout. The way she is looking at things now is wrong, and I could tell by the looks in her eyes, that she knows it, but is stubbornly holding on to them, almost like a lifeline. For some reason only known to her, she needs to believe that what she is feeling isn't real. Eventually, she will wake up to the fact that she has been deluding herself." Sheyleigh pointed out.

"What do you mean?" Kodac wondered.

"You say Tyrus is already of a mind to claim Merika as his." Sheyleigh reminded Kodac.

"I have good reason to think that, yes. But there is the problem of the prospect of Rhys and Merika. That wasn't there before." Kodac replied.

"Rhys won't even factor in the equation in the end, you will see." Sheyleigh chuckled.

"Are you are sure about this?" Kodac wondered.

"Think about it. I am also willing to wager that we could be driving them apart as much with our good intentions, as they are with their obstinate insecurities. Life can be like that sometimes." Sheyleigh spoke his thoughts aloud.

"You think so, do you?" Kodac teased Sheyleigh with an open grin.

"Probably," Sheyleigh responded with a heavy sigh. She knew she was being teased, but didn't care. "Sometimes getting old is not all it is cracked up to be."

CHAPTER XX

Kodac could not believe the distance that existed between Merika and his son during the festivities that had marked Serena and Rodan's marriage. They had shared a dance, as was expected of them, then each went their own way. Tyrus acted cool, but polite to all who spoke to him, and Merika fluttered from partner to partner, like a bright, beautiful butterfly. Neither fooled him, for neither could keep their attention or eyes, from following the other. He noted how Tyrus's lips compressed, every time Rhys led Merika onto the dance floor. When Rhys waltzed with her for a third time with her, Tyrus couldn't stop the glare of anger that everyone could see clearly. The look in his eyes boded trouble, but there was nothing he could do about the reason. Tyrus turned from the scene, and stalked off without saying a word to anyone. In his mind, a plan was forming, and there was a look of determination on his face.

Merika continued to look at Tyrus, as if hoping for him to return to her side. When he didn't, she turned to Rhys with a smile. The gesture, however, was not reflected in her eyes, and even he could see that.

Kodac had wondered what Tyrus had on his mind, but didn't get a chance to ask. It had been over a week since the celebration, and nothing had changed between the young couple. He was ready to throw his hands up in defeat, and admit he had been wrong. Maybe, they were not meant for each other. The only reason he still held on to his hopes, was that despite the pressures he was placing on his son to release her, Tyrus still refused to sever the tie between them. Merika, he was sad to say, was avoiding him in a way that was almost painful to watch, and for that he blamed his son. What was different about her, that he could see, was that she was beginning show signs of thinking about something in a deep and serious way. The expression that she had worn only a week before was being replaced by one of wonder. Instead of looking like an abandoned puppy, she was developing one of determination, similar to the one that Tyrus had left with. Those made him wonder what was going on in her head.

As Kodac watched, and wondered about Tyrus and Merika, people left, until he was one of the last ones left in the clearing. It was time, he decided, that Tyrus and he went home as well, for the weather was beginning to cool, and they needed to turn their efforts to preparing the homestead for the long winter months to come.

Thoughts of returning home, also brought a new problem to the forefront in Kodac's mind. What was he going to do about Merika? He supposed, he would have to open her ancestral home for her. He had wished to give her more than an empty estate, and the cold welcome of a house that held nothing but old memories that didn't belong to her. She needed love and happiness in her life. She needed a husband and family to give her focus and meaning.

As Kodac puzzled out his problem, he grew saddened by the thoughts that passed through his mind. It was going to be a very long and cold winter for them all, well, maybe except for Rodan and Serena.

While Kodac thought about his immediate future, Merika reached a few decisions on her own. She was missing her friend and companion. Too much, she had decided, for her feelings to be a passing fancy, and she decided it was time to find out if Tyrus felt the same way. She figured she had nothing to lose. She couldn't be any more miserable than she was at the moment. If he was gay, as she had been told, at least she would know for sure, and she could move on. She was not so desperate that she would impinge on his choices in that matter. So, before she changed her mind, she sent him a message through their link.

"Tyrus, we need to talk. Please. I will be at our meeting place in amongst the trees, you know the place."

Within the hour, Tyrus and Merika faced each other, deep within the sanctity of the forest. But they were not alone. Kalla and Firth joined them, even before they spoke their first words of greeting.

"We came to shield your meeting as we know how important this matter of your privacy can be at the moment." Firth explained their presence.

"Do you think we are being monitored?" Tyrus quizzed.

Firth spoke. "Not at this time, and no, it is not Rhys that you need to fear. He might want Merika for himself, but if she chooses another, he will give his blessings. Rhys is not petty or vindictive. He knows that someday, sometime, he will meet the woman that will complete him. If there is any trouble from anyone, it would be Meridor."

"We will create a bubble for you so no one will be able to hear you, or see you. If you need us for any reason, we will be here for you. You will also be free to come or go as you feel necessary." Kalla spoke, as the bubble formed.

"You wanted to talk?" Tyrus broke into the silence that suddenly surrounded Merika and him. His voice seemed overloud in the stillness that was almost deafening on its own.

"Yes," Merika quietly replied, feeling suddenly shy and uncomfortable.

Sheyleigh's words had been burning trails through the corridors of Merika's mind, causing her to question much of her beliefs about her relationship with Tyrus. It wasn't the first time she had doubted Tara's description of Tyrus' personality and preferences of partners, but she was at a point where she actually wanted her opinions to be wrong. Had she really been dense enough to believe Tara, and not her instincts? Had she read too much into the conversation than what had been meant? She had to know for sure, so she was going to find out from the man in person. After all, it wouldn't do to compound the problem by acting on the wrong information and making a monumental mistake. In this case, what she was about to do could affect their complete futures.

Although she could think of no reason why, it seemed to Merika, as if Tyrus was sounding somewhat anxious. She did not realize the amount of confusion that she was telegraphing, nor how that was affecting him. He viewed Merika closer and he could see signs of loneliness and anxiety written deep in her eyes. He could only wonder if she had missed him as much he had her? If she was, it wasn't due to Rhys' lack of attention, that man had been at her side wherever she went. Always.

Merika took a deep breath, then began. "I had to see you. There are things that are weighing heavy on my mind, and I need to talk them out to come to a conclusion. To begin with, I find I have missed our time together. Our talks, our friendship, I miss you, Tyrus."

"To be honest, I missed you by my side as well. Our friendship has suffered by our distance," Tyrus was cautious in his reply, but was willing to be a little more open with Merika than he had in the past. as she seemed to be with him.

Merika heaved a sigh of relief, mingled with regret. Was Tyrus being cautious with his words? Or had her earlier suspicions been right after all? Feeling a little foolish she turned slightly from him and looked at the forest floor, to hide her awkwardness.

"I see, I guess my confusion has been nothing but a silly misunderstanding. I tried to tell your father and his friend, Sheyleigh, how it was between us. But they refused to listen."

"Well, that is no big surprise there. But, I might be interested in hearing just what you told them myself," Tyrus confessed to a degree of curiosity.

"I told them how I found being with you so refreshing. There was no pressures, no expectations, and I could understand how some people might have a problem believing how things are between us." Merika explained.

"And just how did you tell them things were between us, Merika?" Tyrus asked, turned her to face him, and gently raised her chin, so he could look her fully in the face, while he spoke with her. He wanted to see the look in her eyes that accompanied what she was gong to say for himself.

"I told them that we were safe with each other. I had been told by someone who has known you for a long time that you were not interested in women as anything more than a friend." Merika confessed.

"I see," Tyrus brushed the forefinger he had used to raise her chin with over a dewy, petal soft, cheek. "And what did Sheyleigh have to say about that? She strikes me as a lady with many opinions."

Tyrus had met Sheyleigh, and found her to be a person that was not afraid to speak her mind, and quite a mind it was too. She had called him every kind of fool and explained why, as she had stood watching Rhys dance with Merika at his brother's wedding celebration. He could imagine she had plenty to say to Merika as well, unless he missed his guess, and he was sure he didn't.

"She mocked me," Merika admitted, as she subconsciously

pressed her cheek against Tyrus' questing finger. "She said you would not be pleased to know that I was only spending time with you because I had been told you had no interest in females. She never took it into consideration that I might be spending time with you because I really liked you. She told me that I was delusional, and that you were definitely not safe for me."

"Who told you I had no interest in women, and that I was safe to spend time with because of it in the first place?" Tyrus wondered.

"Tara." Merika admitted.

"Sounds about right," Tyrus snorted. "That female is lacking the brains it would take to form a complete sentence. How could you believe an asinine story like that?"

"To be honest, Tyrus, I think I needed to at the time." Merika raised her eyes to fully look into his.

"Merika," Tyrus' voice washed over her senses, "do you still think I am not interested in women?"

As Tyrus' hand stretched to cup her cheek, Merika continued to rub against that hand as he moved it to meet her unconscious caress. Her voice grew soft, as she replied. "Deep down, I never believed what she had said. Not even in the beginning, but I was willing to accept the possibility that you were not interested in me. That I wasn't your type. I was more than happy to be your friend."

"That cannot have been all there was to the conversation, not with Sheyleigh there." Tyrus pushed.

"Well," Merika blushed a fire red, as she lowered her eyes, and admitted. "She did say more. She bet me that if I were to dress in something alluring, and allowed you to give me but one proper kiss, that I would soon change my mind about all my preconceptions. She seemed to have a lot of faith in the fact that you could accomplish a lot with one little kiss."

"She did, did she?" Tyrus chuckled, as he reached out to touch Merika's shoulder with his other hand. "So Merika, have you done as Sheyleigh suggested?"

"Done?" Merika sounded vague and suddenly breathless. She could barely keep her mind on the conversation, with her eyes ensnared by the building heat in Tyrus' gaze.

"Yes, Merika. Did you do as Sheyleigh suggested?" Tyrus's voice was smooth as silk and suggested of sultry things that might even be a little forbidden. "Have you dressed like a Queen Goddess under that cape, for my benefit?"

Merika lowered her gaze again, and she blushed harder, as her eyes focused on his lips. As she focused on them, she remembered Sheyleigh's words. 'I bet his lips are the only soft part on that man'.

When Tyrus received no answer from Merika, he placed a hand on either side of her face and guided her gaze back up to meet his.

"I would never in my wildest dreams have considered that you could be shy, Merika. Especially when I take your occupation into consideration."

"This has nothing to do with acting." Merika pointed out.

"True. But, to help you out here, imagine that it does, Merika. If you were Tanya Wade, how would act out this scene?" Tyrus crooned. He then released her to play her part, as he thought would be the case.

Merika thought about Tyrus' question for a moment, then threw back her head proudly and tossed him a sultry, suggestive, smile. Her eyes sparkled with mischief. The effect on Tyrus was immediate, as he felt his pulse race and blood pressure rise. She watched his reaction, then gave a low, husky laugh, as she slowly raised her hands to the clasp on the cloak that held it closed at the neck, and then purred in seductive tones.

"A Queen Goddess, Tyrus? Or something more like this?"

With a flick of her fingers Merika undid the clasp and let the cape fall from her shoulders to pool at her feet.

Tyrus' mouth went dry, as Merika revealed the creation she had made to entice him. She was dressed in a flame colored gown of satin. Sleeveless, strapless, reminiscent of the gown she had worn to Kodac's banquet ball, yet totally different. Yes, he thought to himself, much, much, different.

Merika's smile wavered, as she watched the changes that came over Tyrus' features. His eyes darkened, as they traced her figure. The tip of his tongue emerged, to lick his lips as if to moisten them, when they seemed suddenly dry, or as if in appreciation of a sumptuous meal. His whole body seemed to tense, as if in anticipation of something, and his hands almost shook as he reached out to cup the soft exposed skin of her shoulders.

"I believe the next move is mine." Tyrus' voice was husky and thick, as he slowly pulled Merika into his embrace. "A kiss worthy of not only Sheyleigh's faith in my ability to inflame your senses, but also one that will stand out forever in our memories as our first kiss."

Merika's breath seemed to catch in her throat, as her eyes locked with the smoldering gaze Tyrus was bestowing on her and her lips parted ever so slightly, as she tilted her face up to meet his.

Tyrus was being beyond gentle, yet Merika felt the full force of his possession of her lips. Her spirit floated, and she wound her arms about his neck to anchor herself. He teased and coaxed her lips to part further, and she gave a soft sigh, as his tongue invaded her mouth, to stroke and taste, as his teeth nibbled and nipped at her lips. Her eyes fluttered closed, as her hands trembled around him, and she held tight to the only solid object in an otherwise vaporizing world.

Merika was not the only one who was affected by the kiss, as Tyrus fought to hold on to his control. His arms encircled her, as his hands rose to tangle in her hair, and cup the back of her head. He felt her hold on him tighten, her hands move, to grasp and hold. He noted how her body softened, as she warmed too his touch. Her breasts swelled ever so slightly, as they pressed tightly against him. Her breathing became rapid and shallow, as her lips and tongue sought to return the exchange. His body, in response threatened to burst the restraints he had placed upon it, growing harder and showing signs of a full and painful arousal, which her body seemed to press ever tighter against.

Merika lost all coherent thought mere heartbeats after the kiss had begun. Sure, she knew what seemed to be happening to her, and a part of her even understood why, but this was something that was beyond her experience. At the moment, she had no wish to try to analyze it. His touch was wondrous, intoxicating, and she knew, misleading. Tara had been totally wrong about Tyrus, and Sheyleigh had been right on the mark. For her, Tyrus was a very dangerous man. That, however, didn't matter to her in the least, for, despite the peril, she felt safer than she had in her life.

Tyrus picked Merika up, as he continued his assault on her senses to settle her upon the leafy covering of the forest floor, cradling her in his arms as he did. Her body molded itself ever closer to his, and she became more pliant and responsive. It was with a great test of will, that he raised his head from hers, to view the visible result of his kisses, for they had definitely not stopped at the one.

Merika's lips were wet, and swelled with his possession, and when she opened her eyes to look at him, they shone a deep sapphire blue, as a glint of unrestrained passion peeked through thick highlighted lashes. She smiled at him and wiggled in unconscious invitation, and her hips were tight against a painful erection that he was having trouble controlling.

Tyrus understood better than Merika did, what was happening to her, how her body was seeking the fulfillment and satisfaction only he could offer at the moment. She had no real working knowledge of what sexual desires could be like. Not yet. But she soon would. It was a thought that brought a smile to his face, and with restrained passion making his voice thick with need, he whispered for her ears only.

"Still think you are safe?"

Merika, despite having no memory of how she got to be cushioned against Tyrus' body in such a fashion, just tossed him a satisfied smile and snuggled closer as she replied. "Implicitly, though I am hoping for better."

"Really? And what if I told you that came with strings attached?" Tyrus asked.

"I will assume that I will be able to handle the challenge. What do you have in mind?" Merika almost purred.

"I am speaking of real life, Merika. I am no longer play acting." Tyrus warned her.

Merika just grinned, as she confessed. "I quit acting the moment you took me into your arms."

"You did?" Tyrus grinned.

"Yes I did. I wanted you to kiss me. Not the fictional Tanya Wade. Who did you think you held in your arms?" Merika wanted to know, feeling this was somehow important to the both of them.

"I held the woman I hoped to call my wife someday. It was you I held, Merika, you that I kissed. Do you think you could love me? To accept me as your husband?" Tyrus wondered.

"Yes, but only if you are sure it is me you want. I am not the type to settle for being second best, especially to a fictional character," Merika warned.

"Any man stupid enough to mistake you as anything but the absolute best, would deserve everything you would do to bring him into line. But remember, Merika, if you commit yourself to me, there will be no turning back. No second thoughts. What we promise each other will be for the rest of our lives. If we are to be bonded, it will be until death do us part." Tyrus declared.

"Tyrus. There is no doubt in my mind that you mean everything you say. I also mean what I say. I know you will protect and shield me with all that you are, and that you will love me in the same way." Merika assured Tyrus of her faith in him.

"I guess this means that you have chosen me over Rhys," Tyrus made it into more of a statement than a question.

Merika smiled softly, her eyes gleaming at him, as she confirmed. "Rhys was never more than a friend, and he knew it. He might have been willing to accept me, if you would not have wanted my love, but he always knew where my heart lay."

"You love me?" Tyrus pushed Merika for the words he wanted to hear from her.

"They are scary words to say out loud, aren't they?" Merika stated, knowing what Tyrus wanted from her.

"You know what is even scarier?" Tyrus asked, with a goofy smile on his face.

"No, tell me." Merika teased.

"The moment I saw you, I wanted you for my own, and when you froze me so I couldn't move to chase you, well, just say I was lost. The realization of what that meant terrified me, and excited me, all at the same time," Tyrus admitted.

"We were just too much to fight, weren't we?" Merika teased.

Still smiling Tyrus admitted. "I sure tried. It was, as I found out, a battle I had no hope of winning."

Merika smiled wider, as her fingertips caressed his bottom lip, and he caught one between his teeth for a moment, before releasing the digit to respond. "My first instinct was to tell you to run. To tell you that, for you, I was every bit as dangerous as Sheyleigh warned. I had a feeling that you were even more of a danger to me. I find I don't care any more than you seem to. I want you, Merika. I love you more than life itself. I want you in my life, my world. I want you in my present, my future and right at this moment, especially in my bed. I need you, Merika."

"In that order?" Merika chuckled, as she buried her nose in the crook of Tyrus' neck.

"At this moment, they are much the same thing. There are a few things I think you need to know before we speak any vows between us though."

"Things like, that it was you who were deep in my mind since we met? That you have always been there for me, guiding, comforting, loving me?" Merika asked.

"How long have you known?" Tyrus wondered.

"I suspected a long time ago. I knew for certain for a while. It is why I am here now. It is a part of who we are and why I feel the words we are about to bind our lives together with are a mere formality. In reality, we have been a part of each other for a long time already, and I don't regret our connection. Not for a moment. I believe it is something special." Merika admitted.

"So you are sure of this?" Tyrus double-checked to make sure.

"Tyrus, I have given us a lot of thought, and when I believed nothing would or could ever come of how I felt about you, I was miserable. I have loved you a long time. If you are as sure as you said that you feel the same way about me as I do about you, the answer should be clear to you as well." Merika pointed out.

"Then we can both take that as a yes." Tyrus laughed in exaltation as he rose, pulled her to her feet and he whirled around with her in his arms, as he called Kalla and Firth to join them, announcing as he did.

"Mine, Merika has agreed to become my wife. We will say our promissory vows now, and be joined together from that moment and beyond."

Kalla and Firth looked at each other and smiled; neither were surprised. They also had news of their own to share with their friends. Before they could share it, they had to wait out the exuberant euphoria being displayed before them.

Merika laughed in response to Tyrus' obvious enthusiasm as he spun her around, and around. When he stopped, she clung to him, caught up in the dizzy, spinning moment, and kissed him repeatedly, declaring her feelings between quick exchanges. "I love you, Tyrus, I love you."

"I will care for you, protect you, adore you, worship you, share with you my life and love forever. Merika, my only true love. My wife." Tyrus spoke his vows.

"Tyrus, I am and always shall be yours. I will stand by your side, shoulder to shoulder, sharing my love and life. I will support you. You are my husband. We are united mind and heart, body and soul. Together throughout eternity." Merika answered.

"Mine," Tyrus crowed, as he took Merika back into his arms and kissed her.

Firth interrupted them before they became so carried away in the moment that they disappeared.

"Now that we have witnessed your vows, we would be honored to have you witness ours."

Merika and Tyrus nodded their agreement, and stood encircled in one another's arms, as Firth turned to Kalla with a pleased and proud smile.

"You are my chosen one. The blood of my heart, the completion of my soul, the air I breathe. I have loved you through time, and shall continue to do so through eternity. I am your husband that was, and shall be again. You are the wife I have, and shall always cherish. My love. My life. I pledge all that I am and will be and place it in your keeping."

"I accept and hold the honor and faith of your charge. I am and always have been the keeper of your spirit, as you have been mine. I came into being, belonging to that which is your essence, as you belonged to me. I renew our vow, given at the beginning of time, and acknowledged as it was then, it shall always be. My husband. My world. The light of my soul and life, I place my keeping into your hands and my faith in all that you are, in continuation of our love." Kalla added.

Firth and Kalla's hands touched and held, their lips met half way, as if reaching for one another, and they disappeared.

Merika and Tyrus exchanged a look and a smile, after Firth and Kala left, and then also disappeared. Each couple sought their own refuge. This was their time to be alone, their time of being together in ways that they would never be again.

Chapter XXI

Merika couldn't help the giggles that bubbled from her as Tyrus insisted on carrying her over the threshold of what she figured was probably their new home.

"Merika, welcome to our home. Say you will share it with me." Tyrus announced, and he refused to set her onto her feet, as they entered the foyer of the building they had just entered.

Merika smiled at him and teased back. "Tyrus, welcome to our home." She then noted the serious look in his eyes, and her smile faded as she asked. "What is this place?"

"Your ancestral home. Where your parents lived when they were together. I was hoping we might make it ours. It is a place that has never known unhappiness. Sorrow yes, but it was always a place that was filled with love." Tyrus told Merika the history of the house.

"And love is something you have known too little of. Isn't that so, my poor darling? Well, Tyrus, that is about to change, I have enough love in me to fill your days and nights until forever." Merika promised.

"You are sure?" Tyrus continued to look serious, although he knew Merika would know he was still teasing.

"Come, Tyrus. Show me our home." Merika smiled at him.

"I went through everything in the entire estate, fixed whatever had deteriorated over time, cleaned the house from top to bottom, and stocked it." Tyrus admitted.

"You also dreamed in it, as you surrounded yourself with wishes and hopes of what could be." Merika finished adding. "Put me down Tyrus. I want to see our dream home. The home where love has and will always reside."

"It is not as big as the houses where your grandparents live." Tyrus admitted.

"Are my grandparents still alive?" Merika was astounded. She hadn't spared a thought for the people who had raised her parents. To her, they didn't exist; she had never known them, although she had always wanted to.

"As long as we remain in the valley, we are a long lived people. In the outside world, we are no different than those who live there." Tyrus explained.

They walked together through rooms decorated in blues and whites, pinks and creams, greens and yellows. It was very fresh and clean, so obviously loved. As Merika spent extra time in a sunny, well-stocked kitchen, she smiled, and fingered the things her mother must have used at one time, when she was together with her father. She looked at Tyrus, and gave him a wobbly smile.

"Mother loved working in kitchens, she said it made her feel special, that her talent lay in this direction." Merika shared the memory, as she added. "Standing in the kitchen, where she cooked with my father, I can imagine how it was. He would sit and watch her as she worked, and sometimes take the time to interrupt her work with a kiss and a hug. They loved this room, it was the heart of their house. This is where they were the happiest, outside of the bedroom. I can feel them so clearly here, the atmosphere of the room still holds their memories."

"From all accounts, your parents loved one another madly. I would like to think they are together in death, as they could not be in life." Tyrus admitted.

"Mother would like that idea. She was such a romantic at heart.

It was one of her greatest wishes that she would be reunited with my father some day," Merika replied.

Tyrus walked up to Merika, and taking her into his arms, he kissed her softly.

"Tyrus," Merika murmured, as she stretched into his embrace to wind her arms around his neck to return his kiss. "I want you. I want the happiness my parents shared in this house for my own. Love me."

Swinging her up into his arms, Tyrus wasted no time, as he carried Merika to a room she had not been in yet. When she saw it, she smiled, for it was full of white and red roses.

"How did you know?" Merika asked.

"I didn't," Tyrus confessed. "But I had hopes. Lord, how I had hoped that when you reached out to me, that I would be bringing you home with me. Merika, I have never wanted anything so bad in my life."

"My mother adored roses, as do I." Merika admitted.

Merika's eyes glittered, as she looked at Tyrus, and he felt as if the sun was shining only for them.

"I will give you the world if I can, Merika." Tyrus promised.

Merika smiled up at him softly, as he carefully lowered her onto the middle of the mattress, and breathed a response. "I want more than that, Tyrus. I want you."

With a thought, both Tyrus and Merika opened their minds to their merge, as their lips met and blended in a kiss.

Suddenly, there was nothing beyond the moment, no one but the two of them, as they moved to become one in spirit. Tyrus' kiss caressed, and soothed. His lips touched her eyes, ears, nose, cheekbones, as his hands caressed her body, and slowly made way for his lips to follow, while they bared her skin for his possession.

With the air, heavy with the fragrance of roses, and their minds locked in a single purpose, their bodies moved to complete their vows.

"Touch me, Merika, brand me with the heat of your passion. I need your touch as much as you need mine." Tyrus breathed, as he made their clothing disappear with his powers, and his hands moved to encircle and trace the contours of her waist. She was so very slim, and as he trailed kisses over her neck and shoulders, he stroked her body, guiding her closer, molding her, stroking, caressing, waking senses she never knew she possessed.

"Merika." Tyrus breathed as he nuzzled a slightly plumped breast, licking and kissing his way to the tip awaiting his attention. He was not about to disappoint. His mouth encased the puckered nipple, and he drew hard. She gave a throaty cry, as she arched into him offering more as her hands tangled in his hair, pressing him closer. She gave another cry as he moved on to the other breast, to repeat his ministrations, while his hands languidly continued their exploration of her body.

With shaking hands, Merika continued to grasp at any part of Tyrus she could reach, but he wasn't making it easy as his body continued to slide down the length of her torso, licking and nipping his way down her body. He didn't miss an inch of her satin soft skin on his journey, this was their time, and he wasn't about to rush it.

Merika was trying to hold on to her sanity, but it was difficult when every touch, every velvet rasp of Tyrus' tongue, every sharp nip of his teeth, and every heated touch, shook her to the core. Her legs tangled with his in her restlessness, and when his questing fingers slid into the slick moisture that drenched the parting between her legs, her body bowed to meet his stroking digits.

"So delightfully wet for me" Tyrus crooned, as he continued to use his fingers to build Merika's need for him even more.

Merika had waxed all hair from her body, a habit Tyrus figured she had probably formed as a basic need, in the roles she had played as Tanya Wade. He found he liked it, liked that there was nothing between them.

"Merika, let me in, I need to taste," Tyrus instructed, as he guided her movements, to part her legs, and give him further access to her essence. Then, with a movement both shocking and intense, he lowered his face, to part her swollen folds with the width of his tongue, he made a long pass over the treasure he found below, and she gasped with the sudden heat that flooded through her body.

With a cry, Merika tried to thrust her hips forward, her body bowed, the heels of her feet dug into the mattress as her toes curled, but Tyrus refused to allow her that freedom, as he held her hips captive with his hands. He chuckled as her hands grasped for him, and listened to the soft mewling sounds she made, as he rode the flames of her burgeoning arousal with his tongue and teeth. Through it all, he continued to feed her building need. He licked and suckled, thrusting his tongue into the sheath that he would shortly fill when he possessed her fully. He knew he wouldn't be able to hold on much longer, but fully intended to hold back from joining with her, until it was beyond his power to hold back any longer.

"Please, Tyrus," Merika begged, "no more. I can't take it."

Rising from his position between her legs, Tyrus growled before dragging his body over Merika's, as he caught her hands with his, to entwine their fingers. She was on the brink of release, and he could no longer wait, later, later he would teach her what to do with her hands, and they would indulge in another lesson of loving. For now, they needed to finish this one.

"Look at me, Merika," Tyrus ordered, as he stretched her arms over her head and with their fingers still entangled. Merika opened her eyes, to lock with his. "Now we complete our bonding merge." And, with one slow steady thrust he sheathed himself deep in her body and mind, kissing her as he did. He had fully intended to stop after sheathing his body in hers, to allow for her body to become accustomed to his possession. But, it was not to be. It was beyond his power to hold still, as her cries beckoned him onwards.

"Merika, I can't hold it any longer," Tyrus warned as he began to move within her. It was too much, his need too great, and she was so tight around him. He heard her cries of passion, as his shaft thrust and receded time and again, and he loved her.

With passion filled gasps, and surprising strength, Merika held on to Tyrus, her arms and legs locked about his body. Her hips rose to meet his every thrust, and he wound his arms around her, to ride out the storm of their passion.

Tyrus felt Merika's body tighten, and gritted his teeth, as his responded. He hadn't wanted their first time to be like this, so all consuming that it was questionable whether either would survive it. She had never been with a man before, and she was so incredibly tight around him that he felt she was killing him, even as the experience drove him harder than he had ever thought possible before. Her sheath tightened further as the first waves of her completion washed through her, and she exploded around him. His body detonated right behind hers, as it released his burning seed deep into her welcoming womb. Together, they finished riding the storm that was a sign of their passion.

Finally, released by the mutual satisfaction, from the demands of their bodies, Tyrus released the hold he had shared with Merika since the first day he had met her, as he collapsed over her. He found he could barely find the strength to roll over to the side, so he wouldn't crush her. Their bodies were drenched with sweat, and their lungs fought for air. He smiled at her, and as soon as he was able, he asked.

"Are you alive?"

"Barely." Came Merika's equally breathless answer.

"As soon as I can move, I will carry you to the washroom. I think we might both want a shower after this." Tyrus suggested.

"I never thought it could be like this," Merika gasped, as her breathing began to even out.

"Neither did I." Tyrus admitted. "But, I think perhaps we should rest a bit, before the next round."

"You think you are brave enough to try that again?" Merika teased with a grin.

Tyrus grinned back at her and replied. "You can bet on it."

"It might kill us," Merika giggled, as her breathing returned to normal.

"Maybe," Tyrus admitted, as his smile widened, and he added. "But what a way to go."

CHAPTER XXII

"Where is that boy?" Kodac snarled, as he stormed across the clearing. He had been looking for Tyrus for over half the day already, and still there was no sign of him anywhere. Then again, when he thought about it, he couldn't remember seeing or hearing from him in over a week.

"Boy?" Sheyleigh raised an enquiring eyebrow at Kodac, as he got a little closer. She had been standing near the kitchens, talking with Sephra, when she had heard his grumblings.

"Tyrus." Kodac explained..

Sephra laughed at that as she replied. "Tyrus has not been a boy for a long time, Kodac, if he ever was. That man was born an adult."

"I will believe that when he quits acting like a child. He is hiding from me, as if he has done something to be ashamed of, and refuses to answer my call," Kodac grouched. "Everyone has left. The clearing is empty, and it is time we left as well."

"And he needs you to escort him home?" Sheyleigh teased. "Kodac, I think Tyrus is old enough to know his way home by now."

"He knows his way home. It is actually Merika who I need to speak with, and he is the only person I know who can contact her when she is missing. No one has seen her in days, though they are sure she has been around somewhere. Rumor has it that she has been moody enough, since the celebration, to make people go out of their way to avoid her."

"She has been that way for weeks." Sephra confirmed, making it sound as if it was an ongoing problem.

"Have you tried to contact Merika directly, or is this another attempt to get Tyrus to try to bridge the distance that seems to have grown between them?" Sheyleigh asked.

"I have repeatedly reached out for the both of them, neither are paying any attention to me. He is nowhere to be found in the immediate area, and she is just not there. I hope she isn't with Rhys in his world." Kodac sighed.

"How about further out? Does Tyrus have a hideaway? Most people do." Sheyleigh suggested.

"Yes, come to think of it, although I usually make a rule of leaving him his privacy when he is there." Kodac replied.

"Well, how do you know if he is there or not, if you haven't checked? If you want to speak with him, you may have to reach out to him." Sheyleigh pushed.

"You never know, Kodac. The two of them might even be together." Sephra teased.

"That is wishful thinking." Kodac retorted. He had given up on Merika and Tyrus getting together. It was time to move on.

"Perhaps, perhaps not. But if you really give it some serious thought. It doesn't seem that off the wall to me." Sheyleigh replied thoughtfully.

"What makes you think that?" Kodac stopped ranting, to give Sheyleigh a pensive look.

"Well, I know you have been tracking him almost constantly since Merika showed up. Trying to read their relationship off of him. Tell me, what was the last message you received, before you lost track of him?" Sheyleigh asked.

"He was erratic, confused and frustrated. I got irritated and cut off communications." Kodac admitted.

"And it all stopped at that point?" Sheyleigh enquired.

"I didn't reach out again, and the link went completely quiet." Kodac replied.

"Suddenly? Just like that?" Sephra wondered.

"Well, it wouldn't be the first time. This is Tyrus we are talking about, not Rodan." Kodac pointed out.

"I see. In that case, I suggest you try harder to reach him, especially if this is important. Reach further out and ask." Sheyleigh suggested.

They had a point, and Kodac admitted it. He reached out to where he knew Tyrus went when he was in one of his moods, and found nothing. That meant his son wasn't there. Well, he decided, at this point he had nothing to lose, so he sent out a message on a very wide band. He knew that if Tyrus were in the valley, he would hear that. They only way he could miss it, were if he had left their world, which he doubted if the boy would do.

Tyrus frowned, as he rested his chin on the top of Merika's head, and blocked a questing merge from his father. Kodac, he noted, was searching for him on a very wide band. It didn't matter; he didn't plan on answering, not yet. Merika was sleeping peacefully in the circle of his arms, and he didn't want her disturbed. He also wanted a moment to consider just how he was going to reply to the summons when he knew he would rather not hear from anyone at all. Deciding at the last minute, that it had to be done anyway, he sent back a less than cordial reply.

"You found me, what do you want?"

"I need to see you, where are you?" Kodac asked.

Tyrus could feel a probe in Kodac's questing mind, and blocked it. "I am tending to business. Why? Run out of wood or something like that?"

"Watch yourself young man, you forget who you are talking to." Kodac warned.

"No disrespect intended father, but I can hardly see where my presence is needed. Nor has it been needed for some time now," Tyrus pointed out what he felt should have been the obvious.

"Actually, you are right, nor am I actually looking for you. I need to find Merika, and you are the only one I know who can usually reach her. There are a few things that we need to get settled between us." Kodac admitted.

"Well, as luck would have it, I know precisely where Merika is, as well as what she has been doing." Tyrus replied, as he looked down at Merika's sleeping form with a satisfied smile.

"Yes?" Kodac prompted.

"Merika was dead tired father, and she is sleeping. I am not about to wake her for a decision that could probably wait a few more hours." Tyrus admitted.

"So what was she doing to exhaust herself this time?" Kodac asked.

"Nothing you need to concern yourself with. Notice, there has been no storms? Suffice it to say she has been getting some well-needed rest. Anything else, you will undoubtedly be brought up to date on when you see her." Tyrus stated.

"Well, that had better be sooner than later. My whole world does not revolve around that young lady, you know. If needed, I can send your horse to you." Kodac offered.

"No need, father. I can make my own way there. I will see you later." And then Tyrus severed the merge.

"He dismissed me!" Kodac spoke in shocked outrage.

Sephra replied. "Maybe there was a reason for that."

Sheyleigh added smugly. "And maybe her name is Merika. I still think there is a very good possibility that she is with him."

"It might explain his sudden bout of independence." Sephra pointed out.

"Tyrus has always had an independent streak a mile wide, and he is stubborn as a mule to go with it. As for Merika being with him," Kodac heaved a heavy sigh and added. "It would be a blessing in disguise if she were. But he showed no signs that she might be."

"You can tell this for sure?" Sheyleigh asked, her eyes narrowed as if daring him to evade the question. She wanted to know the answer every bit as much as Kodac, if for no other reason than to say I told you so.

With a heavy sigh, Kodac gave a thoughtful reply. "I used to. There have been times lately that I am finding Tyrus more elusive. He is coming into his power more and more. Usually I find him easier to read when Merika is nearby. His moods tend to be upbeat, and his guard not so tight."

"Maybe he has more to hide now." Sheyleigh suggested.

"Keep thinking like that, Sheyleigh, and maybe all our wishes will come true." Kodac answered.

Tyrus smiled, as he dropped a light kiss on the top of Merika's head, and she gave a light murmur, as she stretched lithely beside him, and then teased sleepily.

"I assume Kodac has found us?"

"You are too perceptive for your own good, my love. Kodac has an idea where I am, more or less, it is but one of his many talents. He seems to have trouble reading your signals though, which pleases me to no end. I managed to block anything pertaining to our time together from him. So, as to that, our secret is still safe." Tyrus informed Merika.

"You really think that matters anymore, Tyrus?" Merika asked.

"No. Our marriage is not something that I feel shame over. That part I don't want to hide from anyone. In fact, I would like to shout it from every rooftop across the Valley. I do get the feeling though, that our time alone here is coming to an end, and I am not ready for that yet. Being alone with you here has been priceless. You realize that from the moment we announce our union, we are going to have to share each other with those about us. Sometimes, great power calls for great sacrifices." Tyrus admitted.

"I am sure we will manage to survive, somehow." Merika teased as she dismissed Tyrus' comment about their having to share their lives with others. It was something that was bound to have happened at any rate. She stretched up to kiss the side of his jaw and added. "Well my love, I guess there is no time like the present to face the rest of the world."

A few hours later, Tyrus and Merika stood face to face with Kodac at the homestead. Kodac took one look at the young couple, and knew the whole story, without being told a word. Tyrus looked downright smug, and Merika glowed with an inner happiness.

"Father. I would like to present my wife, Merika. We would ask that you honor our union with your blessing."

"Not that this isn't the best thing that you have ever done, but I need to know if you ran off to do this in secret because you are ashamed of what you were doing?" Kodac wanted to know.

"Lord no!" Tyrus denied vehemently, as he turned a possessive smile onto his bride. "It would be a poor excuse of a man who would be ashamed of being chosen by anyone like Merika, and you are just as aware of the reasons as I. It might have happened faster than either of us expected when we did come together, but I regret none of it. Nor do I feel any guilt for spending the time alone with her that I did. If I could keep her to myself for the rest of my life, I would. I love her."

"Something I was beginning to think I would never hear you admit." Kodac grumped as he turned to Merika. "And how about you, young lady. What do you have to say for yourself?"

"What can I say? I admit, I have found myself overwhelmed by all that has happened since I arrived in the valley. I feel as if I have lived through a lifetime of experiences and events, in only a few weeks. There are times I have trouble believing that this is any more than just a crazy dream. I have discovered my roots, past and future. Nor do I find or feel any shame in any of it. I have found only love and acceptance in my new life, it is something to be proud of as well. There are some things I might like to know more about, but we have time for that. All things considered, I must admit I am happy here." Merika informed Kodac.

"So what would you like to know about?" Kodac asked.

"My father. My mother never really told me anything about him and the only time I brought it up she cried. I never asked again." Merika admitted.

"I can fill you in on the important things. Your father was a very talented man. His name was Ricard. Your parents met at a gathering and were wed with little fanfare. They were deliriously happy together and so in love, when they lived in the Valley. Your mother was beautiful, very talented, and popular amongst those members of the Valley who knew her. She was very pregnant when your father was killed in a freak accident. His parents took it hard. In their grief, they blamed her, though it had nothing to do with her at all. He had been struck by lightning, as he rode towards their home, during a storm. He had been their only child."

"Your mother had been the last remaining child of her line, as well. Both were powerful talents. Believing herself alone in the world, and scared Ricard's parents would try to take her child from her, she fled the safety of the valley. She was trying to lose herself amongst the greater population of the large cities of the outside world, thinking she would be safe from the powers of those who lived in this world. You were born in obscurity, although we did manage to discover your name, and record it. She did the best she could to hide you, and she did a good job. It couldn't have been easy to keep your developing strengths and talents a secret until she died." Kodac admitted.

"I grew up believing that my parents were just like anyone else. Just ordinary star crossed lovers," Merika replied.

"There are no such things as ordinary people in the valleys. Rather than have a class distinction determined by wealth or hereditary, as exists in the outside world, our positions are determined by power, and how we use it. Your parents, Merika, were far from ordinary." Kodac informed her.

Kodac then turned to Tyrus, and tossed him a lopsided smile, as he continued to speak. "As for my bestowing a blessing on your union, it is well known that I had hoped that the two of you would mesh, right from the moment I first laid eyes on Merika. I am more than happy to welcome her into the family and I am proud to bestow my blessings on the marriage."

"Thank you father." Tyrus responded.

"Now, I must admit that I am more than a little interested in how your children will develop." Kodac smugly commented.

"Our children?" Merika spoke in surprise.

Tyrus went even further. "Always pushing. We have just come back from our honeymoon, let us have a little time to get to know one another before pushing offspring on us."

"Think about the potential," Kodac happily ignored both protests. "Merika's parents were strong and talented. They had not even reached their potential when tragedy struck, shattering their lives. Their union produced Merika, one of the most powerful Prime Alpha Females in our history. You, Tyrus, show the potential to develop into a more powerful Valley Alpha Prime Male than anyone I have ever read about in recent history. Genetically speaking, your progeny should be awe inspiring."

"Father we are not prime breeding stock." Tyrus objected.

"It comes to the same thing in the end." Kodac pointed out.

"You have a lot to learn father." Tyrus didn't mean it the way his father took it, but Kodac's mind was already flying down what looked like a one way street.

"True," and Kodac turned to a stunned looking Merika, as he continued. "I wouldn't let that worry me if I were you though. Think about this instead, you wanted to know the history of your family. Well, you have married the one man in the valley who can teach you everything you want to know, and not just in the bedroom."

"Though I will try to cover that area to the best of my ability as well." Tyrus chuckled, as he leaned over to tease Merika, his voice whisper soft and meant only for her ears. The effort proved unsuccessful.

Merika gave a small smile as she blushed and Kodac choked on a laugh, as he teased. "I think you can count on that, although I would have thought you well educated that way by now."

"We could always invent other methods if needed." Tyrus teased back, thinking that his father would quit at that, and leave it drop, if he saw that his efforts to embarrass them was having no effect.

It didn't work, instead Kodac looked speculatively at the couple, and said, "Really?"

Even Tyrus turned a bright shade of red, as he suddenly had memories of their time together. He could remember very little time during their honeymoon that they had not been in some if not all states of undress. They had loved, and made love, wherever, and whenever the inclination had moved them. Their passions had known no limit, no boundaries, and if Merika had known discomfort due to her inexperience, she had said nothing, and given no signs that she might be. In fact, he hated to admit he had not even thought to ask. The strength and novelty of the feelings he had experienced had often carried him away.

He could only give a roguish smile and reply. "Probably."

Kodac, although he couldn't read his son's mind, could well imagine what was going through it, due to the expressive looks that crossed his features. He just tossed him a grin as he spoke to assure him.

"The intensity of your ardor will cool with time and familiarity."

Running a hand over the back of his neck, Tyrus replied. "For both of our sakes, I hope so. At this time, all it seems to take is a look from Merika, and I am hard. It is embarrassing."

"Only natural and I am sure Merika is no less affected." And the attention of both men shifted to Merika, who refused to pay attention to them.

Looking as if she was receiving a message, Merika stood oblivious to all that was going on. A short time later, she turned her attention on to those about her and smiled.

"My grandparents wish to meet with us. They think we should be alone for a while longer though. They send us their blessings and well wishes. They also believe we should dwell in the home that was my parents love nest, their words. They said they never meant to chase my mother from the Valley, never threatened to take me from her. They were hurt, but would have helped. They said they loved her too and are sorry."

"So what do you think?" Tyrus decided to leave that up to her.

"If you don't mind, I would like to live in the house where my parents loved, much as we have been doing. There is such an atmosphere of belonging, of home to it. Later we will see. There is time, and I think my parents would be happy to know that everything worked out in the end." Merika replied.

Kodac looked at Tyrus, and a wide smile spread across his face, as he said. "So that is where the two of you have been all this time."

Tyrus grinned back, as he wound an arm around Merika, and drew her closer as he replied. "And if you don't mind, we will go back to continue trying for a grandchild for you, as we build our home base into something that will reflect our life together."

"Go." Kodac chuckled. "Get out of here. The both of you."

And as they disappeared, Kodac smiled and added, with a chuckle. "But I want more than just the one. Remember that."

The sound of amused laughter was the only sign Kodac had that anyone had heard him. He rubbed his hands together in glee and laughed, as he also disappeared from the homesteaded clearing to return home. Life was grand, and his future looked rosy. For, he was willing to bet, he would be a grandfather before summer returned, and his family was happy. His was a successful life, for there was no greater reward in the world than happiness and a sense of love in a family.

CHAPTER XXIII

The snows of winter came early that year, as well as fast and deep. The plans that Merika and Tyrus made to travel to meet her grandparents had to be put on hold, as the roads were impassible. They kept in touch with those they knew and loved enough to take time to contact through their talent for telepathy. Rayjan, Tyrus' brother through his maternal side, contacted them, to say he had met a woman in Rhys' world, and intended to settle down to raise a family there. Rhys continued to travel between the two worlds, while he built up favorable relations between his people and Kodac's. He wished them well, and appeared to be sincere in his saying so. Darnell had also settled, and was looking forward to his future. Rodan and Serena reported, very quickly, that they were expecting a child shortly after spring arrived, and it wasn't long after that when Tyrus and Merika found out that they were also expecting an addition to their family.

Kodac was beside himself with glee, as he continued to work his own form of mischief. He had managed to get everything he wanted, and now was setting up new plans. He had been the singular reason winter had set in so hard and fast, as he had called in a blizzard of historical proportions, to blanket the area with several feet of snow. He knew that would keep Tyrus and Merika home, because they would be so busy seeing to their estate that they wouldn't have time to travel. With very little other forms of recreation, they would turn to each other. It was the quickest way he could think of to make sure they were tending to the business of creating his grandchild. He was right on all counts, although he felt a tiny twinge of conscience for setting things up in a way that meant they wouldn't get to meet Merika's own grandparents until later.

With that in mind, Kodac contacted both sets of Merika's

grandparents, with the suggestion that when spring came they would meet, to make the trip to see Tyrus and Merika on their own. He told them about Merika's condition, and they were all as excited as he was about the prospect of becoming great grandparents. They had missed the opportunity to lavish love and attention on Merika, they were not about to miss out on the joys of watching her child grow.

Tyrus fussed over Merika, as she went through the initial stages of her pregnancy. He would hover over her when she suffered through bouts of morning sickness, and tease her when she got testy because she felt like she was being crowded. They couldn't physically travel, because there was too much snow, and the roads were closed. They couldn't use their powers to leave the homestead, because of Merika's delicate condition. When she got moody or temperamental, due to her pregnancy, he would show her how much he loved her, and she would settle.

Merika couldn't pretend to be surprised to find out she was pregnant. There were times when she could swear they spent more time out of their clothing than they did wearing them. They made love wherever and whenever the mood struck them, and often spent entire evenings cuddling together by the fire, as the cold winter winds raged outside. With her pregnancy, came the mood swings, which she doubted if Tyrus was handling well anymore. He could do nothing right one moment, and the next he was holding her while she sobbed against his shoulders, all for no reason. He saw to the wellbeing of the livestock and catered to her indoors, while all she did was cook and clean. She needed to get out and do something, but it was impossible. No one was traveling anywhere by road, and she couldn't use her power to move around because of the child she carried in her womb.

When Merika reached approximately the half way point in her pregnancy, her metabolism seemed to settle. The morning sickness receded, and she began to look forward to the birth of their baby. Serena and her often would reach out to talk to one another, to share their experiences, and she didn't feel so isolated. It was a time that cemented their friendship even more, and brought them closer.

Serena was two months more advanced in her pregnancy than Merika, and she had a better idea of what to expect, as well as the guidance of her mother to help her prepare for the birth and aftermath. She had spent the better part of the winter sewing and knitting, to provide clothing for her baby. It was something Merika had no idea how to do. So, as Merika entered into her fifth month of pregnancy, she began to worry about what she was going to do about caring for her child.

In the world where Merika had gown up, Tyrus and her would have been spending hours in different boutiques, sorting through baby clothing and choosing furniture for the nursery. Here, if you wanted any of these things, you made it with your own hands. Everything had a function, and nothing was wasted. Tyrus could, and did, provide her with everything she needed to create the things she had to, while he did his part. But, and he was the first to admit his shortcomings, he had his limits.

Like Merika, Tyrus had been raised in the outside world, where there were department stores on every corner, and they were more than happy to cater to the needs of their customers at times like this. Here, he was on his own. The cradle he attempted to make was crude, and barely able to stay in one piece. He reached out to his father for advice, only to become frustrated with Kodac's instructions. He needed guidance, not instructions.

Kodac, as winter progressed, reached out to plan the visit with Merika's grandparents that they had planned to make.

"Missive," Kodac spoke to Merika's paternal grandfather.

"Is everything all right with our young lovebirds?" Missive asked in concern. Kodac had told them about the pregnancy when he had first learned about it, and they had been excited about the news. They were, however, apprehensive about meeting their granddaughter. They had not parted well with Teryka, after the death of her husband, their son, and they weren't sure about their welcome. Kodac wasn't giving them any choice about whether they could stay away, or not. He ordered them to make the effort to get to know Merika, as well as Tyrus, for the sake of their family. It wasn't that they didn't want to get to know the young couple; it was that they were incredibly nervous about their reception.

"I am connecting us with Taine, so we can talk together and share thoughts," Kodac warned Missive.

With a moment, the three alphas were linked together, and the conversation began in earnest.

"How is my granddaughter and her husband making out on their estate?" Taine began. He wasn't about to waste time on small talk. There were still a lot of ill feelings between Missive and him to work out, and this hadn't been addressed yet. At this time, he was not prepared to move on that, although he knew it had to be done at some time in the near future, for the sake of the children.

"Tyrus has the estate running like clockwork. Merika has everything under control behind the scenes, and in the house. They love each other with everything they have. They do have a few shortcomings though," Kodac admitted.

"Don't we all," Missive admitted.

"What seems to be the problem?" Taine asked. He wasn't about to respond to Missive's caustic remark.

"Tyrus has no carpentry skills, especially when it comes to making furniture for the baby. He can do the fixing, but unlike the people who remained in the valley, he has never been taught any finishing skills." Kodak informed Missive and Taine.

"What you are saying, is that they could use a little instruction," Taine noted.

"Or do you want us to make the furniture for them?" Missive asked. It was something he was more than willing to do.

"Instruction would be more useful, and bring you closer to them as a family unit. In Merika's case, she has no sewing skills. I doubt if she has ever held a needle in her life, and Serena is getting frustrated with her lack of knowledge. She has been trying to teach her how to knit, or crochet, by telling her through their connection, but it isn't working. She reported that the baby booties that Merika managed to put together are a mass of knots."

"I will let Miranda know that our daughter forgot to teach our granddaughter how to make clothing," Taine chuckled.

"I want you to spend a month or two with this young couple. I want you to teach them the rest of what they need to know so they can survive in our world. I am afraid that if we don't do this, they will leave us. In that case, it would be us who failed them at a time when they needed us most," Kodac pointed out.

"Miranda and I will be there, I will have her begin packing supplies, and we will set out in a few days. I assume the roads are passible, and the weather will cooperate through the journey, am I right Kodac?" Taine both informed and asked.

"I will make sure of it, and yes, the roads are in good condition," Kodac assured them.

"Estelle will be happy to see Merika, as well as Miranda again. Miranda and her were very close at one time, and she says they would like to be once more," Missive stated, letting everyone know he was willing to let the past go.

Taine laughed audibly, as he conceded the point Missive had made. They had also been good friends at one time, and maybe this would be possible now that there were children coming into the family. Either way, it was past time they moved on and let old wounds heal. It wouldn't be the first time that words that were spoken in hurt and anger caused irreparable differences. Their feelings needed to be set aside for, he feared, that if they weren't, even more people would suffer. He didn't want the past to taint the future anymore than it had.

"Perhaps we should try to put the past behind us. Our women have, we should be able to as well. I don't want to lose any more of those I love. We lost our children, we could lose the rest of the family if we continue to hold a grudge," Taine offered.

"We will work together, to guide our granddaughter's family into the future. It may help us grow closer, and reunite our families," Missive agreed.

A few days later, Kodac knocked on Tyrus and Merika's door. He had both sets of her grandparents with him. He hadn't told anyone he was coming, as he wanted this to be a surprise, and it was, just not in the way he thought it would be.

Merika opened the door, in answer to Kodac's knock and smiled when she saw him standing there. He then moved aside, so she could see her grandparents. The smile that had crossed her face earlier faltered, as her eyes fell upon her maternal grandmother, and she fainted.

Kodac barely had time to catch Merika, before she landed on the floor. He lifted her into his arms and carried her back into the house, as Tyrus came running towards them from the barn to see what had happened.

CHAPTER XXIV

"What happened?" Tyrus asked. He sounded panicked, as his hands shook and he tried to brush Kodac aside so he could check on Merika himself.

"I think she had a bit of a shock," Taine answered instead of Kodac.

"Who are you?" Tyrus asked.

"We are her grandparents, and Miranda probably looks enough like Teryka yet for Merika to have reacted to that.

"You should have sent warning that you were coming, so I could have prepared Merika for this. Father, you know better," Tyrus quickly went on the offense.

"I wanted to surprise the two of you," Kodac replied.

"Well, you certainly managed that," Tyrus returned. He was not at all impressed with his father's actions. Merika had planned to take a trip to see her grandparents, and was prepared for that. She wouldn't have expected to face them without warning at this time though. "Damn it Dad, do you know how vulnerable she is at this time?"

"Not as much as you think she is," Miranda interrupted. "Men are all the same, especially when they are expecting their first child. Good thing women are the ones who give birth and not them."

"I totally agree with that. They would never survive the initial contractions, never mind the actual labor and delivery," Estella agreed.

As the two women took over, and pushed the men out of the way, Tyrus opened his mouth to object, only to have Taine shake his head in silent warning.

"Not a good idea son. When our women start on that road, it is better if we head for a safe haven."

"They are in here, so perhaps we should go into the kitchen and put a pot of water on to boil, so we can make some tea for later," Kodac suggested.

"Good idea," Miranda agreed. "Make yourself useful, Merika will need a strong cup of it when she wakes up."

As the men trooped into the kitchen, Merika began to regain consciousness. Again, the first thing she noticed was her grandmother, and she gave a gasp, as she quickly sat up to throw her arms around Miranda and cried out loud.

"Please be real. Please, please be real. I have missed you so much mother."

Miranda closed her eyes, as a tear trickled from the corner of one of her eyes, to run down her cheek. She knew there had been a resemblance between Teryka and her, but she hadn't thought that it was this pronounced. She wrapped her granddaughter into her arms and held her tight, as she crooned softly, to calm her.

"Shush, my darling girl, it will be all right now. I am here, but I am not Teryka, I am Miranda, her mother."

Another cry, filled with anguish, was torn from Merika, as she broke into a fresh torrent of tears, and Miranda began to soothe her all over again.

"Don't cry so hard, Merika, it is bad for the baby, nor would Teryka want you to carry on like this. She was my ray of sunshine, my beautiful daughter, and I loved her more than life. Somehow, I failed her, for she didn't come to us in her time of need. Instead, she chose to run. Please, don't shut us out too, my precious granddaughter."

"Or any of us. We have come to help you, to make things right between our families again, as it once was. Please help us to help you," Estelle pleaded.

"Grandmother?" Merika asked, through the broken sobs that punctuated her speech.

"Yes, my sweetness. Teryka was my daughter." Miranda answered.

"Ricard, was my son. We loved them both so much, which can be as much of a curse as it can be a blessing. When something happened to test us, we failed. Instead of holding strong and turning to each other to make us stronger, we struck out and hurt those we loved the most. Your mother felt she had no choice but to run. For all we know, she might have done the right thing." Estelle admitted.

"Her actions were a wake up call to us. They made us realize what we were doing. Your father's death had been one of those rare incidents when the only blame was in nature. By the time we accepted this, it was too late. Your mother was gone, and we couldn't find her in the outside world." Miranda informed Merika.

"We tried, but she was very good at hiding her tracks," Estelle told Merika.

"The only time we were able to get a fix on her, was when you were born," Miranda added.

"We heard Teryka say one sentence, 'Ricard, our child lives, and I will call her Merika.' There was no more." Estelle replied.

"We took the name of their child home with us, to add to the family tree." Miranda stated.

"We didn't follow her after that. She had a right to live, although we would rather have had her home, where she would have been surrounded by those who loved her," Estelle added.

"She worked in kitchens all of her life. She said she was happiest there," Merika told them.

"Teryka would have been, it was their favorite place. She liked to make Ricard special meals that he enjoyed. I don't think she ever forgot him, ever." Miranda sighed.

By this time, Merika had quit crying and she rose, as she looked towards the kitchen and asked, "Are my grandfathers waiting for us in there?"

"Yes, it was safer for them there. They are trying to make peace with what happened, even now. The rift that accident created between them was deep, and your return to the valley is making them come to terms with what followed. We are going to have to help them with this, all of us." Miranda informed Merika.

"They have been hurting for such a long time, it has become a part of who they are," Estelle warned Miranda.

"Then we will guide them through the pain," Merika stated. She then squared her shoulders, and led her grandmothers into the kitchen, where they found the four men sitting around a small table.

The moment the men noticed Merika enter the room, they stood, and looked awkward. It was easy to see how difficult this was for them, and she decided that she would have to be careful where she trod. She stood before the two older men, and looked at them with a seeing gaze as she spoke.

"Grandfathers, I have two now, where I had none before. My childhood dreams have come true."

Taine wrapped his arms around Merika, as he closed his eyes and spoke. "We have come to make sure those dreams never die. Forgive two old fools who were too proud to admit when they were wrong."

"There is nothing to forgive, Grandfather," Merika admitted, as she hugged Taine back. She then turned, to exchange another with Missive.

"I hear your husband needs to learn how to use a hammer," Missive teased, as he held his Granddaughter.

"And I am dangerous with any type of needle. We are in such trouble," Merika admitted with a watery laugh, before adding, "I am such a watering pot since I got pregnant. It must be a boy."

Kodac chuckled, as he broke into the conversation. "On that note, I suggest we get out some more cups, add a couple of chairs to the circle, and get to know each other, before I leave. You will want to learn all you can, before you settle in."

"Settle in?" Tyrus asked, as he looked at Kodac in surprise.

"Yes, Merika's grandfather has graciously offered to teach you how to make the things you will need for the nursery," Kodac informed Tyrus.

"We will teach Merika how to sew, knit, crochet and other such things, so your children will have clothing, as well as yourselves," Miranda insisted.

Tyrus and Merika exchanged a quick look of amusement, and laughed. It seemed they were going to become part of a larger family unit than they had thought, and they loved the idea. Finally, they had come home.

CHAPTER XXV

"Seven years," Kodac announced, as he danced around the room. He was going to throw a party. He had seven grandchildren, all boys. But finally, he had one that was a girl, and he couldn't be happier.

"Settle down, Kodac, you are worse than a toddler at Christmas," Sheyleigh shook her head at him, as she watched him dance around the house. Earlier, he had been pacing, which made her think that Merika's third child had finally made an appearance. She wondered if it was a boy, or a girl?

"I have a granddaughter, Sheyleigh. Finally, our family has had a female child born in our house. I thought it would never happen, it was been so long," Kodac crowed, as he announced the event.

"I see, I guess this is a matter of eighth time lucky. I thought no one in your family ever had anything but boys," Sheyleigh teased.

"It was beginning to look like this would never happen," Kodac admitted, with an excited giggle. Merika hadn't wanted to try for another child. She said that Serena had done enough for the both of them, when it came to populating the world with her brood of five. She even refused to listen to what he had to say about the subject; instead she told him he was a dangerous man and should be happy with the two grandsons she had borne.

Kodac had eventually given up on Merika, and turned his attention to Tyrus. At first, his son hadn't been much easier to talk to than Merika. He had agreed with her that her two sons were enough of a handful for anyone, but that was a part of their charms. Besides, he tried to point out, wouldn't they love to have a pretty blonde daughter, to give Merika someone to fuss over? He could tell when the idea began to take form in the back of Tyrus' mind. Tyrus' eyes would get that dreamy, far away look in them, and he knew his son was hooked on the idea. A year later, nearly to the day, they had made another of his dreams come true. He now had a granddaughter!

It was at the height of his excitement, when Rhys showed up at Kodac's front door, and his five-year-old son accompanied him. Kodac frowned at the interruption, but couldn't say anything about it. They were here, after all, at his request. He had called a meeting to talk about Rhys' portal. He couldn't imagine keeping his mind on that now though.

"I am going to assume that you will want to cancel your meeting, all things considered," Rhys hummed.

"If you don't mind. I really should go to Tyrus and Merika's estate, to see how she is doing, as well as the child." Kodac pointed out.

"Do you mind if I tag along?" Rhys wondered. He had missed the births of Tyrus and Merika's other two children, and as a friend, he thought the least he could do was congratulate them on the birth of their daughter.

"Come along," Kodac replied jovially, with a wide grin, "I need someone to show my new granddaughter off to."

"From what I have heard of your family tree, having a girl added to all those males would be a good reason for you to crow," Rhys teased.

"Very true. There hasn't been a female born into our family in over ten or eleven generations. I kept hoping to see that record broken." Kodac admitted.

"Is that why Rodan and Serena have five sons?" Rhys wondered.

"Serena had taken after her mother. Sephra had borne one child after the other. Nothing prevented her from getting pregnant.

She was one of those who were lucky enough to be able to go through the different stages of childbearing without trouble," Kodac stated, as he walked through the doorway of Tyrus and Merika's home without knocking.

Sephra approached Kodac, the moment he walked through the door. "Not a sound above a whisper. Merika and her daughter are sleeping, and neither of them had an easy time of this. Merika will never be able to have another child, and the baby came close to dying as she was born. It was a close call. She suffered through thirty-six hours of labor, Tyrus was a basket case, and we had to bring in Darnell to help control him.

Kodac immediately reacted to that, "Why wasn't I summoned?"

"You don't want to hear about that. Now that you are here, I only hope Tyrus has settled down enough not to attack you on sight. It seems you are partially to blame for the problems Merika went through, because you talked them into having another child. I doubt if even he had any idea what he would have done to you earlier. Merika is out of trouble now though, and she spoke with him, to get him to cool down, so things could get back to normal." Sephra told Kodac.

"It didn't take much suggestion to get Tyrus to agree, just the thought of a pint sized Merika. He took over from there," Kodac defended his part in this action.

"Maybe so, but she had been warned before that she would be endangering her life, if she had another baby. Now nature has taken care of the danger in its own way. It will probably be a week before Merika will be in any condition to get out of bed, and even then, she will be weak." Sephra reported. She then turned her attention onto Rhys.

"And who do we have here? Hello Rhys, it has been a while since I had the pleasure of seeing you. Is this your son?"

"It is always busy for the top Alpha Primes. You know how it is. This is my son, Riven. We had come for a meeting with Kodac, and decided to pay a visit with Tyrus and Merika while we were here, to congratulate them." Rhys replied.

Sephra crouched slightly, and addressed they shy looking little boy, who mirrored his father for looks. As he pressed his small body against Rhys' leg, and clutched at the pant leg surrounding it, she greeted him.

"Hello, Riven, welcome to the valley,"

Riven immediately snapped into attention, as he responded with a bow, and rehearsed reply.

"It is a pleasure to meet you."

"He is a darling, Rhys. You must be so proud of him," Sephra congratulated him.

"We are, and he is on his best behavior at the moment. I can't promise how long it will last, but we have learned to take what we can get," Rhys admitted.

"No other progeny?" Sephra asked.

"Not yet, but maybe someday. Again, sometimes you take what you can get," Rhys pointed out.

"So true, well, if you are very quiet, I will allow you to have a sneak peek at our valley rose. But, you must promise not to wake either her, or her mother," Sephra warned.

"They called the baby Rose?" Kodac asked.

"Teryka Rose, after Merika's mother, and the flowers she loved. I must say she is one of the most perfectly formed babies I have ever seen, and I have helped bring a lot of them into the world. You will see what I mean for yourself in a few moments," Sephra admitted.

Rhys followed in Kodac's wake, as Sephra led the way to where Merika and her daughter shared a room. Both were sound asleep, and Sephra took them to the side of a crib that had been tastefully decorated with frills and ribbons. It was the perfect foil for a little girl child, and the baby was snuggled tightly in amongst the covers.

Teryka Rose moved slightly in her sleep, as she raised a perfectly formed fist to her mouth to press it against her mouth and yawned in her sleep.

Riven looked at the baby for a few moments, and then turned to his father to ask, in a whispery soft voice, so he wouldn't wake her.

"Is this a real baby, daddy?"

Rhys chuckled, as he replied, "Yes it is, my son. A very special little girl."

"Girls aren't so special," Riven answered, as he studied Teryka Rose. He had a little boy's disregard for girls that the adults knew would disappear over time.

"This little girl will be very special," Rhys replied, "Especially for you."

"Why me?" Riven wondered.

"Because, she is your future," Rhys answered.

Riven frowned, but said nothing. He scrunched up his nose at that declaration, wrapped an arm around his father's neck, and buried his nose against Rhys' shoulder. He then stuffed one of his thumbs into his mouth. At the moment, he didn't look too interested in his future.

The adults tried to keep their reactions to Riven's response to a minimum, but the sound of their muted laughter managed to cut the silence with enough volume to wake Teryka Rose. She squirmed, as she regarded those around her with a curious expression, scrunched up her face, and burst into tears.

Merika woke immediately and turned to reach for her baby, even as she noted the presence of so many other people in her room, while Sephra moved to calm her. Tyrus came racing into the room, to see what had disturbed his family and frowned, the moment he saw Kodac. When he saw Rhys, shortly thereafter, that changed into a smile.

Rhys noted Tyrus' reaction to their presence, and quickly moved to defuse the situation, before things could get out of control.

"I hear congratulations are in order. Your daughter is beyond beautiful."

"She is," Tyrus replied proudly. He then laughed, as Riven added.

"Daddy says she is my future."

"If she is," Tyrus replied through his laughter, "It won't happen for a long time, and that will be her decision."

Riven seemed to give a sigh of relief when he learned that Teryka Rose wouldn't be in his immediate future. She might look cute, and everyone seemed to be pleased with her, for whatever reason, but he was just as pleased not to have to take on the responsibility of a sister.

TO BE CONTINUED IN TERYKA ROSE

SNEAK PEAK OF TERYKA ROSE

CHAPTER I

Watching them from the edge of the clearing, Kodac knew they were unaware of his presence. That suited him well. This way he could study them at his leisure, for he wanted to see where this was headed, and there was no better way to read their thoughts than through body language. Kodac could read their thoughts easily, especially Rhys, who was watching his eldest son carefully, while Riven spied on Teryka Rose. The young man's face reflected the many emotions fleeting through him, jealousy, admiration and longing.

Riven stood in the shadows as he watched Teryka. It had been ten years since he had last seen her, and he thought she was even more beautiful now than she had been at sixteen. He didn't particularly like the fact that she was attending the gathering picnic at the side of another man, but he couldn't fault her for that. He hadn't been here to invite her to the small gathering in person. That, he decided, was about to change. He should have been the one to escort her onto the fairgrounds, not Darish, and from this time forward, he would be here for her.

It wasn't that Riven didn't like Darish, they were good friends, or at least they had been before this. Now Darish was being relegated to the status of competition for the girl he was sure they both wanted to call their own, something he had never expected. He remembered how they had promised each other that no female would ever break up their friendship, when they were young boys. They would remain comrades for life. They were above fighting over something as silly as a girl. Why did they have to grow up to want the same woman? Damn, he sighed quietly to himself. Teryka was beautiful. Unfortunately, he could tell Darish was thinking the same thing, by the look of admiration on his face. He watched, as Darish said something to Teryka, and she laughed openly. There was honesty in the sound of her laughter. She had nothing to hide from anyone, and they could tell she was enjoying herself. This, he had to admit, was the first time he remembered ever feeling jealous of another man's luck in finding a pretty girl to be with.

Statler, Riven's brother, compounded the problem by walking up to his side and commenting.

"Now that looks like someone I wouldn't mind for myself."

Riven gave a snort or contempt, as he retorted. "You are too young for her."

"I am barely a year younger, and she is hot," Statler exclaimed.

"You are not in the same class," Riven replied.

"Well, we will see about that. Watch and learn, big brother," Statler stated, before he confidently sauntered over to where Teryka and Darish were and pulled her into his arms, to give her a huge wet kiss in greeting.

It was easy to see that Darish was tempted to act on Statler's actions, yet too shocked and civilized to follow through on that. It was something that Statler should have appreciated, for Darish could have pounded him into the ground.

Riven couldn't blame Darish for glaring at Statler. He could barely believe it himself. Statler was asking for trouble, and he had a feeling he was about to get more than he bargained for. He wondered who would deliver the trouncing, Darish, or one of Teryka's brothers. He was half relieved when their father walked up to his side and asked. "How long has that been going on?" Rhys would put a stop to his son's idiocy, and probably prevent him from being killed at the same time. He couldn't understand how his son could be so dense.

"Forever," Riven replied, meaning Statler's feelings for Teryka.

"I see, and I thought you were the one who was acting strangely the last time we were here. Now that I see this, I assume you were just trying to cover for Statler. It looks like it is time for me to take a hand to my baby boy, before someone reduces him to powder. Why didn't you say something earlier? I didn't realize Statler had a crush on Teryka, or that he would take it this far if he did." Rhys stated.

"I didn't think telling anyone would make a difference," Riven admitted.

"I see. Why did you think that?" Rhys wondered.

"Let's face it dad, the last time we were on this side of the portal together, Statler was barely sixteen. The crush he developed on Teryka was the type most of us grow out off relatively quickly. Usually, all it takes is for another pretty girl to cross our path. I guess Statler never got to the point where he had gotten his fill of her, and it has lingered." Riven stated.

"Well, this shows that Statler hasn't woken up to that piece of news yet. He is twenty-six, Riven. That is a long time to hold on to a crush, especially when the woman he was fixated on hasn't been around to hold his attention." Rhys pointed out.

"He may believe he is in love with her, but he will soon outgrow that. She may be the one who has to give him the push in that direction though. I wonder if Teryka has what it takes to do that," Riven asked in his preoccupation.

Teryka was very petite and fragile looking, and Riven wondered, if she had the guts to take on his little brother. Statler could be a handful, but she could have more spunk to her than he figured. That wasn't out of the realm of possibilities. Statler wouldn't retaliate, they had been taught better than that by their parents.

Rhys was about to comment, when he noticed Teryka wiggle free from Statler's grasp, and both Riven and he watched in surprise, as she acted.

"Who said you could touch me?"

Statler didn't pay any attention to the fury in Teryka's voice or eyes, instead, he commented. "I thought I would surprise you. I know how much time has gone by since the last time we saw each other, and figured I would show you how much I missed you, so we could carry on from there."

"I have a news flash for you," Teryka replied angrily, as she pushed Statler further away. "I never missed you, and your attentions are not appreciated."

"You needn't act as if you object to my touch, I could tell by the way you responded that you didn't," Statler answered, as he moved to close the gap between them again.

Teryka didn't think twice about what she was going to do to stop Statler. She buried him in the ground at her feet, right up to his neck, while she warned him.

"If you ever dare try to touch me again, I will make sure there are fire ants in the ground with you next time. Do I make myself clear? Don't come near me again, don't even talk to me."

"Would you like me to move our picnic spot or him?" Darish asked Teryka.

Teryka looked around, to see if there was anywhere else that might suit her better, and then decided she liked where she was. She was not about to move for Statler.

"Get rid of the trash," Teryka informed Darish. She didn't notice how the three men who were watching her grinned in amusement. She ignored Statler altogether, while he objected.

"I am not trash!"

"Matter of opinion," Teryka mumbled, as Darish moved Statler to another location, before making himself comfortable on the blanket that had been spread out for them earlier.

"So, what do you think of Teryka?" Rhys asked Riven.

"I have always liked Teryka. She knows who she is, and is happy to be that person." Riven stated.

"She should be. If Teryka were in our world, she would be Valley Prime. Your aunt would have found her title given to another. Meridor wouldn't like it, but she would accept it, for no other reason than she had no choice." Rhys pointed out.

"Meridor has let the title go to her head over the years. She is a bully. Our people don't need that type of example. We need someone more down to earth to lead them," Riven pointed out.

"And you believe Teryka is that person?" Rhys asked.

"As you said, when we first saw her. She is our future," Riven pointed out.

"Not quite what I said. What I told you is that she was YOUR future," Rhys corrected Riven.

"I remember, I just wasn't sure if the same rules applied," Riven admitted.

"If you want them to, then yes, they still apply. If not, then no, they don't. So, which is it to be?" Rhys asked.

"Wish me luck. It is past time I tried to win myself a bride," Riven declared.

Rhys grinned, as he watched Riven stride towards Teryka and Darish. He was proud of his son. Riven had proven his worth to their world time and again. With that, he proclaimed softly to himself, "That is my boy, may the best man win."

As that thought crossed Rhys' mind, he remembered his own subtle courtship of Teryka's mother, Merika. He had known from the beginning that there hadn't been much of a chance that we would win her at the time. Merika had fallen in love with Tyrus at first glance, although it had taken her a while to accept it. Tyrus hadn't helped her much with that, because he had fought their attraction more than she had. Because of Tyrus' reluctance to accept the inevitable, Rhys had decided he had nothing to lose by trying. He had been right in his first assumption, Merika and Tyrus were meant to be together. By letting her go, when she chose Tyrus, he had accomplished two things that he felt would help with the future. He had made some very valuable friends and allies, and he had opened a pathway to their doorway for his son, if he ever had one.

Rhys doubted if Riven would come up with the same conclusions he was getting, from what he noticed about Teryka and Darish's relationship. His son would be looking at their friendship with blinders. He would miss the obvious points that showed their strong and weak points. He would only see Darish as competition for what he felt was the ultimate prize, Teryka. Because of that, he would miss the rest.

The things Rhys saw, were subtle hints of what could be. Darish and Teryka were familiar with each other. They were very good friends, almost too good to be anything else. The camaraderie between them was one of comfort, which could be misleading. The sense he got was that if they tried to move their relationship beyond this point, they would be content, but nothing more. They had the foundation it took to have a good marriage, but it would lack the passion it took to make a great one. The type of connection Merika had with Tyrus, which was what he would have liked for himself. His marriage was a good one, but the passion he had hoped for was non-existent. He was hoping his sons would be luckier in love than he was.

The lack of potential passion in Teryka and Darish's relationship, Rhys figured, was the strongest point in Riven's favor. Riven was a man who had learned to leash his passions years ago. He could teach her to be more than a friend, and he would light up her world. If his son could get past the calm, cool surface, where Teryka held her more fiery nature at bay, they would have it all. They would be close friends and confidants, as well as passionate lovers and partners in life. Could his son get her to open up to him? He was sure Riven could, but he might need help for, as he could see, Teryka had two extra hurdles for Riven to get past. Her brothers were on their way to make sure no one would take advantage of their family princess. He liked that about them; they protected their own. It didn't matter if it stacked the deck against his son. A little challenge for Riven would make his victory all the sweeter. While he plotted, he quickly decided it might be a good idea to send in a few stumbling blocks of his own.

Teryka wasn't the only one with friends of another gender. Riven had a few that would make her sit up and take notice of his popularity. It was common knowledge that if you wanted a woman to pay attention to you, it often took another female to show her that you weren't a pariah. Rhys knew the person best suited for the task. Tarama. She was as beautiful as Teryka, in her own way, which was apt to make her seem like a rival in the back of Teryka's mind. Where Teryka's beauty was brilliant, in the way of sunlight, when it came to looks and personality, Tarama, was the polar opposite. Tarama was dark as the twilight. Her essence surrounded a man in a cocoon of heat, like luxurious velvet in the night. Her voice was sultry and low, in ways that made men think of summer nights and silken sheets. Her eyes were a dark brown that smoldered, as they slowly burned their way into a man's soul.

For all that, he considered Tarama the sweetest girl in his world. If it hadn't been for Teryka, he would have chosen her for his eldest son.

The thought of Tarama tossed into the middle of the group brought a smile to Rhys' lips. He had a feeling that young lady would soon find herself with three suitors, and not only the one. It would be interesting to see who would win that contest as well.

With several plans taking form in the back of his mind, Rhys turned to leave for his home to set things into motion, but not before he noticed Serena and Rodan's group of children join the group that was growing around Teryka. The crowd that was beginning to form opened up even more possibilities in the back of his mind. He had been looking for ways to bring his world closer to Kodac's. Perhaps he would pay a visit to the Alpha Prime of this valley, so they could plot this out together. Kodac, as he remembered, was very good at that, and he approved of his plans to introduce their people to one another. As luck would have it, the man he was going to head out to see, was the first he noticed as he set out to leave. It seemed he wasn't the only one who had come to the same conclusions as he was, for Kodac was looking at him with an expression similar to the one he remembered from years gone past. Yes, this could prove to be a very interesting time for everyone.

Made in the USA
Columbia, SC
26 April 2017